D0296377

BOURNEMOUTH

410029805

the time is now

By Pauline McLynn and available from Headline Review

the time is now

Pauline McLynn

headline
review

First published in 2010 by HEADLINE REVIEW
An imprint of HEADLINE PUBLISHING GROUP

1

Cataloguing in Publication Data is available from the British Library

Hardback ISBN 978 0 7553 4341 6
Trade paperback ISBN 978 0 7553 4342 3

Typeset in New Caledonia by Palimpsest Book Production Ltd,
Falkirk, Stirlingshire

Printed and bound in Great Britain by
Clays Ltd St Ives plc

Headline's policy is to use papers that are natural, renewable
and recyclable products and made from wood grown in sustainable
forests. The logging and manufacturing processes are expected to
conform to the environmental regulations of the country of origin.

HEADLINE PUBLISHING GROUP
An Hachette UK company
338 Euston Road
London NW1 3BH

www.headline.co.uk
www.hachette.co.uk

In memory of the G Cat –
this one was a lot harder without you

Go where we may – rest where we will,
Eternal London haunts us still.

Thomas More

now

Nothing is worth more than this day.

Johann Von Goethe

january

When she thought about it later she realised it was the silence that had woken her and not the pigeon, she felt sure of that. There was an unnatural hush as if the city was holding its breath, waiting to see if this New Year was worth continuing with. Her first impression, then, was of a lack of sound but also too much light. They had left the curtains open on their return and that was no surprise given the state they had been in. This first day's sun was crystal and insistent. It bothered her eyes and underscored the aching hung-over, drugged-over, everything-over condition she found herself in. Next came the bird sound; insistent also, rhythmic, attention-seeking. But then, 'Tony's not snoring.' A miracle. 'Maybe he's dead,' she thought, idly. She reached a hand behind her to find rumpled sheets and empty space. Not dead then, just gone.

Without turning around she slowly swung out of the bed, ignored the soured vinegar smell of an abandoned glass of red wine stinking on her bedside locker, and pulled on a robe to go in search of water and painkillers. The bird was pecking at the window now, cocking its head from side to side as if to ask a question or wonder why the hell she couldn't understand it

when it was being so plain in its language. The message, whatever it was, was lost on her. She stepped over a pile of clothes
abandoned on the floor and vaguely recognised some as Tony's
but the detail was unimportant at the time. What mattered
now was to stop the thumping bass and drum installed by last
night's revelry and to get back to blessed sleep. Later, again,
she thought that maybe the pigeon was trying to show her what
lay ahead, or behind, however you wanted to look at it. She
pulled the curtains over and in the blessed shade stepped into
the corridor that housed her slim kitchen and even slimmer
loo. She felt like shit. Happy New Year.

The living room was cool and she dozed on the sofa while
new drugs tried to erase the damage of the old. Fitful images
of laughter and excess jolted her more fully awake every so
often, but she couldn't quite sustain the consciousness and
drifted off again. Eventually the smell of her wasted body became
too much to bear so she made for the bedroom again and slid
open the door to her tiny bath and basin. And that's when she
found him. 'Like a Roman emperor,' she remarked to the policewoman and regretted it immediately as if it made him less than
he was or, perhaps, more than he deserved and therefore not
an adequate description. For some reason a level of accuracy
mattered to her now. The water was a most beautiful red and
she knew without touching his blue-lipped, pallid body that he
had long departed her. He looked relaxed and so was she for
a moment, then she turned away and spewed the contents of
her diminished stomach on to the bed: his side, as it happened.

She sat with him, on the edge of the bath, and chatted while
she waited for the police to come. She had phoned the emergency number, not knowing what else to do, but explained

that there was no actual rush: 'he's dead' covered that. She checked a few details with him and he didn't argue and so it was all much of the same stuff she said to the officer when she asked her standard questions, although it was much friendlier and without judgement in Karen's case. The cop seemed unimpressed by Tony and what he'd done. Or tight-lipped, Karen would have said.

'Yes, he was depressed, that was Tony's natural state, his default position.'

The policewoman nodded as if she understood, and perhaps she did, for all Karen knew or cared.

'He always said he'd do it in Moscow, though. He hated Moscow and the Moscow route.'

Again the nods, which were in fact encouragement for her to talk, fill in the spaces on the form that slated her best friend's departure as suicide. The flat was full to bursting with people she didn't know, and buzzing with a strange excitement. She could still hear the pigeon in the background, occasionally underscoring the melee, and from somewhere else in the complex the sound of live music. She could make out trumpet and strings but no more, which gave her red and yellow. Music always offered colour and she thought nothing of it.

'We were not lovers,' she was saying. 'Tony was gay.'

She got 'Ah' for that, as if it explained everything.

'Lazy,' Karen wanted to say, then, but kept her counsel. It was not her place to make a scene: this was Tony's day, after all. And the policewoman needed stereotypes because there were forms to fill and statistics to be boosted. So, 'gay, depressed, suicidal' ticked the requisite boxes. Put like that,

Tony did seem like a massive cliché. He'd probably have appreciated that, revelled a little in helping cement a few dodgy assumptions into convictions. And maybe he had allowed himself to stale into a type. What a waste.

'So, you were friends?'

'The best,' Karen acknowledged. And because it amused her, and she knew it would have made Tony smile, she added, 'I was his hag.'

'They say it's a peaceful way to go, like falling asleep,' the other woman said, as a kindness. That particular cliché hit the spot and Karen was grateful. It was then she started to cry.

Someone must have made tea because Karen was suddenly drinking some. Had she made it herself? Unlikely, she decided. Probably the lowest ranking of the police people. It was too strong and too sweet and she demolished it. She noticed that the policewoman bit her nails quite badly, back to the quick. That's got to hurt, she thought. The assembly had their details now and were simply waiting for someone to remove the body. She was about to be abandoned a second time today. She ached already with the loss of her friend and throbbed with the fear her hangover had produced. Karen chattered in lieu of shaking, afraid to give in to this new, awful situation.

'He was bored with life a lot of the time. He liked fun, though. He was aggressively into that. It could be a little frightening, sometimes, like he was doling out a punishment. Will I just pull the plug in the bath when he's taken out? Am I to let the blood go down the drain? Is that safe?'

The crashing realisation that she would have to talk to his family dawned. Tony, by his own admission, had had a happy childhood. His people were blameless for his unhappy

8

boredom with life. 'I'm just not cut out for it,' he'd whine, then make a joke and take away the sting of hopelessness he could inject at a glance.

The tiny flat was still packed with police personnel. She was stuck in a corner of her front room listening to Soho cranking up outside for another year, quietly, calmly. Her home was the only palpable bustle in the arrangement and wherever the music was coming from. She imagined her neighbours were on the metal walkways, chatting about the incident, getting details wrong, waiting to see the body moved. Body. He, or It, wasn't really Tony any more. He, or It, was a corpse. Her eyes clocked the dust on her fireplace, above an electric contraption that didn't work and looked ugly to boot. There were rings from long cleared coffee cups and drips of old wine staining the once white paintwork. The New Year's light had an ecstatic tone to it and was highlighting far too much. And it was all so random and unimportant.

There was a concerted shuffling from the bedroom. The policewoman looked out and said, 'They're moving him. We'll leave you to it now.' There was a relief in her voice. She could get out of this sad place, nothing more to see. She handed over a card with the name and number of a victim support officer and made for the exit. The bird had taken up residence on the kitchen counter by then.

'We're not allowed pets,' Karen said, to no one in particular.

'Looks like she's quite comfy there.'

'They're flying rats, aren't they?'

'That one is special to somebody. A racer, I'd say. She looks in good nick.'

The bird did look well fed and almost pretty. Sleek, Karen

would have said, and somehow certainly female. The pigeon looked at her with one white-rimmed eye then the other and seemed to try to see into a depth Karen wasn't even sure she had. It also looked suspiciously like the bird was trying to make her laugh, or perhaps she was predisposed to the ridiculous at that moment.

When the posse finally cleared and Karen returned to her bedroom to dress, she saw that someone else had let the water and blood drain away. They will have worn protective gloves for that, she thought. I would not have. I wonder if that is important? She couldn't bring herself to wash in there just yet. It seemed disrespectful somehow.

As a result, her timing was off and she got to Tony's mother before the police.

'Estelle, it's Karen, Karen Dash.'

'Oh.' There was a gulp of air sucked in. Estelle had been waiting for this call a long time. 'Has he done it then?'

'Er, yes, yes he has.'

'Moscow, was it?'

'No, my bath, in Soho.'

'Selfish little git.'

It was odd to cry on one end of a phone while another person cried on theirs, but not unwelcome. She liked the sound in her ear. She hoped Estelle gained similar comfort from her. When she hung up, she looked down and saw that the pigeon was perched on her suitcase, the trolley that she dragged through the airports for work. She saw that it had a ring on each leg and, ridiculously, felt she should tell that to the policewoman. The bird looked completely at home. She wondered what to feed it.

❀   ❀   ❀

I decided to get very drunk. That seemed the only way to get by. My heart was racing wildly through my chest and I needed to slow down the sheer panic of the day. I couldn't think straight about Tony and I didn't want to either. Firstly, though, there was the problem of the pigeon. I repeated the phrase and thought it would have made Tony laugh. He would have invented an Agatha Christie-type jape titled 'The Problem of the Pigeon' and worked on it the whole day. His capricious and brilliant mind was always riffing on brilliant nonsense like that.

I Googled my query and found that grain would do so I offered the bird some uncooked popcorn, which she ignored, and some pumpkin seeds which she nibbled daintily. I put out a small dish of water too and even asked if she'd care to join me in a glass of red wine. She was quite at home but not drinking alcohol, I gathered. I wondered if she was injured but didn't know how to check. She wasn't limping but she wasn't flying either. I tried to shoo her out of the door several times but she was having none of it. She was content to perch close by and watch me, and shit at will on my furniture. I sort of knew how she felt. I finally talked to her about Tony and she listened without judging. I'm not sure I made much sense but again that didn't perturb her. I vaguely thought I should phone work and tell them they'd have to replace him on the Moscow service on the fifth, and me too if I could get away with that, but I couldn't muster the energy to lift the phone and try to explain the tragedy to anyone human. For now, the pigeon would do. The call to Estelle had done me in for dealing with any more people today.

It's hard to describe the new numbness I felt. I was stunned

11

with grief, immobile really, and floored by the wine igniting everything else in my system. I was glad to be at home, at least, even if it was the scene of the awful event. Normally being here would have meant Tony slouching about, complaining, or sneering brilliantly at whatever concern I had called him in to discuss. The place had a strange void to it now, and any shelter it offered was horribly compromised. The bird was company, I have to admit. And she wasn't going to make any dent on my booze stash so I had the wherewithal to get blotted. I realised I was sobbing constantly. I had become accustomed to it throughout the day and didn't much notice it any more. The neck of my T-shirt was sodden and I had globs of snot under my nose. I wiped them off with the back of my hand and wiped the hand on my robe and wallowed. My eyes were almost closed with the crying. The thought of Tony being dead hurt so much, the pain was a visceral stab. At least the slicing light had faded into evening and that was easier on my whole, fragile system.

I thought I might lie down awhile and returned to the bedroom. The sheets were still crumpled from both of our bodies. I could still smell his cologne above my earlier vomit and some sort of disinfectant that the police must have used. It had a carbolic undertone and reminded me of my grand-parents' house. I had a vision of running wildly through tall grass as a child and the feeling it gave me was one of bursting happiness and that proved too much. Suddenly I was puking again, pure wine this time, the red stain slashing across the white linen. When I was spent, I rolled it all into a ball and chucked it into the washer-drier, then lay on the uncovered mattress under the uncovered duvet and tried to still my heart and mind. All I could remember was Tony kissing me, actually kissing with tongues and telling me he loved me the night before. I understood now that he knew what he was about to do. His gift to me was that he felt safe enough with me to do just that. This was the proof of love. I had been the Chosen One. I pulled his pillow closer, breathed him in and dozed. Just as I went over I muttered, 'Fuck you, Tony,' and meant it very deeply.

At some bewitched hour when I woke again I was surprised to feel hungry. At a pinch I'd've declared I'd never eat again, the way this new year was going and with the misery I was steeped in, but there is no accounting for being human so I struggled to the fridge in search of food and cool wine – no sense in halting the poison now, I reasoned. A note was attached by a magnet and, on it, Tony's handwriting read, 'That pigeon seems to have come for you – it's your job to get her home.'

It had always been coming to this, of course. This was the story he had been telling forever. This was the song he had sung over and over. We had always been headed here. Until now a journey, yes, and I suppose foolishly I ignored the fact that one day we would arrive at his prearranged destination, and today was that day. Which is not to say that it was predetermined by fate – no, or at least I don't believe it was; it was Tony's doing, it was his choice. Hadn't he always slagged God off for giving man a free will, saying it was the greatest act of passing the buck ever perpetrated? 'God's off the hook now,' he'd snort. 'As Bette Midler sings, he's watching us . . . from a distance. That's his natural habitat: well out of it.' I wondered vaguely why I had been chosen as the companion for this adventure of his, and why I had allowed myself to be. But such thoughts are foolish ultimately. We know the path we take, as much as we can or may blame outside forces and justify what happens to us from some notion of victimhood. We mould our fate long before it comes to that halt we know is down the line. We expect. We relish the achievement of getting there; it's almost a prize. But then there is the hurt that is, in the end of all, unwelcome, much as it has been anticipated and nurtured all along. It is cruel. And I couldn't help but feel that it would have been braver of Tony not to go the way he had, in spite of it being his life's work, his goal.

I worried also that I had enabled him. I had always pandered to his version of himself and therefore I had somehow excused or helped precipitate this ultimate decision of his, this departure. I wasn't proud of that now. I felt responsible, guilty. And I was beginning to get angry too. How dare he lumber me with this? How dare he pull me asunder, actually? I felt my mind slip away towards a maddened bereavement that I knew would tear me up and that I was not fit for. I needed to regain some control so the best way to start was with a shower in the bath Tony had used earlier to such different purpose. I held the scouring cream aloft and wondered if I needed to use it but there seemed no trace of blood left behind. Amazing how so much had disappeared into the belly of the city and probably on into the river. Father Thames had his human sacrifice today.

I felt nothing of Tony as I scalded my skin and I was grateful for that. I stood a long time under the water, purging the stench I had allowed to envelope me and letting the water loosen the seized muscles of my neck and back. My whole

14

body felt bound up, to be honest, and this was blessed relief. I soaped and scrubbed and emerged looking raw. I was just the tiniest bit happier now. The pigeon cooed at me. It sounded like a birdy purr, and its music seemed dark green and soothing.

He had pegged me for an only child from the off, told me I was not an 'either/or', as he put it. He said he always recognised another particular or solitary soul, that we had a singularity about us those others from a gang lacked. It wasn't the first time someone had guessed it and I've always wondered, when this happens, if only children are so truly odd when we can be pointed out so readily. I think I'm fairly well adjusted (whatever that means in today's fluid understanding of such things) so what is it that singles me out? He was correct, so I assumed he was one of my breed and he let me think that for an age. Tony has two brothers and a sister. He is not, was not, an Only.

My parents were quite elderly for child-rearing when they had me and although I was diligent in keeping in touch, I didn't feel it would do much good to phone them now and upset them with the news of Tony's death. I had wished them a Happy New Year already, listening from their end to the rural idyll I had grown up in as background to the call, and I thought it best to leave them with that. They had met Tony only once and when I realised they were terrified he might be a suitor or, worse, their future son-in-law, as outrageously camp as he was with them and as gay as they knew he was, I never tortured them with him again, much to Tony's disappointment. It was also not an option to turn up on their doorstep and be the gooseberry to their pair (Tony would have had a fine time punning pair and pear so I mentally did it for him). I didn't have anyone to call, really, to tell, aside from work colleagues, and even though some had liked him, there wouldn't be too much happiness out there if I ruined everyone's New Year's Day the way Tony had ruined mine. He had once said, 'No man is an island? Wrong. Everyone is. There's your truth.' Right now my lone status was complete, but for the bird who seemed to be snoozing on the handle of my work trolley. I was blue on blue.

I flicked on the television, for company and distraction, but each channel was showing relentlessly cheery films and upbeat situation comedies or worn re-repeats of New Year celebrations across the globe. There are only so many times you can watch Harbour Bridge explode into coloured smoke or the Big Apple's crystal ball drop in Times Square. I did laugh out loud when Moscow's Red Square came on, in honour of my ex-comrade's feelings towards that town.

I switched on the radio low to take the curse off the silence. The first time I'd met Tony he was listening to very loud music on his iPod, drowning out the world and, I'm guessing, his thoughts too. Noise. He loved noise. Is that why he loved me? Because I can be noisy. I probably talk too much, not necessarily loudly but definitely too fast and possibly lots of ill-considered gushings. And he did love me, I know that, not that it was a comfort then. Was I the sound that saved him for a while from his end or did I simply delay him a tad?

We were paired together in Economy on the Moscow route. He told me that, like Milton's Satan, he'd prefer 'to reign in hell, than serve in heav'n' but he was getting both on this shittiest of all routes. It was true that the passengers could be aggressive and demanding above other journeys. 'I have a BU

16

in 36A and if she gives me any more gyp I'll spit in her gin and tonic.' A BU, I learned, was a Big Unit. 'Must go, Moscow,' he'd intone, telling me that Chekhov had the misery right, that he realised how hilarious unhappiness actually is and how inherently comical man's lot is too. 'Like *EastEnders*, with an edge,' he'd say. 'And humour. And nice clothes.' I was simply struck by how extraordinary Tony's energy was, the life force he exuded. It didn't seem all that negative to me. Yes, it was a certain aggro towards life but that seemed to match his convictions, however pessimistic he said they were. 'Life is terrifying,' he told me, 'which is why I am glad of a uniform: it's my riot gear.'

Essentially he was strong, so why did he not resist his end? Why did he leave me haunted with such questions? Did he think that I was strong enough for this, here and now, and all that it would bring to me? I cried again, easily, drunkenly, and went in search of more alcohol. His mother, Estelle, was right: he was a selfish git. As it happened, I popped a bottle of champagne and drank until I passed out. And when I woke from that bout, sweaty and shaking from unremembered dreams, I also knew something else and said aloud, 'I am so damned glad to be alive.'

The bird needed to be taken care of so Karen shushed it outside in the hope it would 'do its business' and return a little less likely to soil her tiny flat. She also thought it might just fly away and that would be handy and acceptable. She was out on the landing waving her arms about, in what she imagined was a threatening manner, when a hand gripped her shoulder and she all but voided with fright. This was her neighbour, Frank, a man she'd only seen a handful of times but who always seemed to her to be stuck in some sort of time warp, a seventies throwback she'd've chanced if pushed. He wanted to know about the police and she found it easy to be rid of him by telling the truth. Fifteen minutes later he was at her door bearing a casserole of curried turkey, which he'd made and frozen on Boxing Day. He was in and reheating before she could say, 'Fuck off.' In spite of herself she enjoyed the meal and his chat. When he produced some peaches and cream for dessert, she said, 'Eliot. Idiot,' remembering Tony.

'See this peach?' he had said once. 'I dare to eat it, oh yes.' And he had, messily. 'It'll go through me and out the other end and I'll come to no harm. Won't change my life either. Big. Deal.' He waved a hand to ward off argument. 'No time for the wider metaphors and intentions in Prufrock just now, if indeed ever, as Row 46 are giving me the hump. Steerage bastards.'

Frank ignored her giggles and put on some music, speaking glowingly of a track she couldn't quite name, putting this down to too much drink and a sleeping pill she had popped just after he had frightened the bejesus out of her. It made it harder to keep her eyes open although it was a mild sedative and not a patch on some of the stuff she knew was stashed in Tony's washbag. It was almost fun to fight it and to try to keep up with her neighbour.

'I have no idea why he worked in a services industry,' she slurred, 'when he hated people. Said he did anyhow. Maybe he enjoyed being horrible to humans. Though he was capable of great kindness too.' She wondered if that was the truth and decided that nothing in fact ever was, or could ever be, *entirely* the truth. After all, that's what got people killed or crucified. That and being too nice, too caring.

Then suddenly she was waking again, in her bed, almost rested. Frank was gone, along with any trace of his smelly, delicious food, and she was thinking she'd have to get the pigeon home.

She checked the rings and their information. The bird was patient. 'OK, letters, a number, a letter and more numbers on one,' she told it. 'In someone's world, that's gold dust.' She sat at the computer, the bird on the window sill, and typed in helpful words. 'How about a Royal Association?' she asked the bird. 'Seems a good place to start to me. Says here no one mans the helpline site on weekends and I'm guessing that means national holidays too.' The bird didn't look bothered. 'Right, I'm reporting your details but you're stuck here till tomorrow. We'll have to see about better seed or at least a bit of variety. I can't have you going back fat, or bored.' All of which meant going outside.

It was harder this time to step into the bath that Tony had died in. It was just a quick shower but uncomfortable for all that, as if she was dancing on his grave. She wondered if she might have to move, if his shadowy ghost would linger in her mind or in the place. She wondered about events leaving their mark on time. Would there be a haunting? She had often felt this place must be heaving with memories, of lives lived and lost, and that a certain signature had to be found in each of its various cells. Because she sometimes thought that Claxton Court, Soho, was just that: a regular arrangement of near-identical apartments, like cells, and each of the inhabitants monks or prisoners within. She thought about legacy. Tony was right: life was inherently ridiculous. You were born, you lived, you died: that was the sum of it. Pointless. Existing at all was innately foolish. Take Tony – he had left nothing behind except perhaps some memories that would surely die with the rememberer. Why bother at all? And as her stomach groaned and demanded food, she knew there was only one way to deal with this and that was to move forward, if not exactly upward. One damn thing after another.

Somehow time had passed and they were facing a new day. 'They' was Karen and the pigeon now. Not The Pigeon, she scolded, A Pigeon. For all she knew this was as useless a bird as herself.

'If you got lost on a race you're not much good, are you?' she told it.

She listened carefully at her door, needing to be certain no one else was about. She didn't want to be hijacked by any of her curious neighbours as they were, to all intents, strangers she hardly ever saw or greeted. She was now an exotic with news and therefore needed to avoid them. She rushed out and down the flights of metal steps from the top of the apartment building, trying not to clang too loudly and feeling ridiculously guilty that she hadn't brought the pigeon with her. Next I'll be wanting a parrot for my shoulder, she thought. She took a left out of Claxton Court, along Pig Lane and on to Broadwick Street. New Year boulevardiers were strolling, following their breath to pubs and restaurants. They seemed happy, content, muffled in Christmas gifts of scarves and gloves. Karen envied them. What did she look like to these others? A haunted wraith, one of the lost of Soho, a druggie or prostitute on a rare daytime outing to get basic provisions before readying herself for her night's work? Oh, who cares, she thought, I'll be a long time dead and will never even see any of these people ever again. We are strangers brushing past, careless of the others we encounter. Tony was right, we are all islands. Still, she wished she'd worn some make-up to ward off any ill-considered attention. She would remember her shield next time. Also, Tony would not have approved of letting standards slip. 'Fuck him,' she muttered, 'his own halo has slipped.' A woman passing stared so directly at her, Karen realised she was talking aloud to herself. Not good.

She passed some goths, then punks. She saw mods. Emos spoke with rockers. Everyone has a disguise, she thought. So many people were declaring themselves, making statements about who they were. I wonder if they see any suggestion of who I am, she thought. They'd be hard pressed to, she decided, if she hardly knew that herself any more.

Tony's mum, Estelle, was shivering at the gate when Karen returned from the local supermarket. She felt foolish to be carrying a wide variety of seeds for a bird. I don't know what she likes, she might have said in other circumstances to cover it. The walk along Pig Lane towards this grieving mother seemed miles long. Her heart tore to see her raw anguish, plainly apparent for any passers by. But then, why should Estelle hide it? she thought. Why should grief observe some social nicety and cover itself up as if it was bad form to show you cared? Estelle's pale face framed red-rimmed eyes. Black circles beneath told of a sleepless night. Her vapoured breath puffed before her in the rapid gasps of a woman in difficulty. Karen prayed to any cosmic force listening that she might peddle more than hollow sayings that would insult this situation and be unforgivable.

'I've seen him,' Estelle said of her son. 'Or what passes for him now.'

They embraced long and hard, reluctant to leave the spot, to go through the large metal gate that separated the court from the rest of the world and climb the stairs to the place that was now the hub of their small, broken universe.

Finally, Estelle stood by the bath.

'His Ophelia moment,' she said. 'Like that Pre-Raphaelite painting, do you know the one? She's lying on her back with her hair trailing around her in the water.'

'Yes. I never liked it,' Karen admitted. 'Always thought it a bit sweet and manipulative although, if I remember my art GCSE correctly, that's the opposite of what the painter intended.'

'True. And I agree, for what it's worth. Never liked it either. "We know what we are, not what we may be." Shakespeare's Ophelia, and much the better, poor soul.'

They sat on the edge of the bath, as if they were both acknowledging this was the closest they could be to Tony now.

'He really was the most delightful and laziest person I ever knew,' Estelle said. 'He had such talents from the get-go but the moment he realised they entailed any sort of work he gave up on them. Relied on his wit and handsome looks to get him out of any trouble or effort. I don't mean to insult what you do, Karen, but that job gave him every excuse not to make anything of himself.'

'I always thought he could have been a writer,' Karen said. 'Words were his thing.'

'Again, too lazy. And perhaps just a little afraid that he might not cut it.'

'That he'd only hack it instead?' Karen asked in the spirit of the dead man.

Estelle laughed. 'He taught you well.' She paused. 'You're not supposed to have a favourite, as a mother, but he was mine. I feel I have failed him, to let him go like this.'

'Tony was the only one who could possibly save himself and he chose not to. It's not your fault.'

'Perhaps so, but I'll always blame myself.'

'So will I.'

'You've let yourself get stuck in that job too.'

'It was only supposed to be a stop-gap so that I could earn some money but see a bit of the world while I was at it. Suddenly I was years in and facing the prospect that I'd be a mature student if I went to college like I'd always planned. I felt I'd missed my chance. Tony happened along and the job became fun.'

'So, let me guess: you still don't have much money and you haven't seen much of the world apart from the different rooms of its many hotels.'

'A whole lot of similar ones, no matter where we land on the planet.'

'Well, Karen, there is no time to waste. That may be what Tony has left us with. Get out of the rut. Surely it's never too late.' She stopped abruptly. When she had calmed she added, 'Unless you're dead.'

They drank wine and Karen fished out her mobile to show Estelle the last photograph she had of Tony alive. She had taken it holding the phone at arm's length and they looked as fuzzy as they had felt, grinning like loons.

'He used to call me the accidental child,' she told Estelle.

23

'I was born late to my parents and I guess I was a bit of a surprise.'

'He had a bad habit of reducing people's lives to a title. He thought it profound but I always found it ever so slightly trite. I told him that often enough and I'm sure it didn't help matters.'

'Only because it was the truth.'

'As I saw it.'

'That's all we have, though, isn't it? Our small version of a truth, something to get us by, a code.'

The rueful silence let in the sound of the band rehearsing.

'They seem to have been at that tune forever,' Karen said. 'A Stylistics song, I think.'

'Can't say I noticed it. But I do have to ask you, why the bird?'

'Ah, why indeed.'

She tried to piece together last moments from Tony's life, searching for the crucial one when she might have stopped him leaving it. He had kissed her just inside the front door, fully and with passion.

'It's not a turning point,' he'd said. 'Just wondering. And besides, this loving you has become a problem. I feel obliged to you somehow and, as you know, I feel a person should only be obliged to the self.'

'Very cut-price Oscar Wilde,' she'd remarked.

'Bet he wasn't as good a kisser.'

'I wouldn't know, though I've never read any complaints about the quality of his lovemaking, just the nature of it.'

'Nature,' Tony had echoed.

'What a bitch,' they'd said in unison and fell laughing into bed. And unconsciousness.

Karen's phone rang at 10 a.m. and when she answered, a man from the association she'd contacted told her that the pigeon was called Queen Beatrice. 'She's a good bird,' he explained, 'and valuable.'

'How do I get her home?'

'I've contacted her owner and he'll ring you now too. His loft is in Uxbridge. He's Alexander Bulgharov. He's delighted, I can tell you.'

Alex Bulgharov was indeed delighted 'and relieved,' he admitted. 'I thought she might be a goner this time. She's never not made it back.'

'Where was she flying from?'

'Germany. Is she injured at all?'

'Not that I can tell. But she's not inclined to fly away either.'

'She must like you.'

'I'll take that as a compliment.'

'Do. Now, shall I come to you to collect her?'

'Actually, I wouldn't mind coming to you. I could do with getting out of my place. It's been quite a start to the year and a trip might be just the thing.'

Which was how Karen Dash found herself trekking across the capital on the top deck of a red bus with a pigeon in a box on her knee. She had reasoned that the tube, although direct, would be terrifyingly noisy for the bird and besides, it was unnatural for the creature to be in the ground. 'We both belong in the air,' she told it.

They drew stares from other passengers, possibly because Karen found herself chatting softly to let Queen Beatrice know where they were, that she was still here with her and all was well. They changed buses at Shepherd's Bush, a place Karen always found depressing and down-at-heel. Funny, for someone who lives in Soho, she thought, an area most people thought seedy and low. There was a vitality about where she lived whereas Shepherd's Bush seemed hopeless to her. Even the green looked as if it had given up the ghost. The bus started to climb and the trees multiplied. She looked into long, well-tended gardens. She began to get excited. This was a day trip. She was practically in the countryside where no one knew her or could judge what she was or the mistakes she might have made up till now.

The house was a detached redbrick on the bend of a quiet road. Karen skirted the car in the driveway and stood looking through a metal gate at the gardens to the side and back of the property. A small, old man was standing by a bare vegetable patch and muttering to himself. It seemed like gibberish. Karen cleared her throat and he glanced her way and began to shout in a guttural language she couldn't understand. He came through the gate offering his hand and she could see at close quarters that he was ancient. His eyes sparkled in a criss-cross of wrinkles.

'Sergei, Sergei,' he said over and over.

Karen accepted his handshake and said, 'Karen Dash.'

'Karen Dash?' He was incredulous.

What does he know? she wondered. How could I be famous in this sleepy corner of London?

'Karen Dash?' he asked again and when she said, 'Yes,' he let out a series of delighted hoots.

A man in his late thirties had appeared from the back of

26

the house. He, too, seemed amused. 'Miss Dash,' he said. 'Welcome. You have met our elder statesman, I see. I'm Alex.'

'What's so funny?' she asked.

'Karendash is the Russian word for pencil.'

'Ah.'

'*Da, da, da*,' the old man said, nodding, then shook his head at the wonder of it. 'Karendash.'

'I guess it's good to learn something new every day,' Karen remarked, wondering why no one on the Moscow route had ever mentioned it. 'For instance, I know a little about pigeons now, courtesy of Beatrice's stay with me.'

'May I?' Alex asked and gently took the box from her.

Karen followed him into the garden proper and saw that the bird loft was at the back alongside what looked like an artist's studio. Alex took the pigeon out and began to check her, gently pulling her wings out to look for injury. 'She seems totally fine to me,' he said. 'Thank you for looking after her so well. A bath and a snack and she'll be right as rain.'

'What kind of bird is she?' Karen asked. 'Aside from being a pigeon, that is.'

'She's a Blue Bar. See the stripe here on her wings? That's the bar bit and she's blue because she's grey, if that makes any sense.'

'Like a cat.'

'Yes, although I think that's the only similarity.' He smiled and his eyes crinkled.

The pigeon was now preening and leaning forward with her wings spread under an infrared light. If Queen Beatrice could have smiled, Karen was certain she would have.

The tiny man was at Karen's side and he said something quickly to Alex, who laughed.

'My uncle is pointing out that she'll soon be getting more than that by way of pleasure.'

'Oh?'

'Pigeons, you know? Kind of like rabbits in that respect.'

'Right,' Karen said, reddening. 'So there are lots of similarities with other creatures, it seems.'

She was rewarded again with the killer smile. He was so easy in his world. She noticed the wedding band on his finger. Oh well.

'*Chai*,' Sergei announced and beckoned for her to follow him, which she did. The cold air was welcome after the sticky heat of the loft and the proximity of That Smile.

It's the sort of house you never want to leave. A conservatory attached to the back of the house is bustling with people of assorted ages. The air buzzes with chat and there is such a palpable belonging and love to the people there, it hurts my heart, but in a good way. If I fell asleep now, no one would pay any heed, a blanket would be thrown over me and the impromptu party would continue. We drink strong tea, made with leaves not bags. I have rarely felt so welcome. But I do have to leave and, when I see an opportunity, I return to the pigeon loft with Alex to say my goodbyes to Queen Bea.

'Do you want to tell me what happened to you?' he asks and I am stunned that he would bother to be interested at all.

I shuffle a bit, trying to form coherent sentences that would explain Tony and what he's done, but I'm not sure I can yet and it feels a little false to try so I just let it all out.

'My best friend killed himself in my bath. It was an elegant, a peaceful enough, sort of exit but I am . . . shaken by it. He told me he loved me but not that he was going to do what he did. I'm . . . adrift . . . now and so heartsore I can hardly breathe.'

'Were you lovers?'

'No. He was gay so I guess you could say I wasn't his type.'

'Wonderful enough to kiss, though.'

'Yes. It's all a bit confused.'

'I remember reading a quote once that said love was friendship set on fire. Seemed as good an analysis as any other, don't you think?'

I realise that I am standing in this man's arms and I don't know how that happened but it feels the most natural thing in the world. I am acutely aware of his shape against mine. Predominant in my scrambled head is the notion that he fits snugly against me, though there is nothing snug or smug about how good my body finds that. He is a stranger, however, and so the norms kick in and I begin to wonder if he finds this weird. I want this good thing, this unexpected delight, to last but it cannot so I break away and stand on his foot as I do so but he doesn't mention it and I don't know whether I should. I am boiling with mortification. I blabber inadequate thanks for his kindness to me.

'Anytime. And now you know where we are, you must feel free to call by.'

I desperately want to ask about his wife but it's not appropriate. A lot of what's just happened is not. She must have been in the house when I was drinking tea. Which woman was she? A lad is at the door saying, 'Dad, dinner.'

'You are welcome to stay for that,' Alex tells me but I know if I do I will cry in front of these kind strangers and ruin their evening. I thank him and mutter about another time and I wonder to myself if he has any other children. I go to the house to say my goodbyes and I envy these people their situation. I am headed back to the city of the dispossessed, I feel. I am going to my cell, by myself, to be alone. I feel purposeless. So I decide to take the tube on my return journey because I want to be buried. It's also the quickest route and the sooner I get back to my single life in my single state, the better. Dissatisfaction with my lot will be easier to handle in the narrow confines of my two rooms and the sound from outside of the busy street of strangers will fill a void. It is not the hopeful adventure of the outward leg of the day and I am as low as I ever want to be.

Two young girls in fancy dress pass me at the entrance to Claxton Court. The younger, about six years old, is clearly a card. She smiles at me and asks, 'Can you hear the colours?'

I know she means the band's music.

'Yes,' I tell her. 'It's a Stylistics song. Do you like it?'

But they are gone without an answer. I feel less of a freak, now, however. I rarely mention the colours to anyone else because people think I am incorrectly wired when I do. It's nice to know that I'm not the only one.

I miss the bird already. I doubt she misses me. I know that if she's not asleep she's shagging. I wonder if pigeons do actually sleep. I know for a fact that they shag. I'll probably do neither tonight. Interestingly, I am sober now and decide to remain so. I am sharp for all the hurt these days have brought. I decide to relish the ache and cut of these events. I am alive.

I have to return to work. There is no way of avoiding it. I feel sour as I tell myself I should have gone to university, studied philosophy, or some other mindfuck, and given myself over to the world of ideas, imponderables, guff-stuff made up but with standing in certain circles and not the holding patterns above Heathrow. Literature, even, might have yielded a life dedicated to other people's excellence or, at least, their splendid failures. Instead I can look forward to the Moscow route.

It is as hateful as ever it was and lacking in the edge that Tony always brought it. I almost feel we are not doing it justice as a result. I cannot quite believe how I am treated by the other staff. Their reactions are so over the top as to be insane. Alice Mulville says, 'Awww,' into my face with such insincerity I almost gag. She hated Tony more than it's possible to express. The loathing was appropriately mutual and gave my dead colleague much pleasure as a result. 'I feel it has all the emotional urgency of a good friendship, love even,' he once remarked. It gave him great purpose, though not enough to continue with life, clearly.

There is some blame they are tarring me with, those who hardly knew Tony, and I resent that so much I get a metallic taste in my mouth. When I was a child I used to experience that before my worst nightmares. No need to fear sleep and those dreams now because I am living them. Those who did know Tony are treating me either as a pariah who may have brought bad luck along with her or as a dysfunctional widow, the latter meaning they stare pityingly into my face but want to wring as many gory details from me as possible. I hate humans, now, nearly as much as Tony professed to. A BU in steerage gives me grief and I take great joy in gobbing into her vodka and Diet Coke. It is the only time I smile all day.

I am paired with an Irish newbie, Colm O'Callaghan, and he looks worried that he's pulled the shortest straw ever offered by this airline. He's only at the beginning of his sentence here so I go easy on him.

'Relax,' I say. 'I'm not passing the death thing on today. You'll be fine.'

It's the least I can do. I hope I haven't lied to the boy. I am unsure what is true or even interesting any more. And I sure as hell have no idea what's important. Must go, Moscow.

soon

One generation passeth away, and another genera-tion cometh: but the earth abideth forever.

The sun also ariseth, and the sun goeth down, and hasteth to his place where he arose.

The wind goeth to the south, and turneth about unto the north; it whirleth about continually, and the wind returneth again according to his circuits.

All the rivers run into the sea; yet the sea is not full; unto the place from whence the rivers come, thither they return again.

Ecclesiastes, King James Bible

february 2144

Colin heard the Other's voice first as he entered the Claxton Court apartment. Theo was evidently finishing a story with some gusto. This, followed by Alice laughing, spurred an instant, violent grating in him. 'MY wife,' Colin wanted to scream. 'I am the one who should make her laugh, not you.' Instead, he called, 'I'm home,' and slowly removed his acid-rain overalls to allow them time to gather themselves. He smelt food cooking and it evoked a memory so potent, of his parents and his brother, his eyes welled suddenly with unhappiness and a longing for the distant past, or any time pre the Other.

As he entered the main room he saw himself sitting on the sofa, *so* perfectly identical. He would probably never get used to that. He preferred a mirror image, he knew that now. A flesh and blood reality was too much of a challenge. At least when he moved away from a mirror he was alone again and solely himself. Here, he had an unwanted self, he had Theo: his very own clone. Theo, annoyingly, had chosen to dress in similar clothes today too. If asked, he would probably shrug and say, 'I do as you do, you know that. I have no other choice.' And there was the rub: he did have a choice. Theo appeared to be entirely in possession of his own free will but he liked instead to use Colin and thereby divert blame or dilute it. He had been got from kindness, love even, but somewhere a vital component had gone astray.

Colin was caught in his stare. He looked guileless, this Theo, and should have been, but Colin was convinced he was not. His belief that the Other had secret and ulterior motives could not be shaken. Everything Theo did had an agenda attached, he felt, an alternative reason to that given. Above all, Colin hated his suave ease. How had Theo managed that, when he himself could not? Even Theo's identical clothes looked better on. And yet he was made of Colin and entirely in his likeness. How could the perfect match be so unbearable, so loathable?

'Darling,' Alice called and came to kiss him. 'You look forlorn.'

'It's a shitty night.' On cue, thunder sounded and lightning flashed. He felt like rolling his eyes in acknowledgement of the soap opera that his life was trying to become.

'Well, we don't know that, yet, do we?' Alice was saying. She glanced at Theo and they exchanged a smile.

I can just about guarantee it, Colin wanted to say. After all, we have the cuckoo here, nudging us ever towards the edge. The sight of his wife made Colin's heart contract painfully. It had to be argued that Alice was well out of his league, that it actually hurt him to think of his good fortune in winning this extraordinary prize. She was easy with her beauty, would question that it existed as he seemed to think it did. The wonder that she had chosen him never diminished. Theo clearly appreciated her as much and that lurched Colin murderously close to homicidal thoughts yet again.

He stood in front of the picture window looking out on to Pig Lane. He could see his reflection created by the light in the apartment and the darkness outside. Theo stood behind him, an identical echo. And so here he was, and there in the reflection and also, to the side of that reflection, his Other. Three versions of Colin: me, myself and I, he thought. He moved off but his image remained in complex silhouette.

'You need a drink,' Alice said and went to prepare him one. Theo didn't indulge in alcohol, as they had not implanted that need in him. Colin had been selective and now regretted that. Whenever he drank he had to deal with a more alert version of himself across the room. They needed to get Theo a hobby that took him out more. He also regretted allowing his brother's name to be used, however foreshortened for this Other. They should have just called him Teddy in proper mockery of what they had attempted and be done with it, since it was Teddy he was supposed to replace, or help recover in some measure. Recovery? It was a foolish notion. Colin could not do that. He would never recover. Teddy was gone and Theo was a fact of an increasingly miserable life, Alice or no. He wondered at their naive arrogance, thinking they could mend what was unmendable. He had lost half of himself and that half could never be replaced, let alone recovered. He thought about what Teddy would make of him now.

'I am a self-indulgent twat,' Colin said, as his wife handed him a strong drink.

'Whatever you say, dear.'

In the corner, Theo laughed; worst of all, he did so quietly.

✿   ✿   ✿

It had become Colin's habit to get up early and walk to the market on Berwick Street to buy croissants or waffles for the household, deliver them home and sneak away to have his breakfast alone at his desk in the office. He knew it meant too much solitude for contemplating impossibilities but it suited his present mood to be indulgent. It was a present mood that had lasted longer than expected or welcome but his mind was still confused and unhappy and he played a waiting game with it on one side while nudging it into self-revelation on the other. The process exhausted him.

The rain was still just a drizzle so the early-morning shoppers had mostly opted for umbrellas as protection rather than full overalls. He had the choice of shops at the side of the street or the stalls under striped awnings along the middle of the road. There had been an open-air market here for centuries and by all accounts it hadn't changed a lot in that time. People still needed to buy food to eat, bags to hold and clothes to wear. Some simply wanted the chat of commerce and the idea that they'd got a good deal from another human being. The tourists loved the quaintness. Today a man in an apron was shouting out a delivery of fresh fish while another had a special on oranges just in.

A small girl stood fascinated before a display of fabric. She pointed and said, 'Look, oh look at all the colours. It's like a rainbow.'

The effect on Colin was stark and immediate. He broke sweat to think of a multicoloured arc stretching across clear sky. The image was so unsettling to him now that his breath grew jagged and nausea threatened to make him physically ill here in public. He stood completely still, facing a grey wall, to quell the dizziness. Pinpricks of light spotted his vision, projecting beyond on to the wall. His traitor brain began to record their symmetry and pattern as if something beautiful might be made of this moment of awful reminder. Colour was stalking him, insisting that he address it again and put it back into his work. He closed his eyes and watched the rhythm his blood stamped on his lids. His heart, incorrigible, was still beating. Teddy's was not. Eventually, he settled enough to feel able to walk again without staggering or drawing undue attention.

He was turning left on to Broadwick Street when the police screamed to a halt on high-velocity bikes.

'Clear,' they hollered, voices amplified electronically from within their full-faced helmets.

The populace flattened against any available surface or fled in an opposite direction. The sight of the black-suited law-keepers never failed to strike fear and it rarely signalled a happy event. The shining metal uniforms covered the operatives' bodies entirely and probably concealed clones. Any cop worth employing was copied and kept, the original, if he or she was still alive, probably at the controls located under a building by the river. Colin looked at the citizens trying to be invisible and was stunned again at the collective and so-called wisdom of a crowd. Just as the police were camouflaged, so too the townspeople were hiding under umbrellas, using the rain as an excuse to assume an off-event stance, that of emphatically not getting involved. This is how evil might flourish, he thought, when we stand and remain neutral. At the same time, he did not interfere. I am as bad or as mediocre as the next ordinary man, he thought. I am the Crowd. It did little to cheer him.

Each police operative fired off a tazer, blazing scarlet electrical charges forward to snag the running suspect. He was quickly scanned for ID and, having none, was immobilised and made ready for the Slumber Van, which would freeze and transport his body to a place of reckoning. If he was deemed illegal, or dangerous, he might be left in a cryogenic state indefinitely, or harvested for organs and neutralised.

Colin was left low by the morning's outing. February was a beast, the month with more suicides than any other, year after year, short as it was on days. This, of course, was a leap year so there were twenty-nine days of opportunity for the terminally depressed to become a statistic. Colin knew he was not one of those who would take the ultimate step. He deemed himself a coward on all levels. He could not face going into the office so he sat at his home table with Alice and Theo, pushing a waffle around his plate, and glowering.

Colin cannot stand the sight of me and that's a fact of our lives. I offend him in every way, it seems. I cannot tell you exactly what his feelings are or precisely what goes on in his head because, although I am made in his image, I have not been given all of his life experiences so my back story is incomplete in that way. There is a selection process now with clones that tailors us to whatever is needed by our progenitors. I am one of the lucky ones in that I was not bred to be harvested for organs but as a straight swap for someone who is gone. In this case it was Teddy, Colin's twin. Teddy's DNA was not usable but Colin's was so I am Him, rather than his identical twin, though I must be very like Teddy too, I imagine. And, yes, I can imagine. I am a human being, after all. I feel what

42

other humans do although I am, strictly speaking, Other. This is a moot point at times with Colin. I once quoted him Article One of the Universal Declaration of Human Rights during a vicious row. It's ancient but helpful as a moral yardstick. I felt driven to it. I had to raise my voice. 'All human beings are born free and equal in dignity and rights,' I said.

'You weren't born,' he screamed back, 'you were got.'

'I was begot,' I countered, but semantics wasn't going to get us far when he was in this sort of vile mood.

I wanted to follow with more: 'They are endowed with reason and conscience and should act towards one another in a spirit of brotherhood.' These ideals are enshrined for good reason: our basic humanity abides. It must. I am not a disposable nuisance. I am made flesh and must be respected. But Colin has lost his beloved sibling and will be some time returning to the notion of brotherhood even in the wider sense.

I believe he sees me as a mockery of what his life has become and he cannot endure that. He was ill prepared for me, in spite of the well-meaning reasons I was made for him. Alice has apologised many times, for it was she who thought it would be an aid to his recovery. He blames himself for Teddy's death, whether unfairly or not I don't know as he has not spoken to me about it, so I have a steep journey to make to ease his pain or assuage the guilt that stalks him every day. Neither have I asked Alice about it as I've always felt she would say something of her own volition if she needed to. It's an area I am in the dark about but it joins quite a few others in that category and so is not unusual.

Colin has many gifts and I share them, I'm happy to report. He is quick-witted, handsome and a talented fabric designer.

I am all of these things too, according to plan. What I am missing is the pain of his experience. Sometimes I long for it, feel that it would make me whole. Alice says I should be glad I was not given it entirely, that I would be tortured and she couldn't cope with two of us in that state.

'Call me selfish but I'm relieved things are only this bad,' she tells me.

I would never call Alice selfish, no matter what. I love her, as Colin does, but I was not given all of the memories and experiences that attach to that part of his life either, so my love is young, immature, and I probably seem a little teenage and foolish in that area. It is my first time to be in love, naturally. Although I'm physically forty-two years old, as Colin is, I have only been in the world for two years so I'm still learning things, often the hard way.

Alice is in the business of babies. She helps out when humans want to make them the old-fashioned way through sexual conjoining and the mingling within a woman's body of egg and sperm. She delivers the offspring and is called a midwife. She might have made a child with Colin but Teddy's death has affected every aspect of their lives and seems to have set up a blockage to that dream. Sometimes she does dangerous things: she helps the Illegals, which is strictly speaking against the Law. She is fearless, though, and says they deserve their chance as much as any of the rest of us. She is a fair person and the sooner she's called up to serve on the Council for the country, the better for all.

Colin grew in his mother's womb and shared it with his brother. I am a part of him but was grown alone. I wonder if that means anything at all, but I do think it's a fact worth mentioning, the separateness of how I was made. I was grown in a womb too, but an artificial one. Over time, cloning has evolved, like so much else. If I had been made in the early twenty-first century I would have been grown in a human womb, perhaps a surrogate one, and born as a small baby. We have moved on and now the likes of me can be born an adult. I don't have any less time, necessarily, as the babies did back whenever because although they were juvenile they were born with aged genes. I differ slightly from Colin in that my eyes are a deeper blue and, as I've said, he could choose what he wanted my mind to know at the start. My mitochondrial material is from him and if I had been conceived in the altogether more traditional human way, that material would have come to me via my mother. In a way Colin is both parents to me, or largely so. Yet I can't speak to him as I might a traditional parent, particularly as he seems to loathe me.

The manipulation of my memories and mental state is an interesting area. Back in the twenty-first century scientists were working on how the human brain might be stretched or improved. They studied Ordinary Man versus the Super Normals, wondering whether genius was born or made. Was talent an inherent quality or one that could be nurtured? Every time, a definitive solution to this quest has evaded us because that's all part of the glory of the human condition. It can be regulated but only to a certain extent because in the end Man is in charge in all his faulted glory.

Different people are hard-wired to be excellent in certain fields. If everyone were brilliant at everything, the world would be one big boring waste of time. We are various. We are multitude. We should celebrate that.

I want to talk to Colin about hope and what life might hold for me. I want to tell him that I am hungry for my time here to be a fulfilling one. I know he sees me as a pastiche of humanity but I am boiling happy to be alive and for that I need, simply, to thank him. I want to explain that I sometimes despair because I have much less time to look forward to here than an actual child has (I was born aged forty-two, after all). I am lonely, even in this heaving city, but I feel I belong and he should respect that. I question my identity, which is his also, but not altogether. These things remain unsaid, unexplored between us. Colin can never engage with or learn to love me until he learns to love himself. Alice agrees.

He could have me terminated at any time but low as he feels and much though he detests me I don't think he will take that dark path. He cannot just decide to do that off his own bat because I am a clone that was rendered sensate so he would have to apply to the authorities to be rid of me. It's worrying, though, frightening; I'll admit that. Those bred for harvesting are never activated but kept in a state of deepest uncluttered slumber. If Colin were to kill me without permission, it would be a kind of murder but it happens to my sort all the time and mostly goes unpunished. There are potentially lots more where I came from. There is no need to mourn the loss of one, or a few, or any of us.

Humans have opted to stay imperfect, having no other choice, it must be said. They still experience accidental death and genetic throwbacks no matter how carefully they select and refine their tissue. I think that's all part of the splendour of being human and I'm glad I was called up to be a part of it. I get excited to be alive even if my immediate surroundings are soured by Colin's loathing. I want to experience it all and massively too, greedily.

Disease has been curbed largely, of course, but still it gets through. You've got to admire the blind determination of a bacterium or a germ, those tiny little biological machines waiting to pounce when conditions are just right. These pathogens have no agenda, because they have no thoughts or opinions, they just do what they have to, to thrive, to survive. I've looked into history and know that vibrio cholerae, a perfect cholera, was a frequent visitor to these parts down through the centuries.

I made a series of patterns from pictures of the cholera bacterium for our spring collection of fabrics last year. It was one of my first jobs and I found it tricky to portray the rice-like molecules as pretty and oblong rather than small and wormy looking. I used vibrant colours, some quite acid and clashing, to represent the agility and speed of the disease. I thought it a beautifully efficient entity, you see, and I wondered if I could make it attractive. It tickled me that Soho history had informed the designs. They sold well and Alice also installed some cushion covers from the range at home, which was a compliment. I was thrilled by the whole process. For once, Colin did not criticise me but kept his silence. I preferred that to negative comment.

Pestilence and sex have always been part of Soho. It's almost quaint that people still want to experience intercourse with another being, even though there are so many more assured ways of 'getting off', as they say. We can project any imaginings courtesy of our advances in brain science and technology. We can move objects without touching them. We can experience a wealth of sensations independently of others. There is nothing, however, to replace a human touch, the closeness of another person; affection tangibly and physically granted. I crave it.

I am a romantic, you could say. And here's the thing, I was not specifically implanted with this trait. I have evolved it for myself. So in this way I'm progressing as a person and not just an acolyte or spin-off of Colin's, although I am that too.

I meet many more like me every day on the streets of Soho. We are microchipped but that is not what sets us apart as everyone has that sort of identification. We Others have extra chips, of course, but we also have a tattooed number on our forearm that we must try to keep visible at all times so that Hundred Percenters can tell who is who.

My iridological profile is unique to me, however, although I'm a clone, and I like that: it gratifies my need to be seen as properly human, which I am. It pleases me that I have this biometrical marker, thousands of fibrillae forming a pattern to distinguish me as myself and apart, in spite of my ties to Colin and that I am beholden to him for my life. I am in fact unique, like a snowflake. And is it not mind-bending to think that no two snowflakes have ever been the same in the history of time, which is itself of such proportions that, still, even the most powerful artificial minds can only give it that hoary old variation of the power of 'n': the eternal cop-out of the infinite. Though I'll hand it to that infinite that it will never give in and be explainable. I love that and it makes me laugh, it makes me rejoice to the power of 'n'. I wonder if my joke just now would have made Colin smile too, if I could have shared it with him, if he would let me in.

Last night he called himself a twat and something about the way he said it was so deliciously self-deprecating and hangdog that I couldn't help myself but laugh. I did it quietly so as not to upset him. He didn't look pleased. I don't know what I did wrong.

'It is a form of self-loathing, then, you say?' The therapist frowned as he waited on Colin's response, a studied expression and practised. Bogus, Colin felt, but then everything was poisoned and poisonous today. Every day.

'Yes, in essence it is. Well, it must be, mustn't it?' Colin wondered if he hated the sound of his own voice too, as the professional must surely by now. Try having it in stereo, he thought, then you'd know all about hating a voice.

'*Must* it?' The other man had a deliberately sonorated tone, commensurate with his sage profession. Wonder how long that took to perfect? Did he know it didn't match how he looked, which to Colin was goat-like at best?

'Logically, yes,' Colin insisted, amazed again that he wasted his money on a man who didn't care about him or his life and perhaps didn't really understand what the nature of the problem was. These sessions were certainly not yielding the sort of results that sent him home with any less murderous thoughts than he had arrived with. It was always a relief to hear the clock chime and know that he could hand over his money, like washing his hands, and tell himself the lie that at least he was dealing with his lot. His 'lot', of course, was at home waiting, usually with another layer of intrigue added by the time he got there.

'Have you asked this other man to leave?'

'Umpteen times, but he always wriggles out of actually going. And he is my responsibility, after all, ultimately, so I am stuck with him.'

'Yes,' the quack admitted, lowly, reluctantly. 'You did rather call him up.'

Colin swallowed a retort of, 'For this, much thanks.' He was actually too weary to engage with the psych man or himself much more at that point and, therefore, sarcasm was almost totally beyond him. He found the professional creepy, knew he'd avoid talking to him if they met at a party, either for the first time or now after umpteen visits. Like so much of his life, this aspect was somehow a fixture and he had no idea how to shed the situation or to make good again.

Initially he had hoped that simply talking the situation through reasonably, with a dispassionate observer, would provide a breakthrough. I am a civilised man, he'd told himself, reason will triumph and all will be well in my world. Even as those naive sentiments rattled around, he knew that a miracle was the only thing that could help. Replacing a life now lost to him was the only solution that could make any true differ- ence, although the replacing of a life was exactly what had got him to this juncture. What he needed to do was change the way he lived now and he could not see a way through to that.

The therapy was further isolating him, he knew that. At some buried level he recognised it as a deeply selfish activity, especially when all he seemed to do with it was mull over the same problem, letting it fester. He relished the bitching about his lot. He didn't want to move on. It drained him. It afforded him a deeply horrible satisfaction that he knew he would have to jettison. Just not yet. He felt a need, still, to be self-centred.

He took the elevator attached to the side of the building sixty-six floors to the ground, while getting into his protective raingear and trying to see some majesty in the city as he was lowered from on high. He stepped out into the street and heard, then felt, a rumbling just as lightning slashed across the sky. The spindly fork looked like a crone's accusatory point. I'm at the hub of the storm, he thought, with the querulous weather lending a pseudo-metaphysical element to his already troubled existence. The heavens unleashed a late-afternoon onslaught of acid rain. The large drops reflected the sky's light which was green today and so with encouragement from the waning dusk sun, it rendered the spitting rain jade or emerald or, at times, a more brackish moss colour that reflected his mood. He remembered that Alice used it as a face peel from time to time: beautiful and horrid all at once.

He made his way along the high-rises of Regent Street, the classical facades of earlier centuries backing stoically on to tall stretches of fifty storeys and more, the modern inner-city tenements. The later architecture, if it could truly be deemed that, was chrome and dark glass, uniform and threatening. The angry sky was reflected in the glass frontages and therefore rendered endless in its gloom. Others walking the street were also in full rain overalls, the cream fabric covering them from tip to toe against the weather's nasty sting. The headgear, with its clear visor to the front, made everyone look like the beekeepers of the early twenty-first century when bees survived wild, for a short time, without aid from mankind. Then, he knew, this time of day would have been brighter. Now, there were usually only varying degrees of dusk. And rain.

Soho was the last low-rise left in the capital. It was kept

cutesy for its historical purpose, depravity. But notwithstanding that parenthesis, there were still pockets of ordinary citizens, like himself, who lived there, by choice and with as much history pertaining to them, and who did not necessarily support or rely on the major local industry. Colin passed the display windows of women and men vying to lure him to try their wares. He was inured against it, shored up in general, now, to cravings of the flesh. His Other Self had seen to that. Although his wife, Alice, had not complained about the neglect she was suffering and that was a worry that gnawed at him.

They'd had a supremely awkward moment on Valentine's Day when Colin presented his wife with roses and Theo gave her a card he had made himself. Although the roses had been incredibly difficult to source, and had cost a small fortune, it was clear to all three of them that the handcrafted gift was entirely more beautiful and therefore seemed so much more heartfelt.

The fact was, Alice had two of him to choose from now. He shook the thought off as being so reprehensible as to be unthinkable. But it had been thought and it was in the mix now. He wondered how much further he could sink.

Night was fast encroaching and the first of the city wraiths began to appear at the edges of his vision. These were the shadow people, the illegal workers: cheaper, unregulated. There was nothing that could not be bought in Soho after dark. Lewd and whispered entreaties now. What did Sir want? Young, old, filthy, pure, human, animal? 'All for your delight, sir.' A grown man passed by but half Colin's height. Here was the other stream of industry working in the area; the man was a profes- sional beggar. He'd had his legs removed below the knee to suit his way of life. The tourists were keen for this and the seediness of the place, all the local colour they could ever crave, delivered with vehemence. This man would have a wife and children proud that he did his job so well, to the highest standard. Soho had not changed through the centuries. Everyone was still up for the stroke, physical or metaphorical. Everyone was still on the make. Everyone was still turning a bob. Human evolution, he reminded himself with a shiver. Is it any wonder I am in therapy? The grey-cold seeped into his bones as he hurried down Pig Lane and into Claxton Court.

Louise was Teddy's but, once upon a time, I wanted her for myself. When we were callow, and we were, we played one trick on her that led her to hate me but forgive Teddy and then I was no more, didn't figure, in her estimation. I should have seen then how me and Teddy were different though we revelled in our similarities. We would regularly swap while taking to people: even in vision, on Telekit for example, we could get away with it as we had identical voices as well as appearance. In reality it was a subtler state of affairs, but doable. We got a kick out of it and had no thought that it might wound. To us it was a lark and a shared one at that, so all the more desirable.

One night I saw Louise, not Teddy. Early days, I should add, even if that's no excuse. We thought it would be a hoot. It was, until I realised how I felt about her and then, when she found out, how she felt about me. Looking back, my favourite habit, I realise I fell for her because she treated me like Teddy and I was feeling her joy at being with him. It was false all the way through, built on shifting sands. That was hard to stomach, this realisation that I was lesser to someone because I was not the other me, I was not enough, not actually the very same. It felt like the lowest blow at the time but that was before Teddy died, which was a nadir I still find impossible to shake. There are always further depths to plunge, it seems.

I want Teddy back. I want the better part of me here, now. He was the one with the mind, the intellect, something to offer. He was working on things that might change how we live, better our humanity. I create non-essential luxuries, even if Alice says the comfort they bring is important too in our streamlined, chromed age. Why couldn't I have been the one to be taken? Why did death want him yet not me? If we were so close in life, why not also in death? How was it we were denied an identical death?

Teddy was a pathologist who worked on the human brain. It's a part of us that we still cannot entirely explain away. I even see Theo showing spirit beyond him being an offshoot of me, and Teddy would have been fascinated by that. I got the Art and Teddy got the Science but he was insistent that there were vast areas where both move as one. According to him, it was like the poet Keats said: that we move between uncertainties. But he was certain of a few things and one was that although in the vast history of mankind many have believed in another life after this, there won't be one. You can believe any amount of archaic, God-based religions, he used to say, but it ends with us here. And that, he insisted, is actually enough, too, and nothing short of a miracle: that we have lived and loved at all.

A miracle.

I have no reason to doubt him although nothing feels much like miraculous awe or astonishment any more. He always said he envied my joy in pattern and colour but I think he had all of that working on the tissue that makes us interesting and unique, the stuff inside our heads. Science has been able to pictorialise it all for us over the centuries but not what makes us choose what we do: the instant, almost artistic, responses that we make to our every day.

Teddy was an enormously positive force at work and in life. He shared his findings and wisdom easily, as he did his thoughts and affections. I sometimes feel I am more reserved. I loved the times he included me in his research. The brain is such a beautiful, patterned place. I made a whole season's designs from his study on the remains of a great mathematician. It is one of my most colourful and happy collections. So perhaps he was right and we do tread similar, complementary ground, the artist and the man of science.

I can still talk to Teddy. We all have the facility to access our Memory Palaces from wherever we are. Science again has provided the brain with some handy advances to help us humans. Tonight I take myself to the little spare room we use for this, which we all call the Cupboard, to see my brother. I could sit with Alice and Theo but we like to respect a little privacy, even if it feels too little these days, like an old-fashioned notion of decency.

My imagination can make Teddy real, vivify his image. I can call up smells too if I want. It can be a comfort and some-times a strange torture.

He is on to my case immediately. 'Have you seen Louise?'

'No. She doesn't want to see me, you know that. It's too

painful because I look like you. She won't do Telekit. I sound so like you that even if she closes her eyes, I remind her too much of you. It's no wonder she avoids me.'

'You do talk, though.'

'Yes, she will at least talk to me, but it's not regular and the chat is just that, all very general and usually very brief.'

'You need to sort that out. It's been two years so I think you are both ready to take your lives into another phase.' He laughs. 'I know I have.'

He makes me smile with that. He always had that dark humour the Medicals are gifted.

'And what about Theo?'

'What about him?'

'You should give him more to do. He's talented, like you. And he's funny too, you know. You'd enjoy him if you gave him even half a chance. You have to start cutting him some slack. What you're about is tantamount to torture. If he were a dog you'd be reported to the authorities for the way you treat him.'

'Thanks for that.'

'Don't mention it.'

He is maddening positive, this other man, this other me. I can't help it, it seeps into me and I rally. 'If he'd been a dog he'd have cost a hell of a lot more,' I say.

'True. Though I'm not going to call that a good point, because it's not. Now cheer up and get on with your short life. Yes?'

'I'll try.'

'Good.'

I leave the room, and the experience, in better form until

I realise that I can't have been talking to Teddy. Teddy is dead. All I have done is talk to myself, effectively. I have indulged in escapism. But a niggle at the back of my complicated and unexplainable brain also says, 'Plus you weren't so bad to talk to either, were you?'

'How was Teddy?' Alice asks.

I want to say, 'Dead,' and make her laugh with that but a sudden onset of such humour in me might shock her and I'm not certain I'd carry it off properly. My tone has been a problem for quite a while. I settle for, 'A lot like me', and she grins. 'He says I should give Theo more to do in the business and I think he might be right. It would also mean he'd be out from under our feet a bit more.'

'I think that would be great and Theo would be delighted. Why don't you go tell him now?'

We're moving too fast and I panic slightly. I don't want to talk to him at this very moment. 'Actually, I need to sleep on it and formulate a plan so let's leave it for now, eh?'

'But not for too long.'

'No. I'll talk to him tomorrow.' There, I'm committed now. It feels odd and not necessarily good but I have to move on, or sideways at least, and perhaps this will start that. I suspect the Other is listening intently at his door and that annoys me. I feel hemmed in again but must not let it disturb me as much as it normally would. I need to take charge of my life and him.

I heard Alice and Colin talk about me last night. He knew it too and said, 'I know you've been listening.' I waited for the reprimand but it didn't come, just, 'Goodnight.' In many ways this was a small triumph as the man can hardly bear to bid me the time of day so this, even if it was a valediction, was welcome and open-ended: it was not a final farewell or anything. Now, whatever he has dreamt or however last night's sleep has affected him, this morning he is different. He says he wants to discuss work later. He still cannot look me in the eye properly but says to the air, 'I'm going to, em, relate to you from now on and, em, try to do without the, em, therapist.' He 'ems' when he's uncomfortable, unsure how to phrase a difficulty, and it can be a tell of his mood even if he appears level. Perhaps Alice has stepped up for me.

Most extraordinary of all he talks about his twin.

'So how did Teddy die?' He pauses and it's almost like a parody of a joke where I'm supposed to say, 'I don't know, how did Teddy die?' Colin, mercifully, continues without this charade. 'He fell. Such a simple thing to do, you might say. But perhaps the straightforward is good for humans in terms of explaining something, an event, that cannot be accepted, and falling to your death is a pretty uncluttered concept. I can't think that way, of course, because I was there and it was anything but simple or a fine conceptual notion.'

He is over-speaking, aghast to be talking of this at all but determined to get through it as if verbiage will cloak the horror of it and the very act of uttering this tragedy will ease its way into our small Soho world and make it somehow palatable or somehow acceptable, even, as a fact.

And so those facts, as told by my progenitor, are that Teddy and Colin were playing a game of ball-throwing at the time. Colin had thrown to Teddy and, as he reached up and out to catch the ball, Teddy went over the railings at the apartment at Claxton Court and fell to his death. They could have played the game indoors, virtually, but they were on the move to the open air on a rare, good weather day and horsing about as they travelled. Colin speaks quite lyrically as he recalls the sight of his brother balletically stretching his limbs to follow the flight of the ball.

'He began his leap like a dancer and was suspended before me in the air as I laughed and assured him he would never catch that ball. He turned his face back to me, in the slow motion that memory often lends the big occasion, and he smiled and I know now he was saying goodbye right there. He knew his miscalculation.' He shakes himself and with it shakes away the poetry, because this fatality is nasty again now and he feels culpable. 'But mostly I had overthrown and egged him on to his death.'

It is so odd to see my mortal mirror image with such hurt in his face, hardly able to suck in enough breath to sustain him, and these anguished tears in his eyes. Now they are running along his identical face. I want to wipe them away. I want to taste them, which surprises me. But if I so much as flinch I will lose this first, vital moment of true and tender contact I have ever had with him. I dare not breathe.

'Louise is coming to visit,' he tells me then. 'It won't be easy.'

He walks away.

This news is as devastating as it is simple.

Louise.

To say, or even whisper, her name is to invoke the tangled past. It was inevitable that she would finally have to face us, and we her. Louise is about to be made real to me. The idea, the prospect makes me shiver. This won't be easy, at all. I look at Alice and see her rub the inner run of her left arm which aches when Colin is difficult and lashes out to hurt us or push us away. He has done neither here but it hurts all the same.

Louise.

I have always felt my destiny to be wrapped in hers. It might be foolish to imagine it but I think it is no mistake that February, the most romantic of months, has delivered the idea of her to me more tangibly than any other could. February carried the news to me that she will visit. I have waited a long time for this. I have waited my whole life.

Louise.

then

Here's fine rosemary, sage and thyme.
Come buy my ground ivy.
Here's fetherfew, gilliflowers and rue.
Come buy my knotted majorum, ho!
Come buy my mint, my fine greenmint.
Here's fine lavender for your cloaths.
Here's parsley and winter-savory,
And hearts-ease, which all do choose.
Here's balm and hissop, and cinquefoil,
All fine herbs, it is well known.
Let none despise the merry, merry cries
Of famous London-town!

Here's fine herrings, eight a groat.
Hot codlins, pies and tarts.
New mackerel! have to sell.
Come buy my Wellfleet oysters, ho!
Come buy my whitings fine and new.
Wives, shall I mend your husbands horns?
I'll grind your knives to please your wives,
And very nicely cut your corns.
Maids, have you any hair to sell,
Either flaxen, black or brown?
Let none despise the merry, merry cries
Of famous London-town!

Anon (17th century), 'The Cries of London'

march 1854

London is the noisiest and most crowded and foulest smelling place I have ever been. I should explain that I have not been to many places, but no matter, it is still my understanding that this city would rate as very noisy and crowded and foul smelling no matter what the circumstance or comparison. So the Master says, and he is a man who is much travelled. I think that our area, Soho, is perhaps also infamous for being all of these things to extreme and that other parts of London are gentler but I have not been here long and have not seen much else except the streets about the house, like Broad Street, Poland Street, Golden Square and the rest. These are teeming and I fancy when birds fly above us we people look like ants on an anthill.

I am accustomed to the smell of dung, of course, from my father's farm but it is the smell of human dung that is worst in the city. It is everywhere, in the gutters and in the basements of the poorer houses, and some not so poor too. There are animals also in these places, and one man close by has a cow in his attic room, but I think theirs a natural smell whereas the city folk are rank, or that is my opinion at any rate. This place is like a giant cesspit.

My Aunt Nell says my thoughts count for nought and I should keep them to myself. She says I am nothing but a jabberer and should speak only when I am spoken to and not draw attention as it is not my station which is nowhere in the household because I am little more than a skivvy and should remember that and, besides, no one is in the least bit interested what a girl of fourteen years has to say for herself nor would any person ask. But there she is wrong, because the Master asks me questions, from time to time, and sometimes I think he is smiling a little when I answer but I am not sure. Miss Cecily who is but six years old asks a lot of questions too and laughs out loud when the answers please her. She is a most singular and curious little girl and mischief from the top of her head to the tip of her toes. And perhaps I am not so lowly if the Master and Mistress trust me to care for her occasionally, which they do.

Our house is on Pig Lane and it is a grand one. There is a cobbled courtyard through the big gate, with a stable for the two horses that pull the Master's carriage, and the house itself has three storeys over a basement. The household dog, Rex, has a box in the courtyard too but spends most of his time guarding the place from all but the Master and Aunt Nell. He is a mean cur who looks like he could eat you without a second thought or bothering to pass wind thereafter in response to such a deed.

Most houses on Pig Lane are divided into lodgings and have many families living in them but not ours. I say 'ours' but it is, of course, the property of the Master and we live here under his roof and work for him. Outside, the air may be thickly charged with foul odours but here at home we have a sweeter vapour to breathe. We work hard to keep it spick and span. It is fragrant, of course, though anything would be by comparison with the outside street. Every day is filled with cleaning from the dark early hours to the dark of night.

I braid my hair carefully each morning because Aunt Nell is a stickler for neatness and says it must be kept out of the way and woe betide me if she ever finds so much as one single strand of it in her kitchen. It would be easy to tell if it was mine as my hair is white and curled. Aunt Nell says it is messy as a whin bush. Miss Cecily loves to pull a curl out straight to see how far it will reach. Last time it went all the way down my back and sprang back up so jauntily that the little girl laughed for an age and spent the rest of the day talking about how far my hair would reach if we stretched each curl back to back. She decided it would go all the way to China.

Aunt Nell runs the house like a sergeant major does his soldiers. She even has a little moustache. In the mornings my first task is to open up the shutters to let what light there is in and then I see to the kitchen fire. Aunt Nell will give me a cup of tea and slice of bread before she begins to prepare the family breakfast, but I must be quick about eating and drinking. She checks me over, paying great attention to my hands and nails. When I pass muster, I go upstairs again and lay a cloth on the dining table and put the fixings out for the meal. When the Master, Mistress and Miss Cecily are done, I take the plates and so on to the kitchen and wash them. Then I get to cleaning whatever needs doing, under the watchful eye of Aunt Nell and the Mistress.

There is water inside the house, which is quite a new and modern thing. Most people live on top of each other in other houses around us and must get their water from a street pump. We have a proper privy water closet too, though us servants use pots and throw the contents into the privy when it is permitted and seemly to do so. The Master is a rich man and wants the best for his family, and what best they have affects us servants too. He is a merchant man and very handsome and dresses in all of the finery of one who trades in textiles, for that is mostly what he deals in. His name is Arthur Blake. He is a relative of Mr Blake the famous English poet. I am Sarah Armstrong and I come from Kent.

It was decided that I should go into service in the city rather than stay at home to run the farm with my father and mother. My brother, Peter, travelled with me to London and he too works here, at the Lion Brewery, 50 Broad Street, which is just around the corner. When I go out walking with Miss Cecily we call in to see Peter and he gives us both a small sip of his malt liquor, which he is given as part of his wages. He is happy in his work, as I try to be, but there are times when I see him and the longing for home is so great I cannot help but cry. Miss Cecily says shush then and that I mustn't be afraid or lonely because she is my friend. I wish that her kind words could cure me. I have not the heart to tell her we cannot be true friends because she is so far in station above me. Sometimes, at night, I weep until sleep comes with missing my parents and family and then Miss Cecily cannot comfort me. My Aunt Nell must hear me from her room next door but she never comes to ask what the matter is. Sometimes, she knocks on the wall as a signal to me to be quiet. Then I lie in the dark, holding my breath for fear of making a noise that will anger her, and I feel alone and worthless. I must be on this earth for a reason but I find it hard to fathom. God must have a purpose for me and all the other millions here, but what? It is wrong to question Him, I know, and I do not mean to. But did not Jesus himself feel he had been forsaken and he was the very Son of God.

I worry sometimes that the stench of this place will make me ill. Aunt Nell says it would be worse if I were a pure finder, those who gather dog waste to be used by the tanners, or a night soil man who deals with human waste when a cesspool overflows. Worst of all are the toshers who search the sewers beneath the city for anything at all that might be of value. They work amongst the filth and the rats. It is said that sewer rats are the most ferocious of all creatures and big as dogs and they fear no man.

Today Miss Cecily and I dodge past Rex and walk along Pig Lane to Broad Street. Miss Cecily is puffing out her breath to see it in the air because the weather is so cold it makes a vapour. There are mares' tails clouds very high up in the blue dome of the sky. I point them out to my little companion. She says they are made of angels' hair not horse tails. It is a wonderful thought and I hope she is right. I like to see the world through this child's eyes, as strange as that is sometimes.

We pass Mrs Gutsforgarters' house and try not to laugh when we see her in the doorway. We heard her once yell at her son, 'I'll have your guts for garters, young pup, if you ever cheek me like that again. You see if I don't,' so naturally that has been our name for her since. Today she empties a pot of something brown on to the street and I dread to think of what it might be and I hurry us both along.

We take a little water from the pump at Broad Street. It is acknowledged as the best in the area and the water is clear and refreshing. People think it a tonic and it certainly is delicious. Mr Eley, of Eley Brothers Munitions Factory here on the street, is filling a jug for his mother who now resides in a place called Hampstead, some miles to the north, as she swears it is the best water in London. He sends her a jug or bottle by cart every week. He is telling the Reverend Whitehead that business is 'brisk' because there will be a war in the Crimea and the government is buying up guns and ammunition and that it is an ill wind that blows no good.

'Brisk' has a lovely sound and I can guess at its worth but I will be sure to ask the Mistress exactly what it means, later. I have no idea where this Crimea is either and will need to be told that too. There is so much to know. I worry about us going to war. What have these Crimeans done to incur our wrath as a nation? I wonder.

We greet the Reverend, who is a regular visitor to the Blake house, and Miss Cecily makes him swing her about right there in the middle of the street. She squeals and chirrups with delight. He is a tall man with a long beard and kindly eyes and he makes a pleasing sweeping movement in his long clothes as he moves through the frantic streets. You just know when you meet him that you are safe in his company and that he can offer help should it be needed. His congregation are lucky to have such a minister. I feel a little better to have seen him today, a little less upset from this town. I still miss clear air and the sound of birdsong, cattle lowing and the bleat of sheep, the soft rustle of a breeze and the smell of nature's promise as it ripens to be our bounty. I cannot think of a time when I will not miss such things. Here it is machinery and filth and waste, not seeds and fruit and the scent of sweet, soft freshness. Here the livestock are vermin, mostly rats, squeaking boldly and claiming the hard streets as their own. I cannot see beauty in any of it. Even the people, and God forgive me for saying it, look like vermin most of the livelong day. I am a country girl, plain and simple. Oh, and Aunt Nell says I am certainly those last two.

We walk through Soho and it is all a most extraordinary sight and one that I sometimes think I shall never become accustomed to. Firstly, shop follows shop along the way. There are whole premises given over to the quacks and empiricks who would sell you a potion for any ill. Figure-flingers who pretend to astrology and prediction advertise their wares, along with the pettifoggers who will take on any case of law for the going rate. Then there are outdoor hawkers at every turn and stalls of all imaginable things for sale. Each salesman has a shout to bring you to them, women and men barking loudly away, extolling their goods. The fishwives stand in long rows with their baskets shouting, 'Fleet oysters,' or, 'Mackerel alive.' At dusk they light the lanthorns attached to the wickerwork and I will say that is a pretty sight.

Miss Cecily likes to stop and talk to each stallholder in turn so our progress is usually very slow. I would like to hurry through the noisome streets with their filthy gutters and the clamour frightens me, if I am to be honest. Also the children are perturbing, so many homeless urchins, and some so begrimed with filth it is hard to tell if they are black or white. There are drunks spilling out of public houses and lewd women who mock us if we stare (and it is often hard not to). Then, too, there are the beggars, some with no legs but perched on carts and wheeling themselves along using their hands like paddles on the ground. The sea of humanity in all its foulness is not a happy sight and I would far wish to be elsewhere. Miss Cecily loves it.

She asks her funny questions of whomsoever we encounter. 'What is a rainbow made of?' she demanded of a cloth seller one day. 'Is it ribbons or is it music?' People smile and shake their heads and say, 'She's a Blake', as if that explains the matter. When I ask Aunt Nell about that she tells me never to repeat it in front of the Master or Mistress and says that there might be a want in the Blake family but if there is, it is only through excessive kindness of spirit.

As we return to the house today, Miss Cecily stops in the courtyard in front of the horses' stable and says, 'Can you hear it, Sarah? The song? It has yellow in it.' Then she toots like a cornet. I have no idea what she is talking about but I leave it be. She rushes into the house and up the stairs to tell her mother about our travels. I avoid the dog but take a moment to pat the other animals on their snouts. My heart aches for the farm in Kent but this is home now. Life is hard, I think, and I have been reared to expect no less of it but these trials set before me are heavy and they render my spirit leaden. I take a deep breath of the horses' wondrous smell and it helps me along and I go indoors.

The Mistress is reading Mr Dickens' *Hard Times*, which is serialised in *Household Words*. She sits us down and reads the latest instalment aloud. As much as this city is a trial, I think I should hate the industrial north even more; a grim and cold, red-bricked place with huge chimneys belching forth black smoke and malice. I recognise those incarcerated up there might not envy us this London, however.

Today she says, 'You know, Sarah, the newspapers once warned against women reading novels or eating chocolates, especially in the month of May, lest they inflame the blood. Imagine that.' She smiles at the foolishness of it all. I hardly know what to make of it, to be honest.

The Mistress has remarked before that I have a good vocabulary and if I do, it is down to the local clergyman in my Kent parish. The Reverend Farthing, like Mrs Blake, read to us young ones all the time, and Bible adventures and admonishments are writ in such words that one could conjure many worlds with them. May Farthing, his wife, attempted to teach us our letters, or most of them, but I find it difficult to read them as making any sense and my style is not good in the writing of them.

'You must acquire a steady hand on the end of your strong arm, Sarah,' Mr Farthing would say, never tiring of his joke on my name. It could be a tad wearying but he always meant it in good humour and Mrs Farthing found it exceedingly funny, every single time.

The Mistress is trying to teach me improvement on my letters so that I, too, may some day be able to read books all by myself or perhaps make my mark properly upon a page. I realise that I am a very lucky girl and will give God extra praise and prayers tonight.

When I ask the Mistress about Crimea, she says, 'Arthur is the one who could tell you more, my dear, but I can show you where the place is on a map and tell you that the dispute is the dividing up of what remains of the Ottoman Empire.' It is the stuff of Ali Baba and his thieves, a distant place of myth and legend, really, and hard to believe that it is real.

When I am shown the map I see Crimea is so far away I cannot help but wonder why we need any of it. Do we not have enough in our own country to see us by? Will some of us have to go and live there to keep it ours? Do the people there even speak our language? I have as many questions as Miss Cecily.

Later, as I prepare the little one for bed, we see the lamplighters at work. 'Who lights up the stars at night?' she asks.

'Well, God, of course,' I say.

'Of course,' she repeats and smiles like an imp. I know she is teasing me a little and I also suspect she does not truly believe in God. She is an extraordinary caution and I would lay down my life for her.

I cannot always see the stars from here in the city but I trust that they are out there in the black sky and that God is setting them alight each night as he does over the countryside. I must have faith that this is so.

'Sarah,' Miss Cecily begins and stalls. I know when she leaves a pause, as she does now, she is formulating a big question and perhaps one that is also impossible to answer. 'Are the stars lonely?'

I do my best and tell the truth. 'I don't know, Miss, but I think not. They sparkle one to another, like salutations.'

She nods, as if satisfied. 'That's nice,' she says, and yawns. 'They must be sending out their greetings to us also, in that case.'

After Miss Cecily has gone to sleep I am allowed to serve port to the Master and his friend, Dr Snow of Frith Street. My hands shake so much that the glasses and bottle rattle noisily and I redden with embarrassment. I am heavy and artless, lacking in any readiness or grace.

'Steady, child,' the Master says. 'We are in no hurry and you are in no danger.' He smiles kindly and I try to calm myself.

Dr John Snow is famous all over London and, I imagine, the country too. Last year he attended on Queen Victoria as she gave birth to her eighth child, Prince Leopold, and he administered chloroform to her, on which he is the Leading Expert, so the Master says. It is a gas that numbs pain and induces sleep, I believe. Dr Snow is a quiet man and sometimes this unnerves me. The Master seems to know this and takes two drinks from me, one of which he gives to the doctor.

As I tidy, I hear them discuss the foetid air we breathe each day.

'The Miasmatists would have us believe that foul stench alone can kill a man but I challenge them to prove it,' Dr Snow says in his strange, soft voice. 'If this were so, then why do tanners, for example, not die suspiciously early in their lives? They deal with the most noxious of fumes all day long.'

I think about what he has said and I cannot believe that the evil city air is of no harm to us. Surely it poisons our bodies? Nothing which smells so bad could be of any good at all, that much is clear. Surely? The Master must agree with me because next he's saying the same to the good doctor.

'The city odour is unpleasant, I grant you that,' Dr Snow replies. 'And it may make certain of the populace nauseous, but it is unlikely to kill a person all of itself. What it stems from, however, is another matter of concern.'

They discuss the sewer system, 'or lack of it', the Master points out. Dr Snow nods and calls it 'inadequate'. Dr Snow has a wide range of inquiry into all manner of things and I hear but understand little of their conversation as I potter about. I like to listen, though, and the Master allows this. Dr Snow bemoans the number of pickthanks in authority. I know he means officious fellows who do what they are not desired to. He shakes his head and mutters that they are whispering parasites. 'Between them and base newsmongers, is it any wonder the populace is confused and full of hearsay about the world.'

Dr Snow brightens as he says he is looking forward to a talk a Mr Francis Galton is to give soon on his travels in foreign parts, Africa and the like. I must ask the Mistress where exactly that is in the world. I am too shy to ask the Master now and I do not want to seem even more ignorant than I am. It is also not my place to interrupt. But there is so much to learn and I would like to know as much as possible.

The Master takes down some books for us to inspect. I am abashed that I am to be shown things of interest to the great Dr Snow and allowed to admire them at the very same time. This London, with its strange experiences, is not always the scourge it might be.

'First editions,' the Master explains. 'I know many hold that William Blake was somewhat mad but he was also, at the least, a wonderful artist.'

'Agreed,' says Dr Snow, taking a volume in his hands. 'And did Wordsworth not say that there was something in Blake's madness which interested him more than the sanity of Byron or Walter Scott?'

'An interesting point,' the Master says and I can tell that

he is pleased. It is not easy to have madness in a family, however closely it can be aligned to genius. My cousin, John Cooper, is a dribbling fool and an embarrassment to us all. It is a mercy that he does not write poetry or we should be the laughing stock of the parish.

I dare not touch the books, of course. It is enough that I am permitted to be here.

'*Songs of Innocence and Experience,*' Dr Snow reads.

Oh, to be able to decipher the letters with such speed and confidence!

'It's a fascinating process,' the Master explains. 'He left the design standing in relief alongside the text, which was a new process at the time. I rather think he invented it, this illuminated printing. And then the pages were hand-painted in watercolour, as you see, and stitched together to make up a volume. They are exceedingly beautiful, don't you think?'

We do, both the great doctor who has ministered to the highest in the land and me, a farm girl from Kent. I long to read the words of the poems, for somehow I know in my heart I will love them. The Master opens another book and begins to read aloud.

> And did those feet in ancient time
> Walk upon England's mountains green?
> And was the holy Lamb of God
> On England's pleasant pastures seen?
>
> And did the Countenance Divine
> Shine forth upon our clouded hills?

And was Jerusalem builded here
Among these dark Satanic mills?

Bring me my bow of burning gold!
Bring me my arrows of desire!
Bring me my spear! O clouds, unfold!
Bring me my chariot of fire!

I will not cease from Mental Fight,
Nor shall my Sword sleep in my hand,
Till we have built Jerusalem,
In England's green and pleasant Land.

I think it is the most beautiful poem I have ever heard and it makes me cry and I have to flee the room. I crash into the Mistress who is astounded by me and rushes in to ask her husband what has happened. 'She has been touched by an angel,' I hear him say. 'Her soul has been moved.'

It is the truth. I lie in bed, quivering, and my thoughts cannot banish the words. I resolve to learn them by heart. I hear the Mistress playing the piano below for the gentlemen.

Today is the most exciting day of my life yet and I do not see how any after can ever match it either. I seem to rush through my morning chores with the speed of a mythical hero because suddenly it is time to get into the carriage and go to Regents Park. My heart is somehow at the top of my throat blocking air. Miss Cecily cannot stop chattering. We are to visit the Zoological Society. It is to be so exotic that I cannot even fathom a single thought of what it will be like.

The Master and Mistress have spoken of strange creatures and birds but nothing prepares us for the sights to be beheld in this place.

My legs shake as we descend from the carriage. After that I all but forget that I have a body. We go into building after building filled with wonders. The birdsong in the air is nattering and hooting of an order I have never heard till this day. I see feathers that have colours like some of the Master's textiles and that I would never have thought could exist on a living thing without that colour being imagined by Man. One animal is a Quagga and like a donkey but its neck and head are striped. But the most extraordinary thing of all is one called a Hippopotamus. He is the strangest creature I ever did see! He is named Obaysch and he is a slothful, fat, grey-skinned giant who was gifted to the Queen by an Egyptian. The Mistress tells me Egypt is also in Africa, the place she showed me on the map some nights ago. I will need to look at it again when we return this evening, that is if my head does not explode with these new sights before that.

The animal is asleep as we approach and I swear to the Lord God in Heaven Above he has a smile on his funny, grey face, with his bulging eyes closed and crinkled with pleasure. Crowds of people surround the beast's enclosure and some of the children are crying at the sight of this oddity. No one wants to move on in case the creature stirs, and eventually he does, just to grunt and roll on to his side and continue sleeping. It makes both myself and Miss Cecily laugh and the smaller children cry harder that the beast can move because they are afraid he will rise and run after them and kill them. The Master says this will not happen and so we continue to smile and be overjoyed. I never want to leave this place. I want to know all about the animals and birds.

'You would be a zoological scholar?' the Master teases and I am sure that my face is boiling red.

'She is a curious girl, are you not, Sarah?' the Mistress says and I secretly thank her for her kindness. 'That is always to be encouraged.'

The Master smiles. 'Sarah was moved by "Jerusalem", were you not, child?'

I nod, dumbly.

'Not everyone has the patience for poetry,' he says. 'I am glad that you do. May it be a comfort to you all your life.'

We see snakes and reptiles that have scales instead of skin and live in furiously hot houses. And there is an aquarium, which has fishes in it. I think my brain will burst open trying to keep in it all of the new things we have seen. Each is stranger than the next. My head is not a big one and there is so much to learn in the world that I feel unworthy of this life. I am an Ignorant and the fact of how little I know mortifies me. I wish my family could share what I have encountered. They would not believe what I have seen this day, how could anyone?

Miss Cecily falls asleep in the carriage on the way home. We take a route by the river and see the mudlarks go about their business in the low tide. The stink is fearful and we must hold our kerchiefs to our faces, though they are of little use against the potent fumes.

'Poor creatures,' the Mistress says of the river-finders.

They are indeed a sorry sight, their torn garments little more than rags, stiffened with the river's foul grime. They wade amongst the barges scouring for treasure, be it lumps of coal or wood or other paltry bounty. Some are very old, women bent double with age and infirmity, and others are children hardly of Miss Cecily's years. I think of how the animals in Regents Park can expect their meals to be served to them but these poor human beings cannot. Is that not surely a thing that is wrong in the world? And how can a river be a turd-brown colour instead of God's most vibrant and soul-raising blue?

We cross over a bridge and see the huge clock tower that is being built by the Houses of Parliament. I cannot imagine how tall and vast it will be when finished. So far, we can see the elegant ridges of the design as it rises heavenward. God will be pleased with this piece of London reaching towards his Kingdom, I feel. Man is paying Him a fitting tribute by building a thing so beautiful. The Master says that a man called Augustus Pugin designed it and then went mad and was sent to Bedlam and died thereafter. I think of the Master's fore-bear, William Blake, and it seems to me that beauty and madness go hand in hand in our world more often than we might like them to, especially for those who fashion beauty from within themselves. They pay a terrible price for their gift. Perhaps you cannot truly have one without the other. I like the sound of the name Augustus. And Pugin, too. They roll around the mouth. I remember the words of the poem by William Blake and wish I could make my mark better than I can at present. I would like to write words on a page and have them mean something. I can say the Jerusalem poem now as I have learned it by heart. I hope to write it on to paper some day to have as my own actual record of it, though

I will hardly be able to add illustrations also, as the great man who composed it did.

> I will not cease from Mental Fight,
> Nor shall my Sword sleep in my hand,
> Till we have built Jerusalem,
> In England's green and pleasant Land.

I whisper these words into my pillow and resolve to do some good in the world and to try to render a little of this London into some sort of pleasant land, however that might be achieved. It is too daunting an idea for someone of my station to achieve, in all likelihood, and yet a compulsion pulses in me. I must strive my hardest to make some difference in the world, however narrow my own world is. Perhaps the Reverend Whitehead would like help with the poor of his parish. It would be difficult to make the city green, I realize, and certainly these surrounding streets. If I was an educated man like Dr Snow, I could use my skills for good. There is so much to know that I will never learn and so much I could do if only I knew what is unknowable to me. The starkness of this fact leadens my soul and I might cry then. Mr William Blake left behind his beautiful words and prints. I wonder if it will be enough for me to leave some good deeds. They may be all I have to offer. Will living a good and useful life suffice?

The hopelessness is hard to banish. I have been aside from myself, yet not beside myself, since the day I left Kent and am only part of what I could or must ever be. I may never understand why I was given away. Perhaps my parents did not need me. They had two of me, you see: there's me and there's

Martha and she is exactly me and I am exactly her. Did Mama and Papa love me less than my beloved sister? How could they if we are so exactly the same? Perhaps I have more to say for myself; that could be the nub of it.

I never again want to see a sight like Martha lying prone on the ground as I left with Peter, clawing at the soil, howling like a wounded dog. I wanted to echo her movements and cries but I felt I should be strong for both of us. My heart was tearing itself into ragged pieces in my chest and my body stiffened till it hurt. I do not understand how they could rend us asunder like that, or why they would want to. Where is the love in those actions? It is not only the Lord who moves in mysterious ways, though He is Almighty and has higher purpose.

Sometimes, Martha and me would lie in a field gazing at the sky. She loves looking at the clouds and how they move around. Her favourites are the ones that look like cotton balls or giant heavenly sheep. She sees figures and faces and can make up stories to go with the characters she imagines are there. Sometimes, too, we'd lie with eyes closed and reach a hand up to the sky and when we opened our eyes we would see that we had both raised the same arm. That's how I know Martha is crying now, a world away in Kent, trying not to disturb anyone else while she does. I can feel her tears as surely as I can my own.

I want to make her laugh as I used to. I know if I told her about Aunt Nell's moustache she would roll about on the ground begging for release from the mirth.

Instead, here in this hard place I weep as silently as I can manage and resolve to use whatsoever comes my way to rise in the world. The Mistress will teach me to read and write properly and that will be my true start. Dr Snow, after all, was a commoner who bettered himself. I may even try to keep a journal as the Mistress does. The beauty of being alive, especially on this day, is enough to drive me mad and I wonder will anyone ever know that I was here once and felt this way. I must try to record it and that means learning my letters properly. Martha knows how I am, even though she is not here, but if she does not tell of it who else will ever remember me, and the way I find myself right now at this moment? Yet there is so much to be thankful for.

I cannot remember sleep but it comes, as surely as my pillow is still wet when I arise for another day.

Proverbs says, 'A merry heart doeth good like medicine,' and so it is of Miss Cecily. If she was the air we breathe we would not fear disease. She says, 'I heard Mama play the colours last night.'

'She played piano,' I say, as she has mixed up her words again.

'Yes,' she agrees, 'the colours. They were beautiful.'

I say no more on the subject. She is an individual mystery and that is the top and the tail of it. And, after all, she is a Blake and that also seems to explain a lot.

now

Over the land is April,
Over my heart a rose;
Over the high, brown mountain
The sound of singing goes.
Say, love, do you hear me,
Hear my sonnets ring?
Over the high, brown mountain,
Love, do you hear me sing?

Robert Louis Stevenson, 'April'

april

It seemed apt to Karen that April, allegedly the cruellest of all months, began with a day for Fools. She knew Tony would agree, were it not for the fact that he had successfully accomplished the doing away with himself in her bath in the early hours of the year. I have no one to talk to now, she thought, even if I do spend the day in conversation with all sorts. Those were the hollow niceties of the day-to-day and her work, taking shit from grumpy passengers who wanted more alcohol and freebies of any sort, no matter how feeble and useless, as long as it seemed they'd got one over on the system.

Her bones ached and she shivered every time she remembered the past two days at work. Ferrying humans in the air was about as glamorous as a baboon's arse but made all the worse by her disengagement from it all. She was floating parallel to the world of work and perhaps the world itself too, come to think of it. She had fanciful visions of her voyaging high in the clouds, imagining people lying on their backs on the ground looking up at the smoking trail of the aeroplane sketching the vector of the journey's direction then dissipating into the ether. These strangers don't know I am aboard, she thought, few people do; even the passengers hardly notice me. I am here to serve, that is all. I could be anyone.

And then, there had been the incident.

The catalyst was a minor detail: there were no black cherry yogurts in the fridge of the canteen. Simple as that. But it was somehow a last straw. It was as if Karen had been denied a momentous and life-changing item and even though she knew this was not the case, in any shape or form, it seemed to represent an intangible she could not identify but which mattered beyond measure. She stood trying to catch her breath, trying to convince herself of her undoubted stupidity of reaction and then she began to shake, fundamentally and to her core, rigidly fixed in the centre of a tiled floor that had seen too much traffic, too many weary souls trudge past; too much disappointment, in fact. She dropped the spoon she had been intending to use and imagined it clanged like a gate to hell ringing closed, satisfied to have captured another unfortunate soul. A woman who worked for Emirates asked if she was OK and, when Karen tried to answer in gulps and discord, looked around for someone else to share this nutter problem she had brought upon herself. Words strangled in Karen's throat and the sounds emerging were the very personification of agony. What she wanted to scream was, 'I have no hope,' or, 'There is no point to me,' but nothing sensible came except tears in a juddering heartbreak. I am disposable, she thought, not to be missed if removed from the general scheme of things. And when the heaving stopped and the crying faded to a shaky whimper, she could hear Tony's voice say dismissively, 'Catharsis? Uncomfortable but necessary, I suppose.' She was shattered and wide alive.

Later, she dragged her trolley along Broadwick Street, wise to the uneven pavement at the corner of the John Snow pub and the smokers spreading themselves in the cold, lager-filled and unaware of space or how to use it genially. Not even their fug and the vague honk of new and stale alcohol could mask the sewer smell of bad drains, like an outbreak of plague waiting to attack. With her luck, the next human pandemic would originate from the pipes of her small flat a block away.

She put her entrance key into its requisite slot and listened to the languid beep-beep-beep that allowed her in, but as she pulled on the metal gates and stepped through, she was also sure she heard a dog growl. She looked around for an animal but saw none. It was odd because, for one thing, the residents of Claxton Court were not allowed pets and aside from that she had never seen even one stray dog in Soho so it was unlikely to be a mutt that had wandered in by accident. The strays must be swept up quickly if they bothered to come this way at all, she thought. Come to that, she hadn't ever seen a skulking cat, even at night, and surely the place was crawling with all sorts of vermin tasty to the feline world. It was certainly crawling with the human variety from dusk onwards.

A skeletal woman stood by the railings on her landing, new to Karen. The entire cast of the court could have changed, for all she'd notice. A freezing gust whipped at the waif's grey dress but seemed not to make much impression on the woman herself, as if she was impervious to the cold, uninterested in the extreme. If she'd had wings, Karen might have imagined her to be an angel, but she was not sure where she stood on the supernatural and figured it was as well there were no wings in evidence so she wasn't hallucinating as well as cracking up.

91

Still, she wondered if this creature might dance on the head of a pin and how many of her notional colleagues would join her on that miniature dance floor. The woman turned and fixed Karen with a knifing stare of coal-coloured eyes that felt like a haunting. She is so young, Karen thought, and has seen too much already. The woman stood transfixed a moment by Karen's uniform then gave a small, involuntary wail and was gone. It was not the reaction Karen normally got to her work garb. When she remembered it later she had the impression that the young woman had been in black and white.

Cooing on the handrail was Queen Beatrice, all puff-feathered up against the elements, come to visit or lost again. It didn't matter, she was welcome, and when Karen opened her door, she glided to floor level and walked in ahead of her hostess.

'Good to see you,' Karen told her, meaning it. 'I haven't done much with the place since you were here last, as you'll see. No dead bodies in the bath is the major move, I suppose. Make yourself at home, I'll fix us a snack.'

The apartment smelt dusty and musty and she could see that her visiting mouse had been, from the scattering of tiny dung pellets on the stainless-steel kitchen top. She had never met it and hadn't the heart to kill the creature, reasoning that it never did any harm and spent as much time in the place as she did. As long as it resisted inviting its family along to join in the festivities, it was safe.

'Many of our recommended food groups just got a mention here,' she told Queen Bea as the pigeon ate seeds while Karen had a large glass of wine. 'Just as well you didn't decide to ditch in Trafalgar Square, you know: your kind are not welcome there any more. You're rats with wings to some, tuppence a bird or no.' She began to hum the tune from *Mary Poppins* about feeding the birds but got little reaction from her guest and abandoned the entertainment. 'Maybe Frank will give you a blast of one of his favourites. He's playing a lot of Buzzcocks tunes on his ukelele these days. Not that you give a fig.'

I seem to be watching my language around a frickin' pigeon, she thought, and I'm only on my first drink of the day.

'Who was the new lady you were with when I arrived?' she asked. There was no answer forthcoming so she left the subject and reached for Alex Bulgharov's details to phone and tell him of his prize pigeon's whereabouts. She actually knew his phone number by heart, having thought of little else but that man in the months since she had met him. Beatrice was the lucky charm to return her to his attention and she hoped she would not betray her sheer excitement and desire during the call. Facts still stood in the way of any fantasy, the most salient being his marital status. Yes, he's married, Karen, get over it, move on, do not make a tit of yourself. And, for that matter, you've only met the man once so don't be a hysteric. He's just an attractive guy. The world is full of them, apparently.

His voice in her ear made a tingle between her legs. I need to get laid, she thought. When was the last time she'd had sex with a man? There had been a fumbling with a pilot four weeks ago in a spiritless hotel in Hong Kong but it was unsatisfactory and had led to an annoying bout of being ignored and then treated like a pariah by the man in question. It was just a shag, she had wanted to roar, and not a great one at that, pencildick.

She was reminded that her name meant pencil in Russian and it made her laugh.

'Have I said something amusing?' Alex Bulgharov asked.

'I was just thinking that my name is pencil,' she said. 'I don't know why but it makes me happy to know that.'

'Us Russians aim to please.' She could practically feel his grin against her cheek. 'Now, I should come to you this time to collect the feathered one. Would this evening be any good?'

It was almost like being asked on a date, or as close as she was going to get to any such thing today. 'That would be perfect,' she told him, trying not to speak too soon and give herself away.

She spent a flurried hour washing, perfuming and primping to get to a state of casual-looking readiness. And when he appeared at her door, she had to stifle a gasp at the sight of him. In that pause, he leaned into her and said, 'You smell divine', and suddenly she was in his arms. Then they were on her bed. And making love.

'I've thought of no one else since I met you,' he said, much later, as they lay in darkness and sweat. 'A hundred times a day I've wanted to call you.'

'Why didn't you?' Karen could have bitten her tongue off then. She was allowing a wife to appear and an end to this precious moment.

'I had no proper excuse to. So poor Beatrice has been racing her little wings off because I thought perhaps she might land here again if she was flung off course. And, apparently, she has.' He looked slightly puzzled by the idea.

'Where did she come from today?'

'Strangely enough, just from home in Uxbridge; a routine

stretch of the wings. Perhaps she'd got fed up of a moody me in the loft and tired of all the travel.'

Karen laughed. 'So this is all her idea.'

'Initially, today, yes. But not now.' He pulled her hips to him again and as his cock grew steady against her, insisting on its rightful space between her thighs, his tongue caressed her lips then entered her mouth, both acts rendering her hard of breath and thought, and not caring about much except the immediacy of him and the satisfaction it brought.

Karen wondered how she could open up so entirely to this near stranger and why it could not have happened long before this. Their timing was impossibly off. This man was unavailable, he was married with a family, and could never be expected to change any of that.

He showed no sign of leaving and Karen was loath to suggest it. As if reading her mind he said, 'I thought I'd stay but only if that's also what you'd like.'

She didn't dare speak, not trusting herself. It would be so easy to spoil this incredible intimacy with the facts of their lives. She held her breath and nodded emphatically. Time had become precious since Tony's death and although she often felt she had too much of it, it was in fact whizzing noisily past her and she needed to make it matter.

'I don't think Bea will mind,' he said lightly.

'Be still,' he whispers and I know that I will do anything for him, even endure the agony of not responding to his touch, if that is what he wants and, right now, it is. I lie with him behind me, feeling his cock stiffen against my buttock and I could burst with joy that this man wants me. His breath is hot against my neck and his lips brush lightly, maddeningly along my skin. He has found the place behind my ear, the line of sensation that sets me all on fire. He's insistent now, easing into the cleft of my ass, burrowing through to me. I cannot help myself but to moan and I push back against him lightly. His hands are on my breasts, teasing my nipples. There is a direct surge of heat generating from everything he does and the magic between my legs. He is poised there now and with one thrust back of my hips I can have him in me. He knows it too. 'Wait,' he instructs and, as urgently wet and heightened as I am, I do. My breath is in short gasps, anything else and I might pass out. I pant. His hands leave my breasts and make their way down across my belly and between my legs. His fingers are on my clitoris and I cannot hold out a moment longer. I press back to take him and as I do he thrusts into me. Each time I press back he is deeper and deeper in me and as I move forward his hands stroke me and I cannot think straight nor do I want to. I abandon myself to the sensation of Alex taking me and soon I am no longer in control of my rhythms but lost to the orgasm he has brought me to and then weak and exhausted, prone before him as he kisses my back and murmurs words I cannot hear on to my damp skin. I don't care about anything now except this one perfect night with him and I don't give a fuck about consequences as long as I can always have this in my mind and the fibre of me to remember and savour, to help me along. I was once desired. And once, someone acted on that desire. It will do, and more than do.

She wanted, needed, to mark every moment in her mind. Already details were elusive and disappearing. What had he said just as they lowered their bodies to the bed? She had been too much in wonder at the touch of him against her. She remembered how soft the skin on his back had been at first touch and how elegant his hands had looked cupping her breasts. She worried he might find them small, or sagging. I am a 33-year-old woman and starting to relinquish my mortal self to gravity and the inexorable journey south to the grave. She sounded and felt, too, like Tony now and he didn't deserve this human and living thrill she felt: he had forfeited his moment in time. She resented him invading her ecstatic thoughts now. She was engaged again. Too often she had felt out of sync with time and detached from the city, anonymous to both; now she was a part of them and celebrating the new connection. She was present. She was not alone or solitary, as was usual. She heard Queen Bea coo.

'Is that the bath?' Alex asked.

'Yes.'

'We'd best make love there so, to take the curse off it completely.'

Which they did. Make love, she whispered to herself, make love; not fuck, not shag, though they were elements. Make love.

Already she had begun to worry about his leaving, and he would leave, in the morning, or sometime, and forever. Her heart began to palpitate uncomfortably. How am I to adjust now that I have tasted this? The future was rushing in and with it separation and uncertainty. I must try to concentrate only on the now, she thought, and the joy of this union, the awe that it could occur at all, the pleasure that it existed even in the now though also suddenly the near past.

She lay awake later in his arms, feeling him breathe in and out, enjoying his sleep, with a stupidly satisfied grin on his face. I helped put that there, she thought. I can bring happiness. Each minute was marked by his rhythm and each heralded the time when he would notice a new day and prepare himself to take it on. Departure was all it spelt and Karen hated every second it would gift the world. Because it would also remove him. And he might not ever return.

Light crept in and she desperately wanted to banish it to blank darkness to suffer, as she would, in the remembering of this hopeless passion, flattened by the helplessness of pure desire and the impossibility of granting it space to grow or even fade away. It was a high-impact explosion of sudden and unrepeatable ecstasy. It was doomed. And it was dawn. It was over. He stirred and then moved her on to her back and thrust into her with a hunger that made her gasp and grasp and fall into him all over again. It would do, and more than do.

And still he is here, even though the day has begun and the city is on the move. Surely he should be too? Strikes me that I don't even know what he works at.

'What are you thinking?' he asks.

How can I answer this simple question without scaring him to death? How can I say, I'm thinking how wonderful it is to be alive in time right now.

I'm thinking how wonderful it is to be with you.

I'm thinking how wonderful it is that we have collided at all and a miracle.

I'm thinking that I almost belong, that until you and now, I was a ghost in the machine. But you have changed all of that, even if you will soon walk out of that door and may never return.

Instead I say, 'Oh, nothing much,' not daring to reveal the fullness of what I am feeling, to share the enormity of what is happening to me. This burden must be mine alone.

'Liar,' he says gently, but I know he doesn't mind. However, he is now getting out of my bed and I desperately want to cling to him but I can't and I mustn't.

I watch as he washes and take pleasure in having a man in my shower. The one before him was cold and blue and dead. This man is very much alive. I know I should join him but I want to breathe in the odour he has left behind. I think I won't wash today but press my nose to any part of my body or bed that tells of him.

When he is ready to go, we cannot find Beatrice but he is unbothered.

'Here's a strange thing, Karen,' he says. 'If Sergei's not gone entirely gaga, he says the bird was home all day yesterday.'

I am dumbfounded and scalding inside. Does he think I made up the part about Beatrice simply to see him? I splutter as much.

'It doesn't matter,' he assures me. 'Besides, she's a bird, which means she can be in two places at one time, far as I know.'

Something in his tone tells me he means this and I have no need to worry about looking needy or manipulative. I want to press home that I saw her, fed her but I don't want to seem a lunatic or a bunny boiler. I take a deep breath. I point to the seeds and a bit of birdshit on the newspapers I have laid on the floor for my visiting pigeon. He nods and smiles. I am not mad, or grasping. He kisses me lightly and says, 'I'll call you later.' And I think, oh, but will you? Because it is just a line and I am devastated but I must gather my dignity and have the last sight of me in his mind one of a smile and some false confidence.

'I will, you know, Karen,' he tells me, reading me clearly again. That makes me laugh a little and shake my head and I am glad he has got those from me, honest and gentle reactions to his kindness, whether he is lying or not.

I hear him leave below as the metal gate clangs shut and I begin to cry in such a way as to know that this is grief for all that has happened this year so far. I am in for a terrible day and I cannot seem to halt it. In many ways I do not want to. It will be good for me, I reason, though my heart is ripped and the pain enough to hurt physically on a level I have never really known before. How can a happiness unlock so much misery? I think of the nonsense cliché that it is better to have loved and lost than never to have loved at all. I disagree with that bollox so totally at this moment. To taste it at all is to be torn apart and the chance of me being put together again is slim. The man called Alex Bulgharov will not call, he will not return, he's had his illicit dalliance, and with it proof that he is still attractive and vital, and he is now on a journey back to his wife. I nearly manage some pity for the stranger he is married to because I have so much to spare right now. But not quite. I'm going to have to be all about self-preservation from here on out. Reluctant as I am to do so, I wash him off me and then I load my soiled bedclothes into the washer-drier. He is gone, or at least the physical traces of him are. Jolts of how he looked above me, or felt moving inside me, rack me in constant ambush.

I think of old boyfriends and why none of them lasted. Was I too fussy, or were they? Did we just not suit one another and were savvy enough to know that? Were we as well not to stick one to the other in compromise or panic that time was passing us by and we were still single? I've not kept in touch but I think they all found partners, if not soul mates. I wonder how many of us find just that, a soul mate to belong with and belong to. And is it a nonsense to think it can last forever when change stalks us, and our circumstances, so diligently?

Perhaps we just don't want to be lonely in life.

Well, London is the perfect place to learn all you might never need or want to know about loneliness.

And then he calls. Alex Bulgharov calls me, just as he said he would. Oh, me of little faith.

'You are wonderful,' he tells me. I want to believe it but I am probably just flattered. Still, flattery is welcome, it helps a little. 'I had a truly wonderful night.'

'So did I.' It's easy to tell the truth, and liberating.

'I would rush right back to you but I have work early in the morning.' I wonder if this is an excuse. 'I'm an army man. RAF Uxbridge.'

I don't know how I feel about him being a soldier. I am a pacifist though probably a woolly one at that.

'I'm one of the army musicians stationed there.'

How does he do that? How can he answer the concern I have just manufactured silently in my head?

'Well, we're Northolt now, which is a shame because I always used to boast that I served on the same base as Lawrence of Arabia had.'

He's making conversation and that warms my heart. I am falling more and more. I don't want him to stop so there is no way I am going to ask about his domestic situation. He must have some way of squaring his absence with his wife and I cannot care about a woman I have never met, nor ever want to meet. As long as she remains a shadow, I can somehow deal with her. If she is made flesh I will be in trouble. I feel a horror rise about how beautiful she is; very, I imagine. After all, Alex is a handsome man, devastatingly so in my opinion. And I don't think that I merely have the eyes of a smitten beholder. He would pass muster in any circle. Yes, she'll be stunning and smart. She has made children with him. They have laughed together. I am sinking again.

'When can I see you again?' he wants to know.

I have difficulty breathing with any ease, my face is burning and I have a heart-sore ache coursing through me. The heart can finish us off in so many ways.

'Tomorrow evening?' he tries.

'I'll be on a flight to Cape Town,' I croak. I hate my job and wonder if I could call in sick, forever.

'You are doing a Beatrice on me. You're flying away.'

'It's not intentional,' I say. 'I would far prefer to be here with you.' There, even if this opens a Pandora's box of pain, I want this man to know some of how I feel. I will deal with the doomed fallout later. Now, all I can think of is the possibility of being loved and making love with a beautiful other who, incredibly, finds me attractive. I do feel attractive when I am with him, and abandoned. It is a new me and I don't know how long she will be here if she depends on a married man to unleash her.

This affair as it stands, and as early as it is to call it that, can only be this small thing. It can never grow and mature. There is no room for change because we will rarely spend a whole night together, never go away together, never make plans for the future together because the only 'together' is the here and now, whenever it occurs, in this small flat. There can only be two outcomes: it finishes, which it will, or a seismic change happens in the other's life and this love affair becomes the main love, and the latter is so unlikely as to be laughable. The man is married with children and an extended family living all together. Ah, yes, there it is again: 'together'. Belonging, for me with this man, will only ever mean to be longing.

Yet, the joy of now. We must grab what we can as it rushes by. We must not deny the experiences that life carelessly puts our way, unwittingly, as it goes about the business of seeing us born, grow and die. I refuse to regret this. And I refuse to deny it. I will savour each heartbreaking moment because whether it is happy or sad, the moment will rip at me in the beauty of its hopelessness.

I wonder if I am a Mistress now? Is that a label I can go with?

What defines me, at all? Or is that one of those foolish questions we should leave to a drunken and self-indulgent mind? My uniform is navy with white and red details. On some level it could be seen as patriotic. If I were giving a sweeping description of myself I would say that I am English. I am not entirely sure what I mean by this, however. Is it a lazy way of labelling the self? After all, I am not sure how much allegiance I feel to this England and I have little sense of place, travelling as I do throughout the world. My shorthand is my nationality but I don't think it says exactly who I am necessarily. It helps people place me. I wonder why this notion is occurring to me? Do I want a description, and with it magically and automatically a game plan for life. I have been wandering aimlessly, though oddly quite globally, but I have never had a real destination. Perhaps it is foolish to ever imagine you can have that. We have aspirations, hopes, even those clichéd notions of dreams sketched out so skilfully in movies. Now I feel involved again and with it disappointed that I have never seemed to search properly for a purpose. This man has suddenly given me that but with such restrictions that I should stop right now before I break my heart into any further pieces. He cannot deliver me what I ultimately need. In the meantime I know I will take a compromise and be glad of it, anything at all that he can give. I am tingling with the thought of him and wonder if he feels this way when he is thinking of me too. I will drive myself nuts if I keep this up.

'Are you still there?' he asks.

I am so caught up in my thoughts and the impassioned imaginings of what might or might not happen that I have lost track of the now and the fact that he is mine for a few moments on the other end of the phone. I have it bad, no mistake.

'Yes, yes,' I reply. 'Just figuring out when I get back to town.' I probably sound like I am vaguely in charge of myself. If only he could see my trembling hand as it presses the receiver to the side of my face, my shaking legs trying to hold me upright, hear the rush of my heartbeat struggling to break its fragile moorings in my chest.

The days had assumed a blurred edge, which was the way with the repetitive nature of Karen's job. She welcomed people aboard, settled them in their seats, convinced them they were less unhappy than they were with their airline lot, fobbed off the truly vile and waited to feed and water them in-flight. The trip of Cape Town was no different in those aspects but what Karen noticed was that she smelt. This surprised her, as she was scrupulous about her hygiene. Her heart was hammering in her chest at the thought of seeing Alex on her return and, uncomfortable as she found the thundering, at least it had an urgency about it. She was struck by how close the feelings of doom and excitement were: one a persistent hum of dread, the other a hair's breadth from ecstasy. The smell was another matter. It was a pungent odour and mostly from the underarm area. She regularly wiped and deodorised but still it returned. At which point she realised, this is the smell of fear: fear of the unknown and, worst of all, fear of not being good enough.

The stays in foreign towns, however wonderful or exotic or iconic, had finally done for Tony, she felt. She sat in her lonely room, a similar one if not identical to the last she'd had in this hotel, and looked at her life sitting in a small suitcase with wheels attached. It was soul-numbing. The mini bar called, as did a new, male member of the crew whom she'd heard was ticking scalps off his list and had finally come to her name. Well, mate, she thought, you should have had me closer to the top of that list if you wanted to be in with any chance at all. She was restless and wanted to escape these four walls threatening to overwhelm her with their bland lack of promise and vague hint of failure.

She thought to go to the beach, even though it was getting dark, and ordered a taxi to take her to Camps Bay. She stood at the hotel door breathing in the fresh air, watching two drunken locals take unwieldy punches at one another. It was a fight without any discernible malice, just something to do, really. One of them caught her gaze and straightened up a moment. 'Stop this mindless violence,' he said to his companion, 'a tourist is looking.' As she sat in the hired car and drove off, she saw them resume their hostilities and couldn't help but smile.

The sea always calmed her. She took off her shoes and walked in the shallows, feeling the sensations of cool water and gritty sand underfoot. No one knows I am here, exactly in this place, she thought. She wondered if anyone was even thinking of her just then, and if they were, she knew the person was from a select group of very few: her parents, a new lover, a dead friend's mum or the work colleague she had so recently spurned. She had not brought a bag, instead some money and a mobile phone hastily stuffed into her pocket. The key to the hotel was electronic and without its cardboard jacket to say where it might be returned to. She had no markers to tell who she was and where she was billeted. If I were to die here and now, expire somehow, it would take time to establish my identity, she realised. It seemed apt. It would be interesting to hear the who and the why of me, she thought.

She remembered visits to the beach as a child and the joy of running wild through the dunes. She always fell and rolled down at least one and would lie in a happy, crumpled heap at the bottom with her mouth full of sand. Once, she misheard her mother while she nursed away a grazed elbow and thought she'd called the injury a 'hurticle'; from then on it was just that. She remembered the happy abandon of pissing in the coarse, rushy grass. She'd collect shells for her grandmother who would make ugly lamp bases by gluing them to wine bottles. She wondered where all of those hideous ornaments had gone and suddenly wanted one very badly for her Soho flat.

The stars were clear and sparkling in the heavens. I'll be up there again tomorrow, she thought, in the vault of that sky. Here is the church of my life: sea, land and sky. And, for no reason, she remembered that even as she stood on a South African beach at nightfall she was also travelling seventy thousand miles an hour as the earth rotated the sun. She thought of Alex, also hurtling through space without feeling it in any meaningful way. And his wife? She, too, was travelling through space and time. She was unaware that she was being done a disservice at Karen's hand and this disgraceful act was uncomfortable for Karen Dash to admit to. She bent to pick up a shell as a keepsake and kissed it lightly before tucking it safely into her pocket with the money and her phone. She was at a loss as to know what to do next. My average life has consequences, she thought. I am affecting others, impacting on their happiness. It was not a happy thought.

Suddenly it was imperative that she speak to her parents. She needed a system of transmission, proof of love from those she depended on to provide it. In the absence of siblings, she needed her parents. Her father's voice was tinny and far away.

'I'm walking on a beach in Cape Town and I couldn't help but remember our summer holidays when I was young.'

'Cape Town,' he repeated, impressed by the sound and the fact of it. 'The weather is probably better in Africa than any of what we got here on those jaunts.'

'It's funny but I don't remember rainy days when we were away.'

'Oh, there were plenty of them. Your mother wants a word.' He always passed her over quickly, afraid to bore his only child, awkward at the distance between them.

'Mum, whatever happened to those bottles Gran used to make with the shells I collected? Do we have any left?'

Monica Dash laughed. 'Ugly things, weren't they? I think we might have a prime sample or two in the attic still. I know there's an oval mirror she decorated once up there. Entirely hideous. Why?'

'I'd like that for Soho.' Was it continuity she sought here? A souvenir of where she came from: her people, the fibre and make-up of her? It wasn't much of a heritage but it was all she could think of. Her mother promised to hunt out what she could and didn't pass comment on the unusual request or the out-of-the-blueness of it.

Karen walked some more, lonelier now than she had been. She was adrift in the world, travelling for her work and living like an immigrant in London even though it was part of her native land. She was a stranger to the town, as clearly as those who came there from much further away, displaced by her solitary life. Her parents' voices rang in her head with quiet decency. She hoped she had some of that in her, although embarking on an affair with a married man was not something they would condone or want to discuss. She was morally aloof from the consequences of her actions, though, knowing that she could not but see Alex again and lay herself bare before him. Life was short and not to be squandered and she would deal with any consequences when it was all too late to change a thing.

She sat in the back of another moving taxi, letting her mind meander as she watched the landscape. She leant back into her seat as she listened to the radio playing a song she didn't recognise and considered how ignorant she was about African music. She paid no mind to much as she felt a whisper of air pass close by her. It was like the soft breath of a sleeping lover on her face. Then the passenger window of the cab shattered as the bullet crashed through it and the driver jerked the car to a halt. They sat in silence for the briefest moment, trying to figure out what had happened, before both scrambled for the doors to throw themselves on the ground outside. Karen felt her hands and knees rip against the road and suddenly the noise of the gunshot registered, delayed and thunderous, and her ears rang painfully as she realised that she had just cheated death by merely sitting back rather than forward in her seat. They waited, listening for more shots, but none came. She muttered a line from English lessons at school: 'Because I could not stop for Death, he kindly stopped for me.' But she had dodged Death. This had been a random act, possibly even a stray bullet intended for someone else. And whoever it was shot at had also escaped.

'Miss, are you OK, Miss?' the driver called.

'Yes, yes, I am alive,' she said.

I am alive and in love, she thought, and I'll take it for as long as it's offered, but she didn't want to frighten the stranger with hysterical detail so she added, 'I'm fine.' Mortality had reached out but she had evaded its cold touch. That does it; I will live this life to the full. I will have that man if he wants me right back. I am gloriously in the present now and the future will just have to look after itself while I deal with that. She relished the throb of her cut flesh.

She was kept from the passengers on the journey home in case they were bothered by her injured hands. She loaded trolleys in the galley and generally floated through the service to England. Without Tony, there were no taunts of 'earth to Karen' and no reason to engage any more than was absolutely necessary with her co-workers. She knew little of this crew and wasn't pushed to learn more just at that time. She was courteous but distant. For all she knew, they had their own thoughts to attend to and no one seemed put out that she was away in her head. Mostly she remembered Alex. She thought of how it felt to have him close, to smell his skin and how that changed from neck to chest to groin. She tasted his kiss and felt his tongue in her mouth. She thought of how fine his nose seemed from below as she lay in his arms and he slept. She heard his sporadic and gentle snores as he shifted about in the night. She pictured his hands on her body and recalled his praise for the small of her back or her belly or breasts. I am here and yours for the asking, she quietly told him, willing him to hear her across the miles. Her fear and its attendant odour were missing, although she would not have professed to calm about her lot. The acknowledgement of love had rendered the world real again, had arrested her attention, and she was so grateful to be alive still to act on it.

As the passengers slept, she looked out of a portal window over a storm lashing Africa. The plane continued in clear sky under a bright moon, above the angry clouds. She watched moonside as forked lightning sparked up and flew down towards the earth. It was dumbshow, accompanied only by the sighs of the sleeping travellers and the steady hum of the airplane's engines. She calculated they were directly over Congo. Somewhere below, families huddled together listening to the pounding rain, counting the beats between flash and thunder roll to ascertain their position in the storm. They were unaware that others upon high observed their condition from a strange and manmade view. How remarkable it was to be alive in this moment and to experience this odd event. She was temporarily flying through the eternal sky with its wondrous fixings while below her, life on the earth was fleeting and mortal.

Back underground in London, trundling along in a tin tube, a woman gave Karen a beady eye and she was tempted to gurn at her in reply. She reminded Karen of a flamingo with a long, pink neck, beaky face and pale gimlet eyes. She ignored her and read the advertisements tempting her to cheaper car insurance and night courses in economics. Best of all, there was a poem posted. 'I Am', it said, by John Clare (1793–1864):

> I am – yet what I am none cares or knows,
> My friends forsake me like a memory lost;
> I am the self-consumer of my woes,
> They rise and vanish in oblivious host
> Like shades in love and death's oblivion lost,
> And yet I am . . .

She looked about at the strap-hangers and bag-clutchers, the pole-clingers and seat-grabbers and thought of how an almost archaic parlance still explained life in London and that of tube rats like herself, denizens of the underground.

As she rose to leave at Piccadilly Station, she thought she heard the flamingo hag mutter, 'Hoor,' for which she rewarded her with a wide Dash smile. 'Honey, you have called it as it is,' she might have said but did not.

She passed the Windmill Theatre with its promise to patrons that it was one of the world's leading entertainment spots for gentlemen, and further along the National School where the children's elevenses were in full swing and the down-at-heel exotic dance club next to it had to lower its shutters for the duration of the kids' playtime. She walked along Lexington Street, swung past the John Snow pub, on to Pig Lane and into Claxton Court.

A man in a worn, brown suit was on her floor, fiddling with keys. He looked startled to hear her say, 'Hello.'

'Roll with it,' she wanted to tell him. 'This is how it's going today. This is how I am.'

He had settled on a post-war, late forties look but a starved edge left him without the conviction to carry it off completely. Still, she wasn't his stylist, or the counsellor who would tell him to quit whatever narcotics had left him so pale. Safely inside, she texted Alex Bulgharov, 'Be at my face at 8pm', which he was, still smiling from her message.

They made love quickly against the narrow kitchen counter, then moved to the main room and threw themselves on the sofa. It gave a lurch and with a crack a floorboard gave way under the front right leg. They pitched on to the wooden floor and lay prone in each other's arms. When they were done laughing and set about righting the furniture, Karen saw the parchment under the boards. It was clearly old and ready to crumble. A childish and awkward scrawl was written atilt to the edges of the page. Karen laid it, oh so gently, on the clear, modern Perspex table and wondered at the beautiful, transcendant juxtaposition of centuries and materials. She read aloud:

> Bring me my bow of burning gold!
> Bring me my arrows of desire!
> Bring me my spear! O clouds unfold!
> Bring me my chariot of fire!

'Someone's written out "Jerusalem", the William Blake poem,' she told Alex. They stared at the signature and agreed it said 'Sarah' and that the date was 1854.

then

So, men are scattered and smeared over the desert grass,
  And the generals have accomplished nothing.

Li Po (*c*.750), *Nefarious War*

may 1941

'We will be arrested if that is found here,' she hisses, pointing at the Van Eyck. 'What were you thinking of, you fool?'

I will confess that I have never liked the word fool and hearing it referred to myself has not upped it in my estimation. I want to think that we are both exhausted and these arguments, all too common now, are the result of that. But the truth is that I think we have come to the point where we can hardly bear the sight of one another. I cannot guess if this would have happened in a time of peace because we have never known that in our marriage. All I do know now is that I am looking into my wife's face and it is the twisted wreck of what I once loved, a sneering caricature of who she was. And I am probably responsible for that. I can't remember the last time she called me by my name, David. All descriptions now are along the lines of 'fool', 'idiot', and even once an ill judged 'dolt' which made both of us chance a smile: neither of us could figure out where that had been unearthed from. The rare moment of easy togetherness faded as quickly as the fleeting smiles.

On the wall, Giovanni Arnolfini calmly raises his hand in salute to me. He is non-judgemental and I feel he may never have raised his voice in his life. His own beautiful and gentle wife meekly stands opposite, holding his hand, and their beauty and calm is such that the shrill retorts levelled at me from the other side of our small flat are drowned out. This, then, is peace for me now. It is sublime.

My wife, Jane, is spooked by the painting, to tell the truth. She claims that Giovanni is little more than a rich albino and his mealy-mouthed wife, as her description goes, irks her. She claims my voice changes when I speak about the work and that I am a man clutching at a status far above what is ordered for me. She may be right on that last count. I do feel more refined, elevated really, in the company of the Arnolfinis and the comrades that shared their room at the gallery. The rest are in Wales now, our national treasures hidden in a quarry, but I have acquired this beauty and it sustains me through this vile war. And my rocky marriage.

'I wonder how the authorities would feel about the food you get on the black market,' I chance, to even out the argument somewhat. 'It was a chicken last week, wasn't it? Some fruit the week before.'

My wife is making full use of one of my childhood gang members. Ray Rawley is as crooked a man as you'll meet on a London street and he is supplier of her particular, illicit treasure. Something in the look she gives me makes me drop this line of attack, though. There is a signal from her that it may be forbidden territory. For one extraordinary moment my bowels loosen and I wonder if my wife is sleeping with Rawley, and I marvel that I might still care. There's some life in us still, then?

I wouldn't call myself a cultured man but I have grown to love the art I'm paid to guard at the National Gallery. Or I did before Hitler and his German hordes began to wreak havoc with our lives. Then we had to move the precious heritage. For a while there was a worrying notion that the collection be sent abroad, maybe Canada, but Churchill got on board and said not one painting would leave these shores. They've gone to Wales, hidden and safe, but out of bounds to all. That cut me and made the war horribly personal. There was an excitement to the whole situation at first, nationally as well as for us at work. The gallery closed before war was declared, which was a mistake if you ask me but no one did. Then the whole collection was moved in eleven days. That, for my money, was the most enervating time, 23 August till 2 September 1939. It was a fraught time too for me when I realised that I could not part with the Arnolfinis, I could not send them away. Therefore I had to find a way of keeping them here without anyone but Jane knowing. Believe me, if I could have done it all without her knowing too, I would. As it was, I didn't tell her until there was nothing she could do about it. That, surely, should have been a sign to us both that we had a problem, that we had taken the wrong course.

Germany invaded Poland on 1 September, we sent the last of the paintings away on the second, and on Sunday the third, as the nation got together the makings of its dinner, the Prime Minister interrupted the radio broadcast and we listened to the news that Great Britain had gone to war with the Hun again. There was the tingle of a fight in the offing, ancient scores to be settled and the notion that we were a great nation to stick up for the downtrodden of Europe. We felt proud. Less than fifteen minutes later, air raid sirens sounded yet another test but this time it had added significance. We were at war. Slogans screamed at us from walls everywhere, like 'Dig For Victory', so we did. We set to digging up parks to fill sand bags and shore up our houses and town against our unseen enemy. 'Beat Firebomb Fritz – Join the Fire Guard', so I did. Then we endured the boredom of waiting to be attacked. Now the nightly bombings are at least proof that there is a war and a world problem to be solved. It is sapping for Londoners but no worse than being married, in my opinion. We are having a little world crisis of our own at Claxton Court and I can see no levelling off of hostilities on our horizons.

Working at the National was regarded as a good safe sort of position for me and never once did any hard chaw from the area call it poncey, though it was far from art I was reared (if you listen to my wife). A job is a job, no matter what, and this is a secure one, or would be without the war interfering in all aspects. Actually, as kids, me and the gang of inner city pals I hung around with frequently got chased out of the place. The corridors were ideal for games of tag and it was usually warmer than home, and dry if the weather was bad and we'd been turfed out of this tiny gaff of ours.

Paintings were just a given, as a result. We stopped to gawp sometimes and even argued about what was going on in them. Titian was always good for discussion. Lots to look at there: masses of action, with most of the story hidden to us because, in spite of a supposedly classical education with the Christian Brothers at school, Brother Colmcille was more interested in being Brother Comeandkillyou and administering a good thrashing than elevating our young minds very far. He regarded all knowledge as dangerous, I think, and he may have been right. So, nothing in my educational repertoire could cover the singular imagination of any given master artist but that didn't matter then and still doesn't, in a way: the image was, and is, all. As long as we could get something from the picture hanging in front of us we didn't care if we were right or wrong about the subject; all that came later when my curiosity got the better of me and led to an obsession of high order.

The first woman I fell in love with was the Rokeby Venus, lying with her back to me, gazing tantalisingly through the mirror held by a tiny winged Cupid. It is probably the most famous 'Come hither' in art history. Everyone in the gang was taken with her: you couldn't have a pulse and not be. When I tried it on with Mildred Forbes round the back of Hames's Bakery, she couldn't understand why I wanted to pose her and, looking back, I realise she was perfectly justified in thinking I was a total weirdo. As it was, she insisted I put my hand in her pants and I found I liked that very much indeed so it was a win for everyone involved.

I still visit Venus and long to run my hand along her curved spine. I like making love to a woman's back and I think it has a lot to do with Velazquez's exquisite goddess. My wife says it's because I have a fear of confronting women. She extrapolates, therefore, that I have a fear of tackling anything unpleasant. She is wrong. In the first place, women are wonderful, and secondly I have no problem sticking up for me and mine, including this woman in this combative relationship. I have made a contract with her and will stick to it, till death do us part and so help me God and whatever else we agreed to on a day that seems a century ago now. It's just tedious, is all. And, besides, I think the fact that I scrape up unrecognisable bits of human beings every night and try to piece them together in order to grant them a little dignity, though it's not part of my job, is something that makes nonsense of her argument, let alone the job itself. I am fireman to a burning London. In fairness to Jane, she drives an ambulance and sees as much horror as I do, often more. And it is very much part of her job description to try to put the human remains together. The wonder of it is that we all don't go mad from what we see every night now.

I wonder if I was ever actually in love with her. My wife, that is, I am certain about my feelings for the Rokeby Venus, rock solid about those emotions. What I wonder is, was I in thrall to a passion for Jane that could never last unless I was possessed of a madness of the highest regard and had an energy that would fuel the national grid? And 'probably' is the answer. Ours was that worst of all things, a whirlwind romance. At face value there was nothing to suggest that we would not be totally suited to one another but that was perhaps for another time and not when death and war stalk us as they do. Immediate and added stress on a new situation can be detrimental and I think that may be what happened to us. We also let war be a catalyst that was unnatural in the decision to get married so soon after getting to know ourselves as a couple. There seemed to be no time to waste. That's understandable as we live in unnatural times, or 'interesting times' as the old curse has it.

Why the Arnolfinis? Why, indeed. There were other paint-ings that sang to me but the one that called me back always was Giovanni and his wife. It was the first room I was posted in when I got the job and I think that made an impression. I became an intimate of the inhabitants. I saw more of them than anyone else of a day. I loved to say good morning to the man himself, Jan Van Eyck, whose small self-portrait smirked out of its darkness at me, shimmering and cheeky. Look at that guy, wearing a head scarf, no less, and pleased as Punch. I was tempted to take him, too, when the time came but I had such a hard time getting the couple out I had to concentrate on just one escape and it was theirs. And mine, of course. Or should I be using the word 'liberation' so beloved now of all in the world. You'd have to wonder if anyone knows what it means or whether they truly mean to deliver it, whatever it turns out to be. That's to put a cynical bias on things, I know, but this war is dragging on and the results are sparse and seemingly without hope. Salvation and liberation are at the end of a very long tunnel and we are only human and easily discouraged.

The room itself that I guarded was bigger than our flat so that was an interesting factor. The ceilings were so much higher and the space so much freer, somehow. And there in the middle but to one side of a wall was the couple. The painting is a jewel, shining in any light, glowing, glossy. And so much to think about within its frame. I think I became involved with it because it tickled my brain.

Getting the Arnolfinis out of the gallery was more difficult than I had expected, not that I had thought the thing through definitively before I decided I had to go after the painting. It was a compulsion and reason had no place in the equation. For starters, the work is bigger than a satchel so slipping it out by that route was not an option; I really had been naive enough to suppose it might be that easy. Innocent days and foolish, I know. I spent a week in a lather of anticipation and planning. I couldn't eat, sleep or concentrate on anything but the couple coming home with me. My wife put it down to the threat of war and I was more than happy to let her think it. It was a divine order of insanity, of course; I was about to steal a national treasure of immeasurable value but that didn't bother me at all. I was more exercised at the thought that I wouldn't see them if they were buried in the ground in bloody Wales, and I didn't actually give a shit about the nation's cultural privation in their absence, much as I'd like to tell you it was, even in part, a political act. No, this was selfish and just for me. I had no idea where my wife fitted into the plan; not at all, I now realise. And any objections she might have had would have been brushed swiftly aside. We weren't talking much at the time so it hardly mattered. We talk even less now.

It's amazing to me how a face that once brought joy to a soul, made it leap a little, can take on a hard-edged set and then somehow become an annoying and sometimes hated visage to behold. Perhaps I know it too well. It may have been beautiful, and especially beautiful, to me once but it has not aged well and in this brief time of war we have all aged more than we might have in the normal run of things. As terrible as it is to admit, I don't think I actually like the woman now. The hardness gifted us by this war has turned her into a person I do not want to love, cannot love. She is tough, demanding and controlling and I want none of those things from her. I, too, have become a hard thing and cold. I have been made solid by our current, unnatural life and the constant bickering. I will not reach out and ease the situation. I assume I could soften it for us both but I'll be damned if I do. I suspect I may in fact have lost the ability to be kind and loving to my wife, even if I wanted to. It seems mutual. Either way, we are both as stubborn as the other.

On my side of this also is the fact that I am untrustworthy, and it's not something to boast of. I got my people out of the gallery because I was trusted and in a position to abuse that. I was left to wrap the works in my room, one being the Arnolfini, and I took full and awful advantage of that. Whether or not I am proud of it is immaterial, I did it and when I stand or sit in front of the painting now, I feel no guilt about my actions. And it's not something I can blame on the world situation, nor have I wasted time trying to. It is something I felt I had to do and given the opportunity all over again, I know I would repeat it. I don't think it has anything to do with morality and I don't even feel I stole the work, I prefer to think I borrowed it when no one else wanted it, when no one else needed it to try to get through their lives the way I thought I did. And, yes, in case you were wondering, it has helped me enormously. Surely true beauty always does.

The weather is deceptively fine, if a little cold for May. I say this simply because it pays no mind to the fact that the world is in turmoil and just gets on with being weather. It makes no difference to this month that every night we live with the threat of the Luftwaffe pounding the city into destruction. The raids of March and April were heavier than we'd experienced till now but we all gathered ourselves and shielded our nerves and went about the business of making out that we could take it. Each morning the sun rises to reveal even more of the carnage than we suspect we've seen the night before. It shows loss more than anything else; more and more of London is missing, reduced to indistinguishable rubble, a shadow of magnificence with buildings taken apart and cast down. The sunlight is free and unquestioning in its role; the sun simply shines. Double Summer Time was introduced a week ago to keep the city in light until about ten in the evening (I should probably call it twenty-two hundred hours, given that we are at war and everything is regulated) but there is no stopping darkness when it wants in, just as the world is turning with no lip service to what its inhabitants are up to while it does. I am fond of the light, however it is granted us, as darkness simply confuses and creates even more fear than we already live with. To call it Summer Time, let alone double that, seems almost jolly and a misnomer. I hear the Irish are not acknowledging a world war on their turf at all but calling the situation they find themselves in, on the edge of a fractious Europe, 'The Emergency'.

Jane is ready for work and spoiling for a fight. There is something new in her tone that I cannot put my finger on. She wants me to ask her something but I am given no guidance as to what and know I will fail her yet again and a botch will madden her even more than the fact that I have cheated death so far in this war, public and private. So, even our arguments are getting beyond me now.

'You really are a waste of skin,' she tells me. 'Rubbish.'

I don't know why but this does sting, this time, above what else she has dished out in the past.

'Hardly a total waste,' I say, irked. 'I helped some people stay alive last night. I'd say that's something, wouldn't you?'

'You know nothing about life or what goes into making it,' she spits. 'You live in that stupid head of yours with its highfalutin theories and art and useless bloody paintings.'

Ah, we are back to the Arnolfinis.

She stands very close and I can smell hunger on her breath, which is all any of us smells of these days as no one in this godforsaken country has had a decent meal in years. She says, 'You should start living in the real world, start taking responsibility for me, us . . .' she gestures to the small world of our flat, 'this. Be a fucking man.' She pushes me back by the chest and I am startled that she has become physical. God forgive me, my own hand is raised suddenly, on impulse, almost as if I might strike her, and it is then that we both know we cannot carry this marriage on any more. We have almost come to blows.

'Not made of stone after all, David,' she says.

We are both gasping for breath and deliverance from this moment.

'Oh, Jane,' is all I can manage.

'I know,' she says, tenderly.

We stand with tears in our eyes and then I reach out and hold her and it is the most tender we have been in an age. But it is also too late. It is a valedictory embrace to another life. We both know that we, as a couple, are over. The war will be much easier to face than this failure and the void between us is extreme in spite of how close we stand one to the other. Jane shrugs out of my embrace and walks out of the door without another word.

I look to Giovanni and his wife but they have no comfort to offer. They maintain their composure and shine jewel-like in the gloom that is my small home and for once it is not quite enough for me. I am hollow and beyond caring whether I live or die tonight. I almost hope the Hun turn up with added bells on to do their worst because otherwise there is nothingness for me now. At least battle is something. I am alone in this teeming, troubled town. And, suddenly, I am so afraid of that.

The first time I saw a man die I thought I might never be able to face out again but you really do get used to death and the wanton destruction a war can visit on a human being. I have seen us shredded, ripped, broken, cut in half or further pieces, crushed, unrecognisable as people, just flesh robbed of sentience and dignity. The first man was alive with me for a few moments. He was losing blood by the bucketful and I could see that it was important arterial stuff, bright red and essential, and there was little chance of getting him to a hospital in time to save him. He knew it too, I suspect, and was almost serene in his acceptance. Just before his eyes switched off, to show that he had passed away, he said, 'Oh, this isn't at all what I expected.' He died without explaining himself. I spent a long time after wondering what he had thought he'd see or do and what had actually happened, and it almost drove me mad. But then the war kicked in good and proper and extraordinary and unwarranted death became the order of every day.

I remember hearing once about another man who nearly died and the life he thought he'd review as it flashed before his eyes never materialised. Instead, all he could think about was the time he had kicked a stray dog in the street, aged ten or so, and the shame he felt in remembering the deed and how he could never make good on it. Over and over the image came to him. Nothing about his family, those beloved to him, just that damned dog. So, if this nightly bombing is to take me, at least I know that I won't regret not releasing the Arnolfinis into my care because I acted on it and they are here. And I don't think I have ever kicked a dog or cat so I am unlikely to be burdened with that sort of casual, almost cruel, trivia when trying to shuffle off and convincing myself that my little life may have meant something. Or I'd like to think that a distracting detail won't hijack my moment, the one we are all headed to. Each death is an individual experience and one that must be tackled alone, in the end, even if the result is universal to all of mankind, whatever our circumstance.

London's West End long ago stopped glittering. The neon lights of Piccadilly Circus have been dimmed and Eros brandishes his bow from behind a bank of sandbags. Government posters offer the only colour with their slogans and hectoring. The fountains of Trafalgar Square are gone and the pigeons have all but deserted us. Nelson still stands on his pillar but he's not up to much these days. I glance at the National Gallery and feel a troubling rush of nostalgia for my old life and job, upsetting because they will never return as they were, even if we do fight to victory in this conflict. Everything we knew is changed now and can never be properly righted or returned to what it was. Some will tell you this is progress, as painful and seismic as it is. There must be gentler ways of improving our lot.

I make for Waterloo Fire Station, a so-called 'ghost station' because we are out of jurisdiction of any particular authority and considered back-up in case another official station is bombed, then we take over that job. I make a detour by the river, needing to see the Thames take its regular journey as if nothing in the world is amiss. Poor kids are scavenging for wood or planks that may have fallen off a passing ship, anything to sell on for a few bob. Sometimes, at low tide they'll find an enemy incendiary and take it apart to throw on a bonfire later for fun. When the enemy drops a load of these, they form an atrociously beautiful ribbon of fire through the city and with it a whispered 'psst psst psst' like the forbidden caress of an illicit lover.

The city is mostly silent now, waiting to hear the hum of the bombers arriving. It is some sight to see them too, flying along in a file, waiting to drop their deadly loads of mayhem and death.

I often wonder if it wasn't better when warring sides met with their armies on a pre-arranged battle site to pound each other rather than this surprise element, which wreaks such horror on ordinary citizens and misses so much that is military. The Germans are suffering badly too in their country, along with a whole tranche of Europe under Nazi control, not to mention the Russians advancing from the East and all that they bring with them and the Red Menace they represent.

The word is that the bomb you hear go off won't kill you but the one you don't will, so everyone listens very carefully indeed on these nights. I am still light-headed and empty from my encounter with Jane and the realisation that I just don't care what happens to me now. She would be better off if I were to die tonight. Perhaps I'll bear that in mind as I fulfil my patriotic duties. If I die in the line of fire she can bask in the misplaced bravery attributed to me posthumously or, should it be necessary, point to mental instability with the Arnolfinis as proof of my warped mindset.

At the station, someone thrusts a cup of weak, nasty tea into my hand but it is warm and a kindly gesture. The tiny niceties of life abide.

'The match was a draw,' I am told.

Preston North End and Arsenal were playing in the Cup Final today at Wembley, another small semblance of a norm going on in spite of all else.

'Replay then,' I comment.

That's when we hear the dogs begin to bark and know the planes have begun to arrive. The dogs always know first. It is just short of 11 p.m. and air raid sirens begin to wail their banshee cry. We make for the truck. We hear the thump-thump-thump of our anti-aircraft guns as they try desperately to halt the deadly advance. The planes make a furious buzzing, the blind fury of an enemy aloft. The city begins to shake as the first impacts hit. We see the sky light up with explosive fire. London was built on clay so the bombs can sometimes sink to depths of twenty foot or more before going off, or just stick there, malevolently threatening to explode at will. Whichever happens tonight, and it will be the usual strange mix of both, precious people will die, others will go quite mad. Buildings will disappear. Business as usual.

But something about tonight is already very different. Ginger Worth looks at me and says, 'This is it, this is the one.' And that is what we all feel. Somehow this is bigger than the others. And that's how it is.

The Controller roars at us to get moving and someone has understood him because we drive out of there with purpose. People are running for their lives. Some opt to stay above ground in the Anderson shelters for what little protection they provide, and others head into the bowels of the earth, church crypts and the tube system. They will hold each other, make love perhaps, and wait for the night to play out its prearranged carnage. They may even survive it.

The streets are bathed in the glow of fires raging their angry, ferocious red. Above is a cloud of pink smoke. Throughout the smoke I can see bright, flashing specks of anti-aircraft shells bursting forth their defence. It is all anyone can do not to stop and be amazed by this dire beauty.

The stench of burning human flesh will never seem natural to me. But the warm, sickly smell of spilled blood is worse. It should not be exposed as it is now among the dead and dying already beginning to line the cursed streets. It is for inside the body, coursing through a person, giving life, nurturing it. That will be the signature smell of this war for me, blood and dust. We see a man wandering along, smiling. He doesn't realise the top of his head is missing. If he were a dog we would kill him and put him out of unnecessary misery. As it is, he makes it to a post box, red as the blood dripping down his face, standing proudly intact in a mess of rubble. He looks, for all the world as if he can't figure out where his envelopes are. Then he collapses and it is a relief to find he is dead by the time we reach him. Lying by his side is the arm of another unlucky soul who did not make sanctuary in time.

A pregnant woman is crying in the lee of a wall, as if it will shelter her. It is just as likely to fall over on her, I realise, and I help her out. We will find a safer place for her. She clings to me, insisting that she must stay alive for both of them. 'It's new life,' she insists. 'We have to give it a chance.' And something in what she has said, the tone of her voice, shatters my world. Jane is pregnant. That is why she accused me of knowing nothing of life 'or what goes into making it'. Weren't those her very words? When she told me to start taking responsibility for her, 'for us', she gestured to our little home and I was distracted by that and did not listen properly. I thought she meant the two of us, but we are more now. She is carrying our child. That is why she has been even more worried about this war lately, more volatile in all of her reactions. She has been carrying this secret and our baby. I hold this stranger and comfort her but I have no way of finding my wife. I feel I am moving in slow motion for most of the rest of this awful night, disengaged from my actions. Jane, Jane, Jane, is all my mind can think of and it chants the name over and over. I have wasted so much time. I have been a fool.

I save some lives.

Westminster is hit and nearly every fire crew is on hand to fight the blaze. It stands for something, this place. It has significance. A full moon is clearly showing us our symbol of democracy blaze away. We hear later that Winston Churchill cried as he stood in the ruins of the chamber. Big Ben has been silenced. It still tells the time on its blackened faces but cannot chime. The buildings are surrounded by gawkers, the Blitz tourists who have come in from the suburbs to gaze upon the misery and the vast majesty of the city ablaze. It is difficult to tell sightseer from victim. We hear St Thomas's Hospital is on fire.

Somehow we get instructions to head into Soho to try to deal with the many hits it is taking. No one looks me in the eye when we take to the truck again; we are headed into my manor and it is not going to be pretty. I am beyond caring. I want Jane and our baby. I have asked all of the other units if they have seen her. Some think so. One lad says she was at the zoo earlier. The way he says it almost makes me laugh, as if she had called in on a visit to the animals, taking a little time out to enjoy a city attraction. The animals are long gone

to Whipsnade, the fish and birds eaten, the dangerous creatures like snakes all put down. People shelter in the tunnel
linking the north and south of the complex and I hope to God
she has somehow got trapped there and is safely out of harm's
way. That's unlikely, though. It hits home, painfully, how brave
my wife is and how she is prepared to sacrifice herself for her
countrymen and women. I have been a blind fool, wrapped
up in paltry preoccupations while beside me each day a glory
was on show.

Soho is on fire. So many familiar places are in flames on
Dean Street, Old Compton, Wardour, Bourcier; the Ship Inn,
Patisserie Valerie, Café Belgo, the Algerian Coffee House,
Minella and De Rossi's, Luigi's Hair Salon. Nightingale's store
is totally razed. Incendiaries have hit Broadwick and Brewer
but strangely Pig Lane and Claxton Court are untouched. The
Arnolfinis are safe, though no one but me knows that and I
realise that I don't care as much right now as I did a few
hours ago. We try to evacuate as many as possible as the fires
cannot be dealt with in any meaningful way, with most of the
crews trying to save parliament. There is a major fire on
Regent Street, and a high-explosive bomb at the junction of
Soho Street and Oxford has set a gas main alight. Hopelessness
is all I feel but still we must forge on. Jane, Jane, Jane. The
dead line the streets and are unremarkable: seven here, three
there, felled by this plague of war, fire and hatred taking their
lives indiscriminately.

We lose Ginger Worth to an explosion as Harris and
Company, Hatters and Hosiery, Old Compton Street, is hit at
3.45 a.m. Poor Ginger. He will never know the result of the
Cup Final replay. He will never know who wins this war, and

never have to wonder again if it was all worth it. He will never see me hold my child. His last words were, 'I had a hat made in there once. Lost it at a dance up Kilburn way.' His final memory is of a hat.

The all-clear is sounded at 5.52 a.m. with one long siren blast. Ginger Worth is two hours dead. I feel guilty to be alive, but so damn glad of it. I am guilty, too, that I wished death upon myself at the beginning of the night. That was a wasteful and almost arrogant moment, I now feel. Death didn't want me today so I will make the most of what I have been granted and be mighty glad of it too. I need to find my wife and child. I walk back from the station, heart racing faster than ever before, in a thick pall of smoke, dust and petrol fumes. It is like a fog, a manmade fog of war. The flat is empty when I get there, Giovanni and his wife untroubled by the wounded city's ordeal. They are a touchstone, and I sit before them, drinking in the beauty, waiting for Jane to come home. I can hardly breathe for wanting to see her, to hold her, to apologise for being a thoughtless, careless oaf. I concentrate on the couple before me, willing them to help me through.

Their world is calm as they pose for Jan, the artist, and another observer. I can see them in the mirror on the back wall of the room, so beautifully rendered as to be real to the touch, I fancy. The couple are probably dressed in their best clothes and it is clear that Giovanni is a wealthy man. He is a merchant, I believe. I love it that I can talk about them in the present for they will always be in a present tense. They are forever standing like this, frozen in this content and constant moment. As many times as I have scoured this painting for its treasures, I still marvel at the quality of the rendition of so many of the elements within it. The chandelier above the couple is a masterpiece in its own right. Much of the symbolism is lost on me but some day perhaps I will know more about it. The Director has always been helpful when he has passed and I have asked questions. It may be a marriage contract, or a betrothal work meant to be sent to other family members on the Continent as news of the couple's new status. Jan Van Eyck signed it cheekily, using his name like graffiti really. I think he'd be good value on a night out. I close my eyes and see his cheery self-portrait in my mind, as clearly as I saw it each day on my watch in the National Gallery room I guarded.

And then the portrait begins to show me the worst of my situation. I know it is meant kindly but it tears me apart. The beautiful woman is probably the first Mrs Arnolfini, I have been told. She holds her dress up in the fashion of the time but it makes her look pregnant, like Jane is, though it is unlikely that Mrs Arnolfini was. And my eyes are dragged to the chandelier again. A candle above Giovanni is lit, as if to say he is alive, and the one above his wife is extinguished. And that's when the knock comes on the door with news that I am not ready to hear, could never be prepared for, in spite of my friends on the wall.

Jane was at the zoo, as reported, but she did not stay safely there. She drove an injured woman to St Thomas's Hospital. It was bombed and she was fatally injured during that. Her ambulance partner, Michael, sits before me, trying to tell this story without breaking down. I know he feels he owes it to her, to do justice to her final moments. 'She was so brave,' he says, and that is nearly the undoing of him. He takes a moment. I want him to take forever, though it can make no difference, with the outcome of this sad story already decided. But if he stalls, even a few more moments, I can kid myself that the news will not be quite as bad as it surely is. Perhaps he feels this too because he does pause. He looks at the Arnolfini portrait and says, 'Ah, there it is. She thought the dog was all right.' He has used a past tense, though, and it cannot be undone. Jane does not think any more, because she cannot, but I might allow myself and Michael the luxury of thinking he has made a tiny error of speech.

The human mind is a strange place, hoping against all hope and logic that some words will change what history has now catalogued and moved on from. This concept of foolish hope separates us from animals but I am not sure it makes us any better for all that. We make fools of ourselves with it, with our silly imaginings. We cannot change what is done. All that we can change, as time goes on and we supposedly mature, is how we deal with what's thrown at us.

As she lay dying, Jane cried a little and told him about our baby and he wants to stress she called it just that, 'our baby', hers and mine. This man knows the importance of that for me. She smiled and repeated, 'Our baby. Me. David,' and passed away. My wife remembered me at the end, and an Us that I was convinced had disappeared, and not a lost hat or a slighted dog. I carry that with me every day. It is not exactly acceptance but it is a small gift that helps me wake up breathing and sometimes able to get out of bed.

Ray Rawley, black marketeer and childhood mate, appears at my door looking shaken, which is odd to take in as he is the most confident man I know: useful for a trickster. I have always liked him. For all his bravado and deceit he is a generous soul. I once said that to him; he seemed embarrassed and replied, 'Well, it's easy for me to be generous, innit?'

'You don't have to be,' I persisted.

He shrugged and changed the subject.

Now he stands hangdog, upset. 'I heard about Jane,' he says and I am certain he will cry.

Jane getting the fresh fruit and food makes sense now. She was trying to give proper nourishment to the child growing inside her. All I gave her was grief about her black marketeering, me the arch looter.

'I didn't know about the baby,' I tell him, 'but I think you did?'

Rawley nods. 'My own missus is up the duff again so I knew the signs.' He married Mildred Forbes, my teenage, cut-price, mortal Rokeby Venus. 'Long, dark nights, this war, you know yourself.'

He takes in the Arnolfinis. 'Jane talked me through that one day,' he says. He registers my surprise. 'She was worried you loved it more than her.'

'For a while I think I did,' I admit, not without shame. I can feel hot tears begin to prickle.

'She said their fruit made her realise what was up. She craved it. She was jealous they had some and she didn't. And she was jealous that they had you too.'

I look at the Dutch window sill, forever frozen in time. 'They'll never be short of a bit of fruit,' I admit. And they will always be together, I think.

'You'll need to get rid,' Ray says, referring to the painting. 'For when Jane comes home.'

More crushing truth. Jane will be brought here and neighbours and friends will come to pay their respects as she lies dead in her coffin, our baby still hidden within her. My legs buckle to think of it, this further ordeal. Suddenly I have no control at all over myself. I sink to the floor and start to shake with grief and then a howling sound comes, a lament of sorrowful notes that tears from me and I have to stuff my hand in my mouth to staunch it. I convulse with despair and the hopelessness of this world with its cruel turns and nihilism. We mean nothing, it seems; we are expendable. I think those who got out last night were lucky, and Jane and our child are better off somewhere else.

Rawley stays until I calm a little. He offers me a lift to the hospital but I want to walk there, to feel a barren, battered London guide me. I am also stalling the moment when I confront the ruins of my life. I wash as best I can in the kitchen sink to put some sort of order on myself. I dress in my best suit, for Jane, and look in the mirror at a strange parody of a man heading out to a romantic assignation. Before I leave the flat I take the Arnolfinis off the wall, wrap them in a blanket and place them under the bed. They cannot supervise these next days and I must learn to do without them in the long run. They do not belong here. Jane did, but it is too late to acknowledge that to her now. I failed to shelter her.

The first thing to hit as I step outside is warmth. This is summer, after all. The air is dust-filled and smells of fires, old and fresh. Skeletal buildings reach feebly through the smoke to the sky, which is a clear and innocent-looking blue. Silver barrage balloons float and sparkle in the air. Last night that serene canopy hosted the manmade weapons of our destruction, today it bestows light and warmth. Children run and jump in the craters left by the Germans. It's hide and seek now, daring leaps next. They root about for mementos of war and squeal to find their prizes. Their noise floats muggily on the hot air, too stifled to travel any quicker or sharper. I look at the charred earth, know it is only a matter of time till the pink flowers of fireweed, rosebay willowherb, appear as it starts to colonise the ground cleared by fire.

Some lads have located a flat area where houses stood and have put their jerseys down as goal posts for a game of footie. Bombings, war and death are sidelined. I sit for a moment watching them and feel so utterly tired and useless I pray an unexploded shell will somehow find and annihilate me. They are oblivious to the screaming pain I harbour. I am leaden with the exhaustion these last years have wrought and the temptation to lie down in the rubble is enormous. My bones are sore with tiredness and my eyes sting with tears and lost love. Grit from too many fires and bombed upheaval rubs between my teeth, caustic and intrusive. I feel sweat gather on my shirt collar but I am shaking with a chill.

One of the boys is giving me the eye and I imagine I look a rum type to him, all dressed up, gazing mournfully at him and his mates running about. If I were him I'd find a policeman or some other adult to run me off this mockery of a playground. Then the thought that I might be frightening them mortifies me and I shamble to my feet and shuffle off. I hear them give muted approval that I have been seen to. Bully for them.

Jane has been afforded a special resting place at the hospital as she died a heroine. She has never looked more beautiful or rested. There is a slight suggestion of a frown on her brow as if to say, 'Now what's this?' It is so familiar to me, this tiny crease above her nose. I saw it many times as she puzzled over something and often, if she caught me watching, she would let it turn to a smile. In my mind those were the best smiles of all and I am going to have to trust my memory now to provide me with all sorts of details of her. I do not care if they are sentimental or maudlin, as long as they are vivid. I touch the utter stillness of her dead hand and reach over to kiss her marble-cold face. My lips feel marked. I move my hand to the sheet above her belly and try to reach out to our unborn child. 'Are you a boy or a girl?' I whisper. 'Would you have grown to be a fine man or woman?'

I think I make some arrangements but suspect they are made for me and then I begin to walk again. I must break the news to Jane's family. I must get to the station to tell all there. I stumble through the barren, damaged streets, gaining comfort from this torn city. Its condition represents my own. The only difference is that people are already repairing London whereas I do not think it will ever be possible to fix me. I have suffered a blow that I cannot conceive of ever walking away from. I think of Jane and her sacrifice and know that she will be absorbed within the statistics of war. The child she carried will never be acknowledged by anyone but me, and mine is a small life and of no consequence, so few will ever know about us. There is no single story, in life, just as there is no single death. The Government Censor is strict, though, and her obituary notice will only name the month of her death, not the actual date, so casualties of an air raid are harder for the public to guess. We must be kept calm on that front, and managed.

Jane is reduced to a number among many numbers and I am a shadow-man. I stop on Panton Street with a definite halt and

I think to myself that tonight I will be sure to die. Tonight I will join the ranks of numbers of the dead. It gives me enormous comfort. I am stood by the ruins of Stone's Chophouse, once famous for its steaks. I remember that I ate an excellent grilled herring in mustard sauce here once. That feels like another era now, a time of make-believe and heady opportunity.

For the rest of the day I carry that light notion of imminent death in my heart. I will be released this evening. When the bombers come I will help as I normally do and then bow out when my opportunity presents itself. I now have a strength within me because I have a purpose. I find it helps me comfort Jane's family because I carry certainty now. I can be strong for them because I will join Jane soon.

But life is never as predictable as we would wish or want. Even as I am planning my escape, Germany looks East and shifts emphasis. The Russians are now the substantive target. In London at 9.30 p.m. this evening, as Jane lies waiting for me, still and cold in a box in our flat, the usual sirens wail and then there is a hush. The bombers do not turn up and thirty minutes later the all-clear sounds. It is a quiet night. So, in his own perverse way, Adolph Hitler saves my life. And for that alone I can never forgive him.

Preston will win the Cup Final replay 2–1.

Life, football, London, all carry on.

then

Yes, in spite of all,
Some shape of beauty moves away the pall
From our dark spirits.

John Keats, *Endymion*

june 1979

Frank never had a problem walking through any door in Soho. This was his patch. His father before him had been a native and it was in his blood to accept everything these streets had to offer. So, when it came to looking for work in the club, he sauntered in as if it was a relative's open house and he was expected, without a care in the world or a by your leave. Besides, he was twenty-two years old and cocky as all get out. He was also hopeful of encountering an exotic dancer of any persuasion, who might tickle his libido, though preferably a heterosexual woman who didn't look like the back of some worn-out bus.

The club itself was everything he might have expected: underground, cramped, furnished and decorated in red and gold, smelling of smoke and gin and too many abandoned nights. His feet stuck momentarily to the carpet, then made an alarming sucking sound when lifted, as he descended into the bowels of Soho. Although a smallish space (was everything smaller in real life?), the club was empty so his lone voice echoed in a tawdry sound as he said, 'Hello? Anyone home?' Anyone home, he thought, feeling slightly foolish, as if someone might actually live here. Mind you, this was Soho where anything goes and everything went. In spite of his youthful bravado he was keenly aware of being ridiculous at any given time and this was one of those moments. He was glad no one seemed to be here to see or hear it.

He'd wandered in looking for music work, figuring they might need an accompanist for live musical evenings, a hack to strum guitar or plink about on a piano. He was fairly adept at most of the ordinary instruments that might be required and thought he might be handy to take over occasionally when a regular might want a night off. He lived around the corner and could be on immediate call.

He heard a rustling but assumed it to be a rat. In a way it was. A rough type in an expensive suit appeared at the back of the stage.

'Wahaddaya want?' he demanded.

Frank moved forward to give the man a view of him and flashed his best and freshest smile.

'Work.'

'Not pretty enough, my dear,' the man growled.

'I'm a musician,' Frank explained. 'I thought you might need someone to fill in from time to time. Something like that.'

The other man didn't move a muscle.

'I live locally so I'd be on call. Handy, you know?'

Garibaldi, the manager, took another snarling look at him, asked, 'Can you read the dots and change key fast if needs be?' To which the answer was yes, so he started that evening. 'Deep end, darling,' his new boss said. 'Welcome to Lou Lou's.'

Now, months later, he was assembling a combo to debut at the club and times were fraught.

'What I'm saying is that I draw the line at gobbing.'

'I think we all do,' Frank said, reasonably he thought. 'Besides, it shouldn't be necessary and I really don't think it would suit the band's image to spit on people.'

Mike Edwards Smith shot him a look, clearly wondering if he was deliberately pulling the piss. 'I mean them spitting on us, Frank.'

'Oh, right.'

'A gob on to the hand can be a useful lubricant,' Caesar offered, definitely with mischief in mind. Mike wasn't homophobic but he was queasy about bodies and mucus and, sure enough, he turned a little green about the gills. He'd be off to wash his hands again soon.

'Look, chaps, we're playing a drag club on Old Compton Street, not supporting the Sex Pistols,' Frank said. 'And besides, punk is so last year, and even if it wasn't it would hardly have taken such a hold on the queens of Soho that they'd want to shower us with their spit for dressing up in some nice frocks and playing some pretty tunes.'

'And yet—'

'Once again from the top,' Frank ordered, squashing Caesar's line of speculation, he hoped.

He counted them in and began to play the opening notes on trumpet, the jaunty glissando of 'I Can't Give You Anything But My Love.' His brain pedantically registered that it was a rising chromatic scale, which almost made him laugh and miss his sequence. You can't take the classical out of the boy, he thought. He greatly doubted the others appreciated his use of portamento, as he carried the notes up an interval in an elegant slide. However, attention to detail was all and he would give it that. This might be popular and contemporary music but it deserved no less than Elgar if it gave delight to an audience, and he supposed that here, in Soho, there were many casual listeners taking in their rehearsals.

His eyes were fixed on the street beyond in case the girl and young boy passed. It was now a default position for him, the waiting by the window in the hope of a sighting. This time of day was probably going to prove fruitless, but you never knew. In fact, he thought he might not know much about a lot, if anything, any more. There was the question of this motley collection of musicians posing as a drag act in a Soho club to make money. Was that profitable at all or worth it in any respect? It was certainly his idea and he wondered about the brightness of it now. Still, as long as there were female drag queens in the world he needn't feel he'd had such a freaky idea, surely? And there was such a thing as a female drag queen, he had discovered.

His eye was taken with the birds perched on the electricity lines across the road. He jotted down the notes they made on their unnatural stave. It was a habit of his, to mark this birdsong. Today, if he stayed with the key of C, he had C, E, F, G, C. He added two beats to underscore these notes and with a suitable rhythm he thought it might make a good and calming intro to their show: heartbeats and nature's gentle singing then on into a burst of trumpet to announce their arrival onstage and they were sorted for an entrance.

It was a performance of *Peter and the Wolf* that did it. The young Frank, at five years old, could not believe the sounds and feelings revealed to him that evening. It all began with a palpable sense of excitement the like of which he had never encountered before. Even the lead-up to Christmas now palled in comparison, because this was concentrated beyond anything he could comprehend. There was the trip to the Hall, sitting on the top of a red bus and, as they neared the venue, the sense of others gathering for an event, hundreds of others. Then, in the hushed and heightened silence, to hear the orchestra warming up. He almost peed his pants. When the musicians began to play, revealing delights of such magnitude, he started to cry, silently, fervently, with happiness.

He was enchanted. Even if he hadn't heard the accompanying words he would have made a narrative of his own. All of the instruments and musical signatures were playing parts and telling a story. Of course the flute should be a bird and the cat could be nothing except a clarinet. His own grandfather didn't sound like a bassoon but he knew of some who did. It all made sense. For the first time in his short life he felt sadness that was not based on a slight like the refusal of a treat. It was an emotional punch in the stomach. He mourned the duck. He didn't want the bird swallowed by the wolf at the end but at least the oboe still sounded from within the beast because the duck was whole and still alive in there. His tears fell unchecked all the same as he tried to figure out why he was so sad yet so exhilarated.

He had played the random instruments left lying about the Soho flat since he was able to hold them or climb up on them if needed. That night at the recital, sandwiched between his parents, the world of music and instruments began to come together for him. He noticed his mother did not seem as enthralled, particularly during percussive moments, and became uncomfortably agitated at the huntsmen. She jumped at the shots they fired. His father reached out and touched the back of her hand to steady her and let her know she was not alone. Frank wormed his fingers into her tightened fist. Even the wolf, portrayed by melodic horns, made her flinch slightly. It was only much later that he realised why. To him, then, this was perfect excitement. To him it was what he wanted to do. He wanted to make music. He wanted to tell stories with notes. He reacted to each and every gift bestowed by the music and the orchestra and was exhausted by the end of the recital. His father had to carry him home and he was fast asleep by the time they got to Soho.

He had since learnt that the composer of the piece, Sergei Prokofiev, had also shown musical talent from the age of five though probably to genius level, not unlike Mozart, so there the comparisons between Frank and him ended, aside from the fact that Prokofiev also had a Russian mother and played chess, though again at a level Frank could never aspire to or attain. Oh, and he'd composed his first opera by the time he was nine, a thing Frank had yet to attempt. As he led the introduction to the Stylistics' song during rehearsal he remembered that Prokofiev favoured distinctively and highly original diatonic melodies and therefore scales of eight notes within the octave, major or minor, but without chromatic deviation. Thank you, I'm here all week, he thought, and I'll be wearing a dress for most of that.

My mother never enjoyed disaster or war, no matter how accidental one might be or how inevitable the other. I knew this from an early age. She did not see them as fit entertainment. It marked her out from the start. I visited other houses and saw other parents sat around their radios or televisions tutting at misfortune, hungry for the gritty details that would feed their morbid curiosity and make them feel grateful or satisfied with their own lives. Mortality was a turn-on and a great gossip topic. After a report, preferably with pictures to be pored over, they'd set to with their homespun analysis of the whys and wherefores of the situation and whether politics or sheer human bad luck was at the root. Mama seemed wounded by the inhumanity of international cruelties in a way it took me an age to understand and random hurt flummoxed her.

But what does a child ever know of suffering? We are put on the earth to run wild, be spoiled, be utterly selfish without needing to know, until the age of some reason and, let's face it, hormones, the value of responsibility and heartbreak. Until then we learn all the other stuff, the nuts and bolts of life, even a little about sharing, but it's small potatoes compared with the large sweep of history. My mother had all that and the dignity that lends itself to true survivors. And so it was also that people didn't engage her too much in small talk, and certainly not about crimes against humanity or the forbidden joy of natural disasters that you yourself were not involved in.

The subtlety of her situation was lost on me, which was unsurprising, as I was not told her story fully until I was fourteen years old. What I did know was that many families had suffered during, and because of, the war but we, somehow, had an extra layer. I simply did not know why. In the way of children I probably wasn't all that curious about it either, reasoning that if it was pertinent I would have been apprised of it. There is a splendid arrogance to the young and also to the only child, and I was both. I am grateful it was kept from me for so long as it is the stuff that would scramble a brain and send a person mad.

The wonder is that my mother survived it at all with her sanity intact. At times she'd sit for hours in a darkened room, usually my parents' bedroom, and stare at the wall. My father had a framed copy of the Arnolfini portrait there and it sometimes looked, to me, as if she was contemplating it but I learned this was not the case. A burlesque might have happened before her eyes but she would not have seen it; she was watching a dance of death and regret most other people will never know to such depth, and are lucky not to. I knew other mums 'suffered with their nerves' but there was a stillness to my mother's bad times that even I knew was profound. She rarely cried during these spells but neither did it look as if she was breathing either. She was suspended in time. And no other mother ever came at her with advice about it because there was no casual help that could be doled out to Mrs Johnson.

Once, when I crept in and sat beside her, she wrapped her arms around me and said, 'At least the dream stopped when you came along, my little miracle.' It meant nothing to me and simply reinforced my notion that adults were strange and lived on another planet, not one I was too happy to be headed towards. And I rarely joined her in the darkened room, aware that this was private time for her and to be respected as such.

Everywhere there were signs of my mother's past life but as a child I took them all on board without comment because they were normal to me. We never took a train when we went on holiday. I know I created merry hell and havoc about that, not realising its significance to her. She would not allow bunk beds in my room though it would have been a practical solution to the sleeping arrangement, as I shared with my grandfather. I did not realise what kind of reminder they were for her, people stacked upon others, and again kicked up in royal fashion about this incredible privation to me. I was big on injustice for many of my early years and had many examples of the slights done to me within my very own family if anyone cared to listen.

But I did have some inkling one early day that something special was up as I played piano and she began to paint the notes I was thumping out. I can have been no more than nine or ten at the time. She started with a cheerful work, because that was the nature of the piece I was playing, a simple composition to get a child reading music and appreciating rhythm and melody. It was catchy and probably a bit annoying. Obviously at some point I got bored of it because I began to play, from memory, sections of *Peter and the Wolf*. I particularly relished the rhythmic woodsman section and when I was done, Mama was streaming tears and standing in front of an extraordinarily powerful picture. It was painful to behold. The dark, vivid colours were at once gouged in and shredded across the canvas. I think it was the first time I ever said the word 'fuck'. She did not reprimand me but rather nodded in agreement. We stood in front of it, catching our breath, and then she hugged me and said, 'Thank you.' I knew it would be the first of many such sessions down through our lives. That painting now hangs in a permanent collection in a stately home and is always an unscheduled stopping point for tours, though no one can ever quite explain why.

My mother carried herself with dignity but also an elegance no others appeared to possess. I think every man wanted her, rattled though her demeanour and beauty made them, and every woman was jealous without wanting to swap with her.

157

Mostly what I noticed was that she rarely raised her voice. She didn't need the drama of picking a fight with anyone the way some other mothers needed to pass their ordinary day. In the petty competitions of life between neighbours and acquaintances, the pissing contests if you like, my mother won hands down so she was rarely included in them. She was also actively 'arty' and that was of another, alternative mindset. But, then again, she was Russian so what could you expect?

I liked to call her Mum when anyone else was around, in spite of the fact that we were surrounded by mongrels such as ourselves. I saw it happen to lots like me who were bred of diverse sources and cultures. For example, Marty Fabiano was half Greek half Italian, all London, and his parents were Mum and Dad for those who lived outside of his four walls but within they had their proper Fabiano names of Pappy and Mammo. We were searching to create a new conformity in our public lives, an even playing ground. I guess that's the way of it when you live in a proper city melting pot and Soho was all that. It *is* all that. It always will be.

What we had in our household that others lacked was the grimmest of hilarity. Everyone living in London in the aftermath of the war was a survivor of some sort. I was the child of survivors and so it trickled down to me. Humour was the currency with which you dealt with your lot. As I grew to learn of my mother's horrid misadventure I also grew to appreciate her wit. I've heard it called mordant and morbid and it was those things but also very funny in its ghastly way. For instance, she had her lucky numbers and didn't ever need to worry about forgetting them. I remember as a child brushing my fingertips along the small blue tattoo on her arm and having her say, 'Never forget these, Frank, they are important for all of us.' Later in life she would proudly declare her lottery numbers sorted and, yes, each time we'd smile. Hers had been a happy ending, after all. If asked what she would do with her winnings, she'd say, 'Spend it very unwisely, I hope.'

And, strangely, I don't remember being embarrassed by her as a teenager, though I thought my dad was a total asshole for no reason other than that he was breathing for large parts of the day. I was busy wearing adventurous trousers and feeling that no one had lived a life quite like mine ever before in the history of living. To my developing eyes Mum seemed to understand that, whereas Dad always looked a little more sceptical.

Mama was not the only one with a sad history in our family, of course. Dad had lost a wife in the war. 'Almost carelessly,' he'd told me once, and I knew he was not being flippant. His was not an unusual story for Soho and I knew of no household that was lucky enough not to have been touched by a war death. I've heard that there are towns and villages throughout the country that are cursed with the title 'lucky' after various wars because all the soldiers came home. We seem to need our dead and the monuments we give their memory. Mama always insisted that we remember ours but never lose any joy because they were gone but rather celebrate our own lives and relish what time we have here. This, she would say, was paying tribute. We must also tell our stories in the light, she insisted, as darkness and muttering within it was what kept whole nations down.

Then there was my grandfather. I shared a bedroom with him for most of my childhood and formative years. He was an unlikely elder sibling to me. Konstantin, Kostya, Dedooshka, Pappy: Russians are like cats, I realised; they have many names. He would call my mother Natasha as well as Natalia, and all the other diminutives of family and loved ones. His story was different to my mother's in that he experienced a different kind of prison camp, the sort that was not entirely designed to wipe out whole generations, but to contain and punish. He continued the punishment he saw fit to dole out to himself for most of his life, breaking his body to give London back its visible dignity and grandeur.

His favourite job was to be involved in building houses or apartment blocks for ordinary citizens, as the egalitarian in him was never far from the surface. Just after the war he was watched closely and with suspicion by authorities and neighbours alike. After all, he was the Red Menace, the spectre of Communism nestled within the community. He would shrug that off and say, 'I try to be fair, that is all.' He was rarely fair to himself, always taking ultimate blame for his family's misfortune and suffering during the war. He missed his dead wife and daughter and regularly cried for them at night. He was the first man I knew to show emotion of that momentous sort, my father being more of a stiff-upper-lip type. My grandfather was demonstrative in his foreignness too and I grew up thinking nothing of hugging a person in greeting, which marked me out from the crowd and often brought taunts.

Because we had an Auschwitz survivor in our household we also spread the real word of what had occurred in that place. That was our duty to history. Good people had been snatched from the world unfairly and that action and those lives needed to be acknowledged. It seemed to me our little collective did more to inform Londoners of the Holocaust than any Government initiative. If anything, those in power were reluctant to dwell on the atrocities, or encourage the populace to do so, perhaps fearing that questions might be asked as to why Great Britain had been tardy in its rescue and had failed to act in time to save over six million souls.

And yet, even as my mother lay dying in her London bed, she still had call to ask, 'Did I do enough?' That is the burden of the Survivor.

Frank wasn't sure what his preconceptions were, if he had any at all, but he was fairly certain he'd thought each drag queen would be a man. Was it not, after all, a man done up to look like a woman, or at least a very theatrical version of a woman? So, how could a woman pretend to be a man pretending to be a woman? And why?

Sal laughed into his face on that first day and said, 'We're not exactly legion so don't get your knickers in a twist.' Already that notion made him uneasy but there was no doubting that he had been looking at very large versions of women's control panties and would own at least one pair imminently. Strapping his manhood down was the order of the week. Sal was oblivious to his discomfort, having probably seen it all a thousand times before. 'We help out with the vocals, for one thing, because the girls might look the part but sometimes their singing voices let them down.'

Sal was a trained actress, currently out of 'legit' theatre or film work, and therefore swirling about Soho as a drag artist. When the real women were in full regalia it was a challenge for anyone not in the know to pick them out as anything but an actual queen.

'Tons of slap, false lashes, gold lamé and a smile and, hey presto, I'm practically a transvestite!'

They were sitting on the tiny stage selecting fabrics and embellishments for their costumes. Actually each member of the small company was fussing and hissing, chests primped forward, hooked on this new, camp finery.

'I know we are all a tad hysterical right now,' Caesar said, applying unlikely understatement for him, Frank noted, 'but I cannot stand idly by and allow the cavalier use of exclamation marks where they are not deserved. So, some ground rules: they may be used for unicorns and sequins.'

'Might I posit a case for feathers also, especially when used in tandem with unicorns or sequins?' Mike asked.

'You may,' Caesar allowed.

Smiles all round. It's good to see them play off one another, Frank thought, relieved that the group had gelled.

'Run me through the names again,' Sal said to monopolise the order and copper-fasten the calm.

'I'll be Goldie Horn,' Frank explained.

Without looking up, Sal smiled and said, 'The lass with the magical trumpet.'

His face heated but not uncomfortably. He imagined it was quite a sight, as they had spent over an hour experimenting with their make-up and he was heavily disguised by what felt like a ton of coloured cement. It was a condition he would just have to get used to.

'I am also happy to introduce Nica Lastic, Shirley Knot and Wanda Fruit. Well, if Eric were here I'd be happy to point to

Nica Lastic. Last we heard he was muttering about his hair with what sounded like dark intent.'

'He threatened to shave his head when Thatcher got elected last month,' Mike reminded them.

'A hairy moment indeed,' Caesar conceded, his Glaswegian accent thicker, as it always was when politics were discussed. 'He's not the only one concerned about it all and to be honest I don't appreciate his high moral tone lecturing the rest of us when he knows fuck all about deprivation or having to fight your corner to survive.'

Sal met Frank's eyes but he gave her an imperceptible shake of the head to warn against engagement here. Caesar was a gay, black, illegitimate Scot who boasted jokily of having most of the minorities battling away inside him and Frank didn't doubt it. Caesar had been beaten most days of his life by his pissed-up mother or one of the many low-rent men she had to visit or live with them. He was also a highly politicised leftie and anyone who simply took the fey, pretty transvestite he now played as the full story was in for a big shock.

'We're hardly Bette Bourne and the Bloolips,' Caesar moaned, invoking the legendary and daring drag company who were the talk of London and any other place they performed. 'They are the Grail, the artists.' He issued a theatrical, but clearly heartfelt, sigh. He wore a rose satin gown cut on the bias and was painting his nails to match.

'Not everyone can, or even wants to be, the Bloolips,' Sal explained. 'Besides, there's room for everyone. You do some great, gentle covers of recent classics, all with a spin, and I think punters will love your style and how you're going to look.' She put her sewing down. 'Tart trap,' she said.

'Perhaps,' Mike remarked. 'But what exactly is so wrong with that?'

'No, *discuss*,' Sal said, pointing upwards. 'It's time you learnt about the other bits of the club you might like to use in the act. That, gentlemen and ladies of the company, is the tart trap. From thence we have lowered many a prop or semi-nude person. The proscenium arch has been purpose-built for such airborne entrances.'

'Next we'll be shitting glitter,' Frank remarked.

'That's the spirit,' Sal agreed.

Caesar shrieked and grasped a newly padded and embold-ened chest. He pointed to the figure at the door. 'Hair do? Hair don't! Eric, what is that upon your head?'

'I have decided to be a New Romantic in what little of my real life is left to me outside of this spangling charade.'

'I preferred the punky urban hedgehog of yesterday,' Mike admitted.

'But not in a gay way?' Eric said. 'Just checking, you know, that this lark hasn't turned you.'

'No, clearly not.' Mike had a sweet, tiny blonde fiancée called Bianca who doted on him and he was unlikely to change his mind about his sexuality any time soon. In fact, Bianca had made some style decisions for him that included a corset, which gave him an hourglass silhouette the envy of Lou Lou's. He stood with hand on hip, unconsciously highlighting his newest asset.

'Hair fail,' Caesar said, sadly assessing Eric. 'Thank heaven for wigs.'

'The Bloolips use mops,' Eric said. 'Their costumes are made of cracked wash baskets and found objects.'

Sal took charge again. 'Ladies and gents, can we leave the artistic arguments aside on the understanding that you have an audience paying good money to see you within forty-eight hours and if you look or sound crap they'll not be pleased and might even have cause to notice they are also being ripped off on the price of the mind-alteringly disgusting hooch available in this venerable establishment. In other words, exactly the sort of nasty incident we'd prefer to avoid.'

'OK, OK,' Eric conceded. 'Have you heard about the dyslexic transvestite?'

The company dutifully shook its head.

'A man walks into a bra.'

I am a classically trained musician, Frank thought, and the son of a survivor. This whole venture was my idea. What would my mother have made of it all? Then he remembered her lottery numbers and felt there was a chance she would have smiled benignly and told him simply to do what he had to. 'Life happens, you know?' she might say.

'Like shit.'

'Precisely.' And after a pause, 'Oh, and Frank, language.'

They were a gentle Thursday evening entertainment. They would do two sets, one at 9.30 p.m. and the other at 11 p.m. They would be followed after the second show by the house burlesque spot starring, among others, Miss Sally Manda.

'Easy-peasy, lemon-squeezy,' as Mike so annoyingly put it, more than once, many times more than that. It was his cack-handed way of calming the troupe and had a predictably alarming effect on Eric.

'A Conservative witch has been ushered in to ruin us, and that clown is speaking in faux nursery rhymes . . .'

There were times when Frank wished he knew less fiery harp players than Eric but he did not and, in fact, harp players in general were scarce on his patch of ground. Especially harpists with access to a full-sized concert instrument. Which totally looked the business show-wise. Which access Eric had. As well as the talent to play like an angel. Which Eric did.

I want to study for a masters degree, Frank wanted to point out. Instead I'm worried that this livid blue eye shadow is clashing with the rather unsubtle tones of my pink and white gown. And my shoes pinch. Different strokes, folks.

Caesar gave a deep Scottish growl and told Eric to get on with business. 'We'll worry about the Tories tomorrow.'

'We'll worry about them for fucking years from here on out,' he was told.

'Take a leaf from Thatcher's barnet book,' Mike said, reaching towards Eric with a giant can of hairspray. 'Liquid cement. Nought shall move.'

'She certainly won't, now she's got her feet under the table at Number Ten.'

'Can we remember she might not be all that bad. She did support Leo Abse's bill to decriminalise homosexuality,' Mike said.

'That was sixties Thatcher who also supported the retention of capital punishment and wanted to restore birching,' Eric spat. 'It's akin to the Hitler Was A Vegetarian So He Can't Have Been All Bad argument.'

'She also wasted no time having kids,' Frank said. 'She had both at once: twins. Ruthless efficiency.'

Caesar pitched in again. 'In her science days she was part of the team that discovered a method of doubling the amount of air in ice cream, allowing manufacturers to use less actual ingredients and reduce costs, while still charging the same amount. Now that, if you ask me, is ripe for metaphor. 'Nuff said.'

Sal announced, 'Ladies, this is your five-minute call.'

That silenced them.

Eventually Mike spoke. 'I have a bad feeling about this.'

Eric nodded. 'I know. It's a sad day for the country.'

'Well, I don't think we're that bad, though I'll admit I'm nervous and I don't perform well under strain.'

'You really are a fuckwit,' Eric told him although, from Frank's viewpoint, Mike didn't look too upset to be told it.

Garibaldi appeared and stood dangerously close to Frank. He was wearing his usual uniform of sharply pressed expensive suit and too much Old Spice aftershave. The man was not happy. 'Why didn't you tell me Ray Rawley is your godfather?'

Frank shrugged his padded pink and white shoulders. 'Why would I?'

'We go back a long way and it's nice to do a mate a favour.'

'Exactly. A lot of people feel like that about Ray but I wanted to do something off my own bat,' Frank said, squashing the urge to add, 'Even this.'

'Independence,' Garibaldi snarled, making it sound foolish and dirty all at once.

Frank felt a bead of sweat travel along his spine. It wasn't due to the boss's proximity so much as the tiny space coupled with the nylon mix of his gown in horrid partnership.

'We'll talk later,' was the threat left by the manager. Frank watched his departing back through the heavy, hairy curtains on his eyes. Will I ever get used to false eyelashes? he wondered.

The club filled to three-quarters capacity for the first set, with a murmuring crowd not yet tipped into alcoholic oblivion. The lights went down and the notes of Frank's bird composition mellowed the clientele with the base notes of heartbeat and gently above them the song spelt out recently by the birds on the electricity wires on Broadwick Street. When hush settled, a spotlight picked Frank out as he began his trumpet intro to the Stylistics number, to be joined by Caesar, moving through the small auditorium on percussive maracas, and Mike onstage on keyboards. Eric was the singer for this number and he took centre and belted it out, but towards its conclusion he also whipped a red silk cover from his harp and took over the trumpet's rising signature scale to applause. He was quite the showman for a man wracked with a social conscience who thought this frivolous. Still, even leftie politicos have bills to pay. So far, so good, Frank thought.

Without hesitation between numbers the band headed straight into their version of Thin Lizzy's 'The Boys Are Back In Town', with Frank playing trumpet instead of the original's lead guitar, Eric and Caesar sharing vocals while playing harp and xylophone respectively, and Mike filling everything else in on keyboard. This time the appreciation was more vocal. They began to smile though relaxation would be weeks off. Frank slowed things down with his take on the Buzzcocks' 'Ever Fallen In Love With Someone (You Shouldn't Have Fallen In Love With)', strummed languidly on ukelele while swinging in a basket chair suspended from the ceiling. A mirror ball scattered sparkles on to the walls and faces of the happy punters.

Between sets Sal came to give them a tutorial on audiences.

'OK, girls, listen up. Already I have spotted no less than four notorious tranny fuckers in the crowd, so be aware that you will have strange men approaching you with a view to taking you home for sex, should you wish to avail yourselves of that. There is also a snake charmer here, name of Norma, who likes to bring a ladyman home to fuck while her husband, a magician called Ian, looks on. Julie Noted, of my own troupe, had to stage an epileptic fit only last month to distract them and run for the door, and freedom, from their council flat in Stockwell. I shit you not. You have been warned.'

'Oh, brave new world that has such creatures in it,' Mike muttered.

'Hallelujiah, sister,' said Caesar. He was a dark Audrey Hepburn tonight, with a pair of killer pins no one had ever suspected lurked under his trouser legs. Frank's money was on him to be the honeypot for admirers and he hoped the Scot kept hold of his native common sense. He was aware that he made a big woman himself, and didn't expect much in the way of wooing.

'Hey, handsome,' Sal said to Frank. 'Will you stay for our show? We can have a drink after.'

'If I can go back to being a man.'

'It would be best for both of us if you did.'

'And will you go back to being a woman who is not pretending to be a man pretending to be a woman?'

'As you wish.' Sal stood on tiptoes and kissed his extra smooth cheek.

They would shed their disguises and be themselves again,

whoever anyone ever was these days. It was almost a date, though conducted at odd hours when most of the rest of the city was asleep. Frank smiled. There were no rules any more. But he was on a promise and the world was good.

'You see, there's music everywhere.' I'm slurring now, Frank thought. Doesn't matter; some things have to: Just Must Be Said. 'I can see notes in the way people leave their bins out if I arrange them on a hypothetical grid in my mind. So, the wires the birds sit on are just like the lines of the stave we write the notes on, therefore the birds are making music with their bodies. Well, potentially they are, if anyone cares to see it or hear it. And of course they have their actual birdsong too. A blackbird adds new trills and variations each year of its life. It has a bird symphony by the time it's done. The Aboriginals hold that we can be sung to a place or a thing, like water, say. We must follow our song lines too. They can be our story.' Am I a boring gobshite now? he wondered.

'They also say we must have our dreaming, don't they?' Sal observed. She was still talking to him, on subject, so maybe he wasn't as crashingly dull or incoherent as he thought. Her eyes were drooping slightly but no less beautiful for it. There were traces of glitter still on the lids and on her pert high cheekbones. 'If you have no dreaming you have no story which means you can have no love, ultimately.'

'I think I love you, Sal.'

'What do you really want to do with your life, Frank?'

'I just said I love you.'

'I heard you. We'll deal with that later. Answer the question.'

'Is it relevant to what I just said?'

'It might be.'

'OK. I've been watching a deaf girl walk by every weekday for the past two months, bringing her brother to his school around the corner. Same one I went to in my day, as it happens, and my dad before me. He lived here most of his life before he moved to a house in Uxbridge with my mum. The flat got passed on to me.'

'You're rambling, Frank.'

I don't want to seem lunatic to this woman, he thought.

'The girl and her brother?'

Here goes.

'I want to help her "hear" music in some way. So, I am trying to make a machine that will portray music in colour so that she can see and therefore appreciate it.'

Sal leant in and kissed him gently on the mouth. 'Good,' she said.

Her second kiss was a lot more fervent. 'Now, about this love business.'

The third was the proper start of their life together. He was glad they'd left the club instead of having that one last drink 'for the door'. Sex in public was fine in Soho, often rewarded with money, but romance was another matter and love something private and worth guarding.

They had strolled home in daylight, buying fruit on Berwick Street from a codger who'd been at his stall for fifty odd years and could trace his business back many more decades. He threw in some grapes 'for the pretty lady' and they fought jokily over which one of them he'd meant. A grey pigeon roosted on the railings by the door to the flat and was quite indignant when refused entry.

soon

Music, when soft voices die,
Vibrates in the memory –
Odours, when sweet violets sicken,
Live within the sense they quicken.

Rose leaves, when the rose is dead,
Are heaped for the beloved's bed –
And so thy thoughts, when thou art gone,
Love itself shall slumber on . . .

Percy Bysshe Shelley, 'To Emilia V'

july 2144

Teddy died on one of the finer days. The weather had been manipulated to give sunshine without any of the usual hazards that required safety clothing. Instead, anyone venturing out simply had to wear their sunscreen. The day started with the rainbow we had been promised. I think most of London came out to see that rare treat. Although we get constant rain, we seldom see what used to be its glorious aftermath in previous times, as sunlight reflects off or bends through the drops of water to create an arc of beautiful colours. In a grace note, the meteorologists also managed the echo rainbow, dimmer and parallel. It was breathtaking, heart-halting. Afterwards, the sky was clearer than usual but still tinged with the crimson and green reminders of the toxins moving around up there, proof of man's bad attitude to the planet through the centuries.

These days were always intended as pick-me-ups for a jaded city population, tired of the endless near darkness and acid rain, or worse. The sky has been angry as long as I can remember. Colin and Teddy were puckish. They had originally planned to go to a soccer match but instead decided on a game of throwball between themselves.

It was strange and almost comical to see their identical faces whitened out by the screening agent to a featureless blank, opaque and chalky, to resist the harmful rays: two ghostly spectres laughing as they exited. The sound of their enjoyment continued, fading slightly for a moment or two, then a palpable silence, which I now know was the very sound of time standing still, followed by Colin screaming. It was the oddest sound I have ever heard him make, a high-pitched howl of warning segueing to a keen of purest horror. I knew, without seeing it, what had happened. He hadn't even managed the cliché of yelling 'no', a detail that haunted him afterwards, as if the word might have stopped the action or prevented its outcome taking hold and becoming real.

When I got to my husband he had hunkered down outside our door and was peering through the bars of the railings at his brother below. Teddy was splayed at an impossible angle, broken, his hand incongruously clutching the oblong ball and his head oozing bright red blood. His white face was a clownish mime mask but serene, his soul clearly absent now from our lives. I was thankful his eyes were closed. Blood continued to pool and ooze, as if it was alive and moving, though its host was not. There was no need to rush down the stairs, he was dead, and he had said often enough that revival would be unwelcome. Like ourselves, he felt our time here should not be prolonged unnaturally.

The Federation sent their people to deal with Record and Removal as Teddy was one of their medical stars. In the meantime, Louise came and sat with him, cradling him and talking gently, though she probably shouldn't have disturbed his body. It didn't matter, as she pointed out, nothing was going to bring him back now. She whispered endearments to her dead husband as mine cried quietly, inconsolably, in our front room. When the authorities took Teddy away, I brought Louise in and washed her and then she calmly walked out of the door.

Her composure was extraordinary, as if she'd been waiting for this day a long time. It was almost the last we saw of her for two years. It was certainly the last time we had any meaningful conversation although I have no idea what we talked about, probably the blandishments associated with sudden death: soundbites of shallow comfort, well meant but ultimately useless, disguised by our minds as helpful.

The weather suited Colin's tragedy. Wind beat the city, wailing around the buildings and whistling its eerie ululations. Storms came and went as regularly as his fits of grief. At times he sat still and soundless, staring out of the window. Sometimes he paced and shook his head so violently I worried for him. He would get up in the middle of the night, agitated, talking about a child shouting 'yellow' and a dead woman lying in a plain, wooden box in our lounge. He was convinced an ancient Dutch painting was hanging on our bedroom wall. He saw a dead man in our bath and hummed strange tunes. He was entirely deranged while seeming to make cogent sense of the surroundings that he could see and I could not. He remembers very little of that period, as if his brain has shut a section off. It can be a capricious and untrustworthy instrument when it wants and it's grimly fascinating to see what it leaves us to work with and what it deems out of bounds.

It's hard to watch the man you love tear himself apart. It's tough to have your offers of care rejected. It's painful to feel that you have failed as a wife. Yet, this is my life, and has been for two and more years. My man is grieving and must be left to that for as long as it takes, but it's still rough as hell to be left on the edge when you want to be in the middle battling for your beloved and their well-being. All I could do, most of the time, was to hold him whenever I was allowed. There was no point in trying to reason the problem away; that was never going to wash off the stain of this death.

He went through a period of incoherence as he tried to make sense of what could not be explained or borne. This was followed by a vile period of shouting. He made it clear that nobody else could possibly know how he felt and should therefore back the fuck off. He roared that no one understood his suffering. He swore. His face twisted with bitterness. He said cruel things, regretted them, cried for forgiveness. It was snotty and ugly and without much dignity. He was incapable of asking for help or reaching out at all. Then he became inarticulate, still plagued by a restless misery. He could not be consoled.

I tried to be patient throughout but it was impossible to remain even-keeled all the time. I am no martyr, no saintly creature by any means. Far from it, and I broke on many occasions. I was exasperated with him. I snapped. We bickered. I began to see his unwillingness to engage in an argument as an annoying appeal to the sentimental and that irked me hugely. It made me unreasonable to a point and I resented that too.

Finally he stopped speaking altogether, which is when the plan to replace Teddy in some measure began to take hold. I was at the end of my emotional tether then and desperate to make a change to our lives. Before Teddy's death we'd talked of starting a family, a new phase to our lives together. Now, everything was on hold. Making Theo, or calling him into being, as it were, was not a substitute for a child but I did think that if the necessary building blocks were almost back in place we might get back on course with our plans. My head was akimbo and I now see it was a lunatic approach. But it means we have Theo and he is a delight, if only Colin could see that.

My husband became exquisitely attentive to his own pain and when that state persisted, as it has, it became our biggest shared problem. He doesn't quite see that all three people living in our Soho home share it but we do. I realise that there should be no stigma attached to sadness but Colin has immersed himself in it to the point of it becoming unwanted baggage. Yes, he has been debilitated by grief, and that is to be expected, but he has also let himself enter a loop of woe. He has allowed the fact that he came to grief morph into abiding depression. He needs to break this ruminative cycle he's in, which only extends his negative mood. It is tedious for those suffering beyond his personal zone but also, ultimately, tedious for him, too.

Colin's depression is almost textbook. The condition has been with Man and documented since we learned to write and record our ailments. Darwin, father of evolutionary theory so long ago, was crippled with it and 'not able to do anything one day out of three'. Colin displayed all of the signs required: he lost his appetite, his interest in sex, had difficulty sleeping and began to obsess about death. In fact, he was morbidly worried that he would die, immediately, and afraid for all of us in general because we will all die and that is still the only thing we can rely on in this life. At least he didn't ever seem

181

to consider suicide, that I know of, though I am sure he wished for his own death a number of times when he was lowest.

He needs to shed his fixation with the darkness, with pessimism. He must fall out of love with his pain, because it is as if he's in love with all the passion, focus and torture that his sorrow brings.

The way he has treated his new double until now has been disgraceful but we have tolerated it because of his grieving. It has been hardest for Theo, born into this emotional maelstrom. He arrived as ill-equipped as any of us to deal with the situation but has been patient, sanguine almost, about our lot. He is a very even-tempered and fair man. Colin must be made to see, in a genuine and meaningful way, that this other is not a robotic construct but a proper person and worth knowing. Theo is a sentient being with feelings and emotions. He can make rational decisions. A brain that cannot feel can never make up its mind; we know that from scientific experiment. We need emotions in order to reason. Feelings and emotions are signals from the brain and they describe us as clearly as our eyes or bodily shape. Complex decisions, and Theo makes those every day, are never just about rational analysis, but stem from everything that makes us wonderfully flawed and human.

I have lost myself in work a lot to compensate for the gap in my life at home. I'll admit that I have done some dangerous things in that respect too. I have helped Illegals. They have rights like the rest of us. I know they may be here without sanction but many of them have good reason. In fact, even if it's only to better their lot I see that as good enough justification. This city has provided sanctuary or camouflage for the persecuted and displaced through many centuries so why not now? We have room for refugees. What is the government so afraid of? Change? Or a healthy influx of new ideas and cultures because, as uniform as the world is becoming, there are thinkers out there and traditions that still abide and there is a swing to them as our weary population searches for truth and meaning. Perhaps that terrifies the powers that be.

I don't believe in any of the gods touted by the various resurgent religions but I do want to live my life well and leave behind some kindness and a few stories of some-or-other good done. There were times, mind you, during the worst of Colin's grief when I would have been grateful of a sacred or religious topography for us both to cleave to. It might have brought comfort, solace.

Mostly, I help deliver the babies. It's what I'm good at. I have been offered a few in my time too and have placed some in other lives than they might have had, with the blessing of their biological parents. It's all deeply against the law but I feel compelled to make a difference and I hope it is for the better.

Colin has been impervious to my activities. Before Teddy's death he would have noticed what I was up to and cautioned against it. Now, I am more peripheral. He doesn't know about the fake identities hidden in our flat waiting to be used, the fake tags and chips for those seeking their new life. We all seem to want that in some measure: change.

I'm seeing signs of a softening in Colin and that's to be welcomed. Anything but this cycle of self-recriminatory lashing that he gives himself over to. His life has miscarried but we must make something of it and move forward, baggage and all. He regards himself as a failure, not only because he feels his work is frivolous but also because he thinks he caused his brother's death. He'll deny the latter and assure me it was no one's fault because he thinks that's what I want to hear. I don't want to hear that: what I need is for him to believe it.

Bit by bit over the last few months he has stepped up and tried to regain his former self. It's a long process. He finds it hard, I can tell, but he is trying. He sees his therapist less, and tries to deal with his problems more in situ and I think that's an improvement. Talking to a stranger was helpful for a while, now he needs to act on whatever he established in those sessions. He isn't as selfish. These days, he treats Theo with a degree of civility.

We have started to make love again.

I found it best to keep Colin on the move through the worst of his lows. Distraction helped him. Theatre proved a particular saviour in that regard. It got us out of the apartment and kept Colin's mind stimulated with fresh ideas for a few hours. I love the live performance. Everything is so lazily convenient in our lives. We can get the latest movies direct to home. If you wish you can watch television on the back of your hand as you go about your daily business, courtesy of a tiny implanted screen. Everything can be miniaturised. But theatre is big and it happens in its own designated cathedral before a crowd of strangers gathered to share the energy and delight it offers.

We've had our hairy moments. *King Lear* was a case in point. I worried that Colin would be too moved by it, thrown too roughly back into the world of emotions. When it came to the storm scene, with Lear on the heath bashed by the elements, my husband was physically in pain. Strangely, though,

I think it offered his mind respite for a while, as Lear's is also diverted in the play just then. But the line that resonated most for him was earlier on in the play: 'Who is it that can tell me who I am?' and he would mutter it for days after.

Tonight we walk along Pig Lane, on to Broadwick Street, head along Lexington towards Shaftesbury Avenue. The rain is light and the darkness benign. Our eyes track the neon signs advertising musicals, plays, live sex shows while details are whispered in our ears using biofeedback. The resident company at the Rylance is presenting a season of twenty-first-century dramas and we see a play called *Jerusalem*, which sends me rushing back to look at the poetry of William Blake. I wonder if we will ever regain a green and pleasant land.

Louise dipped out of every scheduled visit for months. Teddy was increasingly agitated as a result whenever Colin visited him in the Memory Palace. For Teddy, read Colin, my husband. They shouted at one another a lot. Most people would have been worried at the seeming psychosis of it all but, remember, Colin had been a twin and those of us involved in such a situation know it comes with a different set of circumstances than most will ever appreciate. What went on in the memory room was unsurprising to Theo and me. We could not help and we did not intervene. We just hoped for a workable outcome.

At least things in the household continued to improve, slowly but exponentially. Theo was given more to do within the design firm and he proved a boon. He has the same excited eye as Colin, or that Colin has on a good day. I find one range he's working on mesmerising. It's based on clouds. He has worked with images almost lost to what I now know is the nimbostratus we endure daily; it provides our incessant rain.

'Ah, Alice,' he might say in admonishment, 'let's not forget the towering thundercloud that is cumulonimbus; dull for design but a frequent visitor in our modern, exciting lives.'

Theo has been teaching me the names of all of the forgotten clouds, the shapely ones he loves; it is a new fascination. It's also fun to learn with him. He has a dry sense of humour that I enjoy. Laughter is always welcome and has been in short supply on Pig Lane.

I have always had a strangely uneasy relationship with Louise. As the brothers' wives we were thrown together. It could be argued that we were both married to the same man, though that was not the case. The twins may have been identical but they were not the same. If they had been they would have just married one woman, either Louise or me. It's an uneasy notion and not one I dwell on because, in reality, they didn't do that: they were separate people. I am, however, bound to this other woman in a more unusual way than most who are related to a family through marriage to siblings. Now that Teddy is dead it's even more heightened and all the more so because she doesn't want to see us. I can understand that last part. We are the living, breathing reminders of her lost love, none more so than Colin. I think she knows, on the most basic level, that his suffering might affect her and be reductive. She must have great difficulties of her own dealing with the loss and little enough left over to deal with an identical brother in trouble.

She finally named a date and swore she would not default on it, then surprised us by turning up a day early. We were unprepared and perhaps that was a good thing as it would have been stilted in the extreme if we had been sitting around counting down the moments, which is exactly how we would have prepared. I was the first of her encounters as I answered the door. Although I had not seen her for the guts of two years she had hardly changed. She was trim, alert and extraordinarily glowing. Her dark hair was longer and shone in what little light was available; it looked like it was attracting all available light, actually. Her face had always been inclined to a smile and she gave one now that looked genuine.

'Alice,' she said and reached to kiss me.

'Louise, it's so good to see you. You look magnificent.'

'And you.'

When she looked past me she saw Theo and immediately knew who he was. She could tell the difference just as she'd know Colin and Teddy apart. She cocked her head sideways and took him in some more. 'You're not Colin.'

Theo was delighted. 'No, I'm not.'

I was happy for him. He deserved this.

It was extraordinary to be there and to feel their instant connection. The scene was painfully intimate although all they did was look at each other. I felt surplus, intrusive, but in a really good way. This was a happy moment and as welcome as it was unexpected.

'I met two little girls as I was coming in. They said they were off to buy ice cream. The Federation isn't allowing children to live here again, is it?'

Teddy and Louise were relocated to the edges of the city when they started a family as Soho is considered an unsuitable environment in which to raise the young. The giant biospheres created in the suburbs are deemed more conducive to a healthy childhood.

'No,' I tell her. 'Policy hasn't changed so they must have been visiting someone.'

'They alerted me to the music. You have noisy neighbours.'

We listen but cannot hear anything. 'Must be on a break,' Louise says.

Theo cannot take his eyes off her although he is trying to be circumspect about it. I can't blame him as she is a great beauty and is also such a curiosity for him, given her history with our family. She seems entirely at ease with herself and that's a very attractive quality.

'You're keeping your work up?' she asks.

'Oh, yes.' Louise is very aware of my extracurricular activities and it is these she's inquiring about. Teddy introduced me to many useful people within the system, people who want to see the right thing done, even if it's against the law as it stands at the moment. I have access to officialdom and the mavericks within help me with problems of false identification or burying discriminatory evidence or information.

'Teddy would be pleased,' she says. 'Gratified, even.'

I make us some mint tea though I suddenly long for something stronger. She asks how Colin is and I tell her. She looks pensive but unworried.

'It sounds like he's breaking the circular thought cycle and that's the most important step for him on the road back to some sort of happiness.' Louise trained as a psychiatrist and still practises part-time. 'Make sure he's eating well and taking exercise,' she adds. 'How are you finding him now?'

It is a difficult question to answer and I don't want it to be about me but about Colin. 'He is less flattened out emotionally with us,' I say. 'That has been the general mood until recently, a kind of absence, really. He's coming back to us. His work is improving, although he did a beautiful series of muted fabrics when he was at his worst, so creatively he was still firing on some great cylinders.'

She smiles. 'The old suffering-for-your-art adage. There's something in it as an idea, but it shouldn't be mandatory, if you ask me.'

'I'll let Colin know you're here,' I say. I wonder, briefly, if she was hoping all along that he'd be out if she called in a day early.

In the hiatus, Louise admires some fabric samples and Theo talks her through the new ranges. He revels in her attention, blossoms in her kindly gaze. She's responding well to him, which is no surprise: he is a lovely man. I feel a twinge of something that I'm surprised to identify as mild jealousy.

Everything changes when Colin arrives. He brings a heightened energy, certainly, but there is another charge present. Theo retreats into his shell, Louise is suddenly on her guard. Colin decides to barrel through any awkwardness, rattling off questions about the kids, spilling out sundry details of his work, filling the air with noise, anything but name Teddy. Theo slinks away, eventually, and I make an excuse to go check on a midwifery appointment. I sit at my desk in the next room, looking at the sky through the window. Darkness is encroaching again and we can be certain of rain within the hour. I can still hear Louise and Colin.

'We've missed you,' Colin says.

Louise has no comment for that.

'I miss seeing the children too.'

Again Louise lets the statement hang between them.

'I don't mean that as a criticism,' Colin adds, anxious to keep the atmosphere civil.

After another lengthy pause he says, 'I miss him so much.'

'We all do,' Louise says, softly.

In time I can make out the gentle sound of sobbing. Colin is crying. Louise lets him. Finally he wrestles out the words that have been tearing him apart for years. He says, 'I killed Teddy.'

'You didn't, you know,' she tells him. He starts to protest and she cuts him short. Her voice is full of disbelief as she says, 'Is that what you really think?'

'Well, of course.'

'Oh, Colin, you poor man.'

It is lovely to hear her voice say his name. Louise rarely gives Colin his name, his identifying title. This woman is gracious. I don't think I could be that fair if the tables were turned. I know Colin wouldn't be. Though Theo probably would. He is more like Teddy than we know.

Louise takes a deep breath and releases my husband. 'Teddy had a range of tumours including a particularly aggressive one in his head. That extraordinary brain of his was poisoning itself. He refused any invasive treatment and I agreed with him, much as I did not want to lose him. He wanted to die. You gave him a beautiful way out. He went away as he wanted to, with you there to see him off. He was happy.'

I wonder why she didn't tell us this two years ago. Why has she let Colin suffer?

'I thought you knew,' she is saying and there is truth in her voice. She sounds amazed that the man sitting before her has tortured himself for so long, needlessly. 'Please don't tell me he didn't say how ill he was.'

'No.'

'Bloody Teddy. Scatty bloody scientist nonsense behaviour.'

'Maybe he didn't feel the time was right,' Colin says, defending the other half of him and therefore himself. He is also slowly figuring out what happened on that day. I can hear his brain cranking it out. 'He seized his moment, didn't he? It arrived accidentally but he recognised it and acted. You see, we were supposed to go to a soccer match, not play throwball between ourselves.'

'Whatever it was, and whyever it was, I want you to know you helped him, Colin.'

Colin is crying again. 'He never said goodbye.'

'Sometimes goodbye is unnecessary,' Louise says. 'Sometimes it does more harm than good.'

It wasn't me. I did not kill Teddy. It was cruel happenstance. What this knowledge has done is odd. Instead of a weight lifting, I now feel I have wasted time and am panicked that I have lived the last two years under such a misapprehension. I trod water, ticking off the days, hours, minutes regardless of how precious they were. The ground is falling away.

The truth doesn't solve everything nor has it in any way set me free as it might in some clichéd song or fairy tale. Teddy is still dead. But I have the opportunity to release myself from the morbid guilt I have carried around so long. I know it won't be shed immediately. There will always be grief and a slicing sorrow that he is gone but I know that I did not hurry him on his way. Ted chose the manner of his leave-taking. It should be a comfort but it will take time for me to look at it in that light.

I have a new and strange perspective on my life and I don't know where to go from here. I remember the rage I felt initially after his death and then the maw of hopelessness I descended into. I felt him with me all of the time, because that is how we were made from the start, but he was physically absent and the fact that I would never again touch him or speak to him properly nearly drove all reason from my mind. Then, for so long a flat emptiness was my natural state, an endless straight line of nothingness stretching far away into the future. I am now adrift, so much so that the walls and fixtures of the apartment appear to move and bend when I try to pin them into logic with my eyes. The anchor of grief is removed and I am flailing. I am a little ashamed of myself too. I have been devoted to a myth and treated those closest appallingly as a result. How can I ever make amends? My heart beats unnaturally fast in my chest. I am dizzy. My limbs tingle. I want to retch.

Alice comes back into the room. She sits by my side and puts her arms around me.

'I know,' she whispers. 'I know.'

Safe in her embrace I am certain this woman will save me, yet again. I am so lucky. I do not deserve the riches my life has held on to for me.

I sit in my room clutching a pillow to me. I try to smother the happy sounds I am making in it so as not to disturb the

others or draw attention. Louise knew I wasn't Colin just by
looking at me. It made my heart soar in a way I have never
experienced before. Louise. She is beautiful beyond any of
the images I have seen till now. Even the three-dimensional
holograms could never capture her energy, the soul that is
animating her. I expected her eyes to be azure but they are
deepest violet and I know I must use this unique colour in
my work. She radiates health, generosity. My skin is clammy
and I am feverish to have been close to her. I need to talk to
her, let her get to know me, but I don't know how to go about
this. I have no experience of dealing with a woman romanti-
cally, and this is what I assume I am entering, a state of
romance. I do not dare to think Louise might ever feel that
for me but if she knew me she might at least like me. How
can I spend time with her? I can hardly breathe now and it
is tearing away at me. Is this falling in love? Should it hurt
like this does? There is so much I don't know about, and so
much I cannot do because I just don't know how. I don't know
how to proceed. I don't know how to conduct myself. Alice is
calling me and I hope she will point me in the right direction. I feel I am approaching my family, properly at last, as I
open the door and step out into a newer life.

In a few short hours everything has changed again, or might
it be truer to say that everything is regaining a course. I feel
my husband is returned to me and with that is the prospect
of living again. We will take small, cautious steps but I feel a
stirring in my belly that tells me we can hope again. I can
imagine us having our children now. We can at least try.

I look at Louise and Theo and I wonder if she might, in

part, get her husband back too. Theo will see her to her transport and she is wondering if he might like to visit her and the kids one day soon. Of course he would, and he will; he says as much. My heart grows huge for them.

Something very positive has been granted us in this little home today and it is precious and not to be wasted. We have our second chance to do what we must with our lives and each of the four of us, in a silence, looks one to the other and realises this. Then we smile in acknowledgement and we all start to move forward. I remember an ancient rhyme about the animals moving two by two into the Ark. On cue, a heavy rain begins again.

now

Earth in beauty dressed
Awaits returning spring.
All true love must die
Alter at the best
Into some lesser thing.
Prove that I lie.

Such body lovers have
Such exacting breath,
That they touch or sigh.
Every touch they give,
Love is nearer death.
Prove that I lie.

W.B. Yeats, 'Her Anxiety'

august

It was odd to be hit by a wave of intense heat getting off the plane in Heathrow, of all places, even in August, but that was the case. Normally, the crew were first to feel it when they opened the doors in Barbados, say. Today, London was a contender.

Karen had been posted in Business and was still trying to find a huge difference in passenger mood between here and Economy. If anything, the atmosphere was more voluble in this section, with recession stress rife and everyone wanting their money's worth. She dutifully smiled and bade the passengers a goodbye and safe onward journey in a voice that didn't sound like her own and a sentiment she mostly did not feel. When they were decanted, she did a sweep of the cabin with the young Irishman O'Callaghan, binning books and magazines as they went.

'Shit-lit,' she declared as she tossed a few of the more luridly covered novels away.

'Shizz-lit, if we wanna be hip with the kids,' her companion informed her.

'I like it,' she said.

Within an hour her uniform was stuck to her skin as she shook through the bowels of London on the tube. A free newspaper told her Florence Nightingale had died in her sleep, peacefully, at home in London on this day, 13 August, in 1910, aged ninety. I wonder why I never became a nurse, Karen thought. It's what I wanted to do when I was a girl. Probably too late to start now. It seemed inconceivable that she'd remain a trolley dolly all her life. She couldn't really see the point of that but would it be such a waste? What else did she have to offer the world? She had been promoted to Cabin Supervisor but felt it was by default. It was simply her turn to be fully in the firing line. She was moving through the ranks by virtue of age and time served, like a sentence. All she could look forward to from the job was an ever-expanding uniform and the prospect of relics of past travel glamour eroding steadily over time. Dissatisfaction was general with her today. It was not a good feeling. And it was getting meaner all the time.

As they cleared up, she had asked the O'Callaghan boy why he was in the job.

'Didn't have that much choice,' he said. 'I'd have liked a career in the arts but I don't have any noticeable aptitude or ability in that area. Like you, I have a talent for people though I'm not as good as you are, not by a long shot.'

He had to be mistaken, or mocking. 'Me?'

'Yes. Look how much happier that woman in 10E was after you'd talked to her.'

'She did seem to be, I guess.'

'It's because she spoke to you, she shared her problems with you.'

'She was drunk.'

200

'That too, but don't underestimate what you gave her. She left the plane with a bit of vigour about her, and a bit of hope. They say you kept Tony alive a lot longer than anyone expected. He stayed around because of you.'

Could any of this be true? And was it enough to have going for the self?

What did she have to show for her life? A dusty, rented flat in a laneway no one ever noticed. A dead-end job, steeped in servitude and humiliation, that paid poorly and didn't require much skill. The part-time use of a married man who probably only wanted her for the sex which was, admittedly, awesomely good. She had four hundred and seven pounds saved in her deposit account in the bank. Her best friend and confidant was a pigeon who couldn't be relied on to visit regularly. The previous incumbent to the Best Friend title had killed himself in her bath. She was in love with the married man and that was a hopeless state of play.

I am in love.

I am not sure he loves me in return.

Eight months of wondering and hoping.

I am a fool.

She felt bile rise and palpitations set in. I have no decent future to look forward to. I have no past to relish. The present is simply to be lived and got out of the way. She gagged drily into her hand and tried to steady herself. I am a worthless piece of humanity. And I am actively afraid of what's in store for me.

The woman in 10E on the earlier flight had cried all the way from New York to London. When Karen consoled her she said, 'Never give all of yourself to one of them,' flicking her head at the businessmen surrounding them. 'You will always lose. You may even lose yourself. I feel like I'm going mad. He's divorcing me. What hope do I have of meeting anyone else ever again? I'll be fifty next year. I don't want to be alone, even if I don't actually like the bastard that much any more. What's wrong with me that he needs to be rid of me?'

It had a dual effect on Karen. She worried about her tenuous affair, thinking, I don't want to be lost to it or, in general, lost in time, and she felt guilt-edged to be intruding on another woman's life. Alex Bulgharov had a wife. Has a wife, she reminded herself. Has. Present tense. Nothing so handy as 'had'.

'You will, you know, meet someone,' she told the woman. 'There are lots of people like you out there. This is just the beginning of the next phase. Now you get to be yourself and not a satellite within some worn-out arrangement. You need to believe in yourself and embrace what's coming at you and for you.'

Whenever we speak, she thought, we acknowledge a situation and make new truths, new rules by which we operate, rules by which we can or need not abide. She wondered how to make this work for her. The blues she was experiencing were rapidly becoming red. She thought of the 'mean reds' Truman Capote had described for Holly Golightly. They were based on being afraid of the unknown. The blues were easy by comparison. They dealt with being disappointed. Disappointment was gentle compared with fear. Fear was a slippery customer that terrified a person and could lead them to taking to the bed and never coming back out of it.

Rattling through tunnels she thought of the abandoned stations all over the city. They were sad ghosts, once useful, now forsaken. They had heaved with life, ushered workers on and sheltered those on the run from whatever demons followed them, political or personal, general or specific. There were theatres and cinemas throughout the town in similar crisis: places people had been taken on journeys away from their regular existence, had felt enjoyment and connection. Audiences had travelled to places of imagination and escape. If such places of delight could be abandoned, what hope did she have?

The train did not offer any words of wisdom today. A rival airline wanted her to discover Europe at surprisingly low fares and an antiperspirant promised men maximum protection. She missed the poetry. Instead, she was advised by the signs not to eat pungent food in consideration for other passengers and to keep her feet off the seats.

Karen moved around a lot with her job so the affair was conducted in her down time. This ensured it was intense and concentrated. It was excitement ratcheted to the highest level and the resultant whirlwind was the most enervating she had ever encountered. She had lived so timidly till then, this was turning her world on its head. Until now, that had been welcome. However, the spectre of a Wife waiting at home for Alex was increasingly popping up and it made her feel hidden and dirty. Karen was the secret. Karen was the disposable woman. She did not want to lose this man but the situation was tearing at her and her self-esteem was low. In which case, how could anyone find her attractive? She wasn't displaying

much moral fibre either. She was allowing this to mould her
and she wasn't sure she liked the results.

Alex would visit tonight so she loaded the washing machine
with her soiled clothes and the bath with her soiled self in
preparation. She had forty-eight hours before she could look
forward to a journey to Los Angeles, City of Angels. No one
tells you just how ugly most of that place is, she thought as
she lay back into the bubbles. A song on the radio asked, 'Do
you want the truth or something beautiful?' I am tired of ugliness now. She closed her eyes and tried to get happy but all
she felt was low-level crankiness. The Beloved was in for a
rough time. Her heart rose and grew fierce to think of him.

He spotted her mood immediately. 'What can I do to help
you out of this funk?' he asked.

'Funk all,' she replied and tried her best to smile with it.

They made love watching themselves in the mirrored doors
of her wardrobe. There was no denying how beautiful that
looked and how well they fitted together. Of a sudden she
could not shake an image of Alex with a stunning wife doing
much the same in his Uxbridge home and it made her eyes
tear up. She could skirt the issue no longer. He turned her to
face him and asked, 'What's wrong, Karen?'

'This is hopeless.'

He asked a cautious, 'Why?'

'You know.'

'I'm sorry, sweetheart, but I don't.'

She wanted to scream at him. How dare he be so deliberately obtuse. 'Well, you have the best of all worlds, don't you?
You get to keep your cosy home life but have the best of sex
on tap here with me, no strings attached.'

He let the words settle. 'There seem to be some things we need to clear up,' he said. 'Let's have a glass of champagne and see if we can't work this out.'

How dare he be so maddeningly calm and reasonable.

'I don't want this becoming an ordeal rather than a courtship,' he was saying.

And while she was at it, she couldn't look at a glass of fizz any more without an image of him appearing in her mind's eye. Would it always thwart her long after this was done? She began to seethe. She accepted a glass of champagne. Courtship indeed.

'Now, let's start at the beginning. What's bothering you?'

'What would your wife say if she knew?'

There, it was said, and with it the beginning of the end had entered the equation, surely.

'I don't think she'd care.'

'That's such a standard fob-off, Alex. You might as well go the "she doesn't understand me" route.' She sounded, even to her own ears, like a nagging whine. Why am I doing this?

'Why would she care?' he asked.

'Why wouldn't she?'

'Christ, Karen, she's been gone five years. She couldn't give a shit.'

'What? What did you just say?' This could not be happening. She could not have heard what she thought she just had. She had conjured it, pure and simple, because it was what she wanted.

'My wife? She left me five years ago. We've been separated since then. She doesn't give a flying fuck what I get up to. The kids are happy. She gets her maintenance money. End of.'

✿　　✿　　✿

I feel the world has fallen away from under me while the wall is accelerating towards my face to slap me, stingingly. I jerk my mind back to this altered reality. He is not married. Or at least he is not as married as I thought. I am exactly the fool I suspected but for very different reasons to the ones I tortured myself with. Now I look at this man's face and everything is possible again, which is even more frightening than the notion of failure I had become so enamoured of. I am in trouble here. I have to deliver to a good man who seems to like me.

'I love you,' he says.

It's far worse than I thought: I have to deliver to a good man who loves me. I am terrified. The only immediate answer is to reach for his beautiful face and pull it to me and kiss it as if my life depends on it, which it probably does.

We lie on sweat-soaked sheets later and talk about what it is we might do with our new life together. I feel abstracted. A song line echoes with me about most important decisions being made between two people in bed. So be it. Alex will finish his army career soon. 'I'd like to travel the world,' he says. 'I want you to come with me.'

'I'm a bit jaded with the world and travelling it,' I reluctantly point out.

'You might see it through different eyes if you're with me.'

'True. Do you think we might avoid flying wherever possible? That might help.'

Might. This happiness might kill me. I might burst with it. I want to run down the street shouting it out for all of London to hear. I want everyone to know how good it feels and how daunting. I never want it to end.

'Do you want to hear something freaky?'

'I'm not sure. Do I?'

'Well, my family lived in Soho for years. Right here in Claxton Court. My grandfather, David, was here during the war with his first then second wife before they decamped to the burbs, and my dad took the flat over for a while in the seventies before he married my mum, Sally.'

It's hard to know what to make of all that. Life's a strange old riddle. 'I wonder if Queen Beatrice knew that when she flew in here.'

'Stranger things have happened. So, it seems I have come home.'

Home. Yes, this place is home properly now. I have my soul mate. I am on the cusp of being complete.

'Karen, there is a question I have to ask.'

I feel my heart quicken nervously as I turn to him.

'What's with the shell-covered mirror in the loo? It has to be the most hideously bizarre item I have seen in a long time.'

The artwork was in the studio at the back of the garden of the Uxbridge house. Karen had noticed some small, original works on the walls of the house but this was a treasure trove.

Alex explained the provenance to her. 'Sergei is a distant cousin and the youngest of the Bulgharovs. He was given some of my Great-Grandfather Kostya's work to guard. He managed to squirrel them away safely although he was only a child when he was entrusted with them. Then, when he crawled out of the Urals and over here, he brought the works along. Papa Kostya got to see these before he died but he looked worried by it all more than anything else, according to my father. We know there are pieces in the Savitsky collection too. It's in

Nukus in Karakalpakstan. That's one of the places I'd like to visit. An extraordinary man called Igor Savitsky collected a vast selection of Russian avant-garde art, most of it banned by the authorities as subversive, so Kostya's work is hanging with the likes of Voloshin and Kramarenko.'

'I feel a bit ignorant. I've never heard of that country let alone those artists.'

Karen stood before the paintings. She found them moving and if pressed would have described the style as muscular, without knowing why. The colours were vibrant within the spectrum employed in any given work, and thickly applied. Alex held up a small canvas and told her it was called 'Icarus'.

'Konstantin painted this when he was on the run. We think it may be his last picture. He refused to paint ever again.'

They stood in silence before it, taking in the reds and yellows, the orange fire of a man's heart breaking and his world coming apart in flames: the ultimate fall to earth, the end of a life and a way of life.

'It's impossible to browse, if you know what I mean,' Karen said. 'These grab you and shake you up. They're deeply unsettling but incredibly moving and beautiful.'

Natalia's work was more mixed in the materials used but no less striking. She had her father's knack of confronting the viewer fearlessly. Karen's favourite was a plank of wood with nails and rags attached, stains deeply ingrained and an air of despair and solitude that spoke to her. She said as much.

'By all accounts, this is my grandmother's first work of art. I love it too but it can be a lot to encounter every day on the stairwell so we hang it in the house from time to time but not permanently. It should probably go to a museum.' He thought about it. 'Would you like to give it a home for a while?'

'I'd be honoured.'

'Working it through, she will have painted it in Soho, so it'll be a return to base for it. There's something circular I like about that.'

'Do you paint?'

'No. I am the musical end of the clan. My father played and composed. That's what we leave behind: music. Sometimes only the memory of it; I can't say I've been celebrated in recordings for posterity.'

'It's still more than I'll ever gift the world.'

'You don't know that. You make me so happy, you know, and that's got to count for something.'

'It does.'

'So, is it not good enough to leave joy?'

'I hope so, in case I have nothing else to offer.'

Alex watched as Karen smiled and her face became beautiful by any standards. She would never accept that so he wouldn't press her with it just yet. He felt it should be noted though, so he said, 'You are stunning,' and kissed her immediately to quell any protest.

'Why the army?' she asked later.

'It was really a case of why not? I was your typical, know-it-all, wide-boy Londoner. I was drinking too much, dabbling in drugs, getting into trouble with the law, all the usual. Instead of letting me go completely off the rails, Dad kind of press-ganged me into signing up. I think he knew that the music would keep me out of active combat, which it did. It's not like

I was going to be ruined by handling guns and the like, 'cos I already knew my way around anything a gang might get its hands on. I was a bit of a knob, Karen. My favourite party trick was to take a weapon apart and put it back together again with my eyes closed.'

She found it hard to imagine a younger Alex as an arse but he was unlikely to lie about it. 'Did the army work for you?'

'It supplied a bit of discipline. Then I became a dad and got married and repeated the process of becoming a dad.'

It cut her to be reminded that he had once loved someone else enough to marry her and have children.

'Bad reason for getting married, by the way, but worse things could have happened to me and it's a wonder they didn't.'

How long were you happy then? she wanted to ask but was too afraid of the answer. He told her anyhow.

'I was twelve years into it all before I recognised we were in a life rut and we'd have to get out of it. She left so that decision was made for me, taken out of my hands. Anyhow, I was a ditherer so fair play to Janice for going.'

So that's the name of the faceless woman I've been so bothered by, Karen thought: Janice. The name gave her a shiver. She was still unsure of what was going on and didn't trust her new elation. How could it last? Was it not absurd to think it could? Oh, for goodness sake, why stop there? Being alive was absurd. If the essential fact was ridiculous, why wouldn't associated details be too?

'Suddenly I'm years down the line and looking at retirement from the forces even though I'm relatively young. I've done my time.'

Karen could hardly concentrate. I have got to get my mind

off Janice. She is the past no matter how close they were. I am now. I am also the future. Move on. Ask him something. Anything.

'Have you ever fired a gun at anyone?'

'No. Nor will I, in case you're wondering.'

There was a commotion in the garden led by a flurry of Russian from Uncle Sergei. 'Alex, Alex,' he called. 'Mama.'

'Ah, time to meet my mother.'

And therein lay another surprise. His mother was Sally Cameron.

'He never said,' Karen told her.

'No reason for him to,' Sally said. 'I'm Mum first and foremost, not just some famous bint off the telly. Has Beatrice been winging off course again?'

'I'd call it very much on course, Mum,' Alex said and Karen felt herself glow.

'Yes, she is a homing pigeon, after all,' his mother said. 'She's trained to find her way. I hope you'll stay for dinner, Karen. Or longer?' Sally said before disappearing into the fabric of the household. There was no way of knowing how many more people were in the building as it always seemed to be shifting personnel, swallowing some while producing others, some family, some not. It was a moving, living entity.

Alex led her to a glass of wine and a sofa where she could sit comfortably in the crook of his arm.

'That means your father is dead, doesn't .it? I read about Sally's husband dying in some magazine. Or maybe it was a red-top. I read whatever headlines jump out at me from the passengers' newspapers and rags.'

'Frank. Yes, Dad passed away.'

'Frank? I have a neighbour called Frank, or had at the beginning of the year. He was very kind to me.' She turned her face to him, eyes alight. 'You don't think . . .'

'No, I don't. Coincidence, Karen. He's been dead a while and he lived in your building in the late seventies when you did not.'

This was all true yet didn't seem altogether the explanation, but Karen could not put her finger on why not. Alex was right about one thing: life was made up of coincidences but that didn't make them true or pertinent. Everything was oblique, after a fashion, and needed embellishment by lies and half-truths to show itself properly. So, add enough layers and vehemence and you had yourself a fact sometimes. I have begun to think like a tabloid, she realised.

'That also means your dad was one of the great drag queens at Lou Lou's.'

'How do you know a thing like that?'

'Tony, the late, great, kill-myself-in-your-bathtub best friend, was an expert on the queens of Soho.'

'Did he know my mum was also a drag artist? That's how they met.'

Everyone has a disguise, Karen thought. Some have formal uniforms, the shorthand by which people might know them at first glance: hers was an airline outfit, Alex had his military garb, his parents had been in their own version of motley. Getting to know who was beneath the layers was the trick.

Sally sat on the edge of the double bed she now had to herself. She looked at her reflections in the three-mirrored vanity console before her. Her multiplied face, echoes of an actor's many roles and identities, was wonderfully maintained by the best that money could buy. She couldn't help but wonder if her painted, coloured-in features had more of the drag queen now than the subtle elegance she aimed for.

It was hard to see this wrinkled woman was once an urgent, sexual being. Seeing Alex with his new love made her miss Frank all the more. It was like watching a younger version of themselves starting out, hopeful and willing. And she did miss Frank, every single day.

He had died in this bed but while they had lived in Soho. She remembered he'd been tired that week and had spent a lot of time sleeping. She was boiling the kettle in the kitchen when she heard him shift in the bed and begin to count the band in as he had done when they'd rehearsed in the flat in the early days. Then she heard the music as clearly as when they'd played it. 'I can't give you anything but my love,' he sang. By the time she reached him he was dead.

I hope Alex tells Karen about the Bulgharov family legacy sooner rather than later, she thought, so that they make the most of time.

then

I wander thro' each charter'd street,
Near where the charter'd Thames does flow.
And mark in every face I meet
Marks of weakness, marks of woe.

William Blake, 'London'

september 1854

The weather is so stiflingly hot it is hard to stay upright. Even Miss Cecily, usually so sunny, is fractious with it. She tires easily of counting the freckles on my face and arms, which activity usually gives her endless mirth as she makes up new numbers and words in the process. She does not want to wear her clothes, any of them at all, but I tell her it is unseemly to run about naked even if it is, she says, 'as God intended me'. She is finally persuaded into a loose cotton shift and it is already sticking wetly to her back when we leave the house. Outside, the weather presses down on the multitudes like a lethargy. No one moves quickly. Everyone shuffles, even my young charge. She sighs and shakes herself in an attempt to be rid of the cloying heat.

'I do not like this,' she moans.

'None of us does,' I say and buoy her up with the reminder that the Master has given us money to buy an ice cream from the Italian seller. Miss Cecily loves ice cream and having tasted it myself I cannot understand how any living thing would not.

The London air is even more thickly charged these days with the stench of noisome decay and it feels more difficult to breathe than is normal. We have barely covered the breadth of two lanes in our travels today when we have to stop to rest. We would like to take a sup of water from the pump at Broad Street but there are too many people ahead of us. The water looks tantalisingly clear and delicious. No one there, filling their buckets and jars, has it within them to talk much as this boiling heat has sapped all spirits. Even the lurks who use this captive audience to beg money are only partly interested in their business. One is half-heartedly trying to extort alms with a sad cotton spinner's tale of travelling all the way from Manchester to try for work but to no avail. This particular lay is a lad I have seen stage fits on other streets to elicit funds. It is unusual that he be allowed two walks, which are like the costermongers' pitches and closely guarded, and I can only assume he is making a good living from them both.

The fuss of the city is absent. The streets have a strange quiet to them and an unease, it seems to me. The buskers who normally bawl out their songs and tunes are missing. We pass by the King's Head on Compton Street which my brother tells me gives a prize of a gold repeater watch to the dog that can kill fifteen rats in the shortest time. Such animals are highly regarded and valuable. A drunken yeoman howls at some injustice outside and I fear Miss Cecily will ape his foul language but for once she hurries on and I am glad of that. A strumpet tries to importune the sailor but he is uninterested and she has not the energy to pursue the matter.

We buy our ice cream and I realise what a lucky girl I am to have a Master who will allow me to partake of it too, even though I am a servant and have no place being treated in such a way. He has told me that the Blakes believe in the equality of women, no less, but this should not extend to the lowly depths of society, I think. I am grateful that it does, at least in our household, and also that he has almost called me a woman. I have not yet begun to bleed but it cannot be far away. How awful if today should be that benighted day, in this fug of heat. I somehow think my aunt will not be pleased if it is and though she should help me, I have laid in my own rags in preparation. Perhaps I will never have to tell her of the event. It reminds me, oddly, that William Blake, the Master's famous cousin, ate no meat. How strange a family they are. Aunt Nell cannot fathom it at all, at all.

'No meat! What order of man was he, I ask you? I wonder he had the strength to sit upright and no meat in him. Whoever heard of such a thing?'

I glance at Miss Cecily who is smiling, as I am. An Irishman is standing by us, having the iced cream for the first time and I stifle a laugh to see his face contort with the pleasure of the taste and the unexpected pain of the cold. 'Jaysus, that has me kilt altogether,' he exclaims and Miss Cecily immediately echoes him word for word and sound for sound. Then I cannot hold the mirth and I think I may fall to the ground with laughing. I am worried the man may take insult, but he is engrossed in his new experience and puzzled by it beyond measure, and so oblivious of our attentions.

There is a commotion on the corner of Dean Street and I see the Reverend Whitehead is in attendance. A crowd has gathered and Miss Cecily is trying to push her way through to the front of the action. Something in me says this is not to be encouraged and I tug at her to stay here on the edge. I just know that something is terribly wrong, although I do not

221

always have the capacity to tell even partway into the future, which would be a kind of curse, really. There is a tone about the people here that tells of something other than the run-of-the-mill misery these streets can visit on their lives. One old woman has blessed herself and begins to recite prayers in a language I do not understand. The Reverend sees us and motions to me that we should go. For the briefest instant the crowd parts and I see a bundle of rags on the ground. Then I realise it is a small child and I also know in that instant that the poor mite is dead. A combination of starvation and this crawling heat, and the vile-stenched air of London I have no doubt, has snubbed out its life. I cannot tell if it is a boy or a girl and it hardly matters now, which is a cruel detail I think. There is no mother here to implore heaven for mercy, to wail at her loss and accuse God, just a group of strangers standing over this lonely little body. How can this be just?

A man is raising his voice and pointing, complaining about our lot.

'This may not be the time, Mr Marx,' says the Reverend.

'If not now, when?' the other asks, in a foreign-sounding voice. 'How can your God allow this? How can our society let it pass?'

I have these thoughts myself, God forgive me, and I want to hurry away before He hears them in my head and smites me with His justified rage. An ignorant girl has no place criticising God or His manifold ways. I will burn in Hell, no mistake, alongside this man with the curious accent. Flies buzz about the little corpse and that seems like the worst insult of all to the departed. I am saddened beyond words by the scene and eager to be gone from it. My traitorous mind mocks me with the Book of Job. 'Stand still and consider the wondrous works of God,' it taunts. At that very moment the Reverend Whitehead catches my eye and I know he sees straight through to my soul. He looks a troubled man as if the thoughts in my head might match his own, though that could never be, as he is a man of the cloth. I can no longer bear this place and fear I may faint. I grab Miss Cecily's hand and march her home. She is listless and I do the walking for both of us. I want to lie down now and sleep and never wake again to this brutal place with its ugliness. I am a daughter of the soil, I want to cry out, not a child of this barren, cruel city.

The Mistress is in the courtyard when we return, clearly waiting on us. She hurries us indoors as if to shield us from the outside world. I go to the kitchen for my instructions from Aunt Nell. She is tearful and when I ask the matter, she merely says, 'Cholera.' It is enough. The very mention of that scourge makes goose pimples rise on my skin, hot though the weather is. It is most unsettling to me to see an adult afraid. This is not the natural order of things and I feel the world sway uncertainly beneath me. Later, my aunt tells me that dozens are already dead and the yellow flag has been raised in Soho to indicate that the disease is at large. I look out of a window later again and see carriages piled with people and their possessions taking their leave of town. Then Aunt Nell orders that all the window shutters be drawn.

Dr Snow visits the Master in the evening. I hear him say that he has been taking samples of the water from street pumps as he is convinced they are where the solution will be found.

'My theory is that this disease is waterborne, as you know, but I have yet to prove it sufficiently and render it fact.' He gives the Master a half-smile to indicate that he is regarded as a bit mad for thinking as he does. The Master returns his smile. 'Of course the scientific community and the chattering classes will hear only of the poison emanating from the earth or the sky, a deficiency of ozone or electrical theories based on atmospherics. No, the cause lies elsewhere. I am continuing to knock on local doors and question the populace about their water. I am making a map of my discoveries and I think that should sway my doubters in time.'

It is true that Dr Snow is at large throughout the area, asking his peculiar questions. Aunt Nell says he has done so in other wards south of the river where she has friends and they all think him a singularly odd fellow.

'Take my advice, Arthur,' he further tells the Master, 'do not let your people drink from the public pumps but only from your own private supply.' He turns his eyes on me. 'Did you hear me, child?' he asks, in that quiet voice of his.

I nod my head, unable to speak. He has this unsettling effect on me.

'It will be no harm to exercise caution,' the Master agrees.

I cannot wait to be released from serving the gentlemen so that I may find my brother and warn him of the danger. Aunt Nell does not want me taking to the streets at this hour, let alone with death stalking the area, but I am so upset that she allows me out, with dire warnings to be home as quickly as I can.

I step out of the door and the heat knocks me back a moment. My breath cannot catch and find its rhythm and when it does, the air smells of rotting mortality. I hurry and sweat to Peter's lodgings in Golden Square but his landlady says he may be drinking at a hostelry in Dean Street so I change course for there. Why is he mingling with others when this curse is upon the streets? Since no one knows exactly what causes it, might he not be in danger of catching it from others as I did measles when I was younger? Every other door is disgorging a coffin, although in tandem with this the area seems strangely deserted and wretchedly decayed.

Peter is not in the pub but above it and I hear him cry as I climb the narrow, reeking stairs. My feet stick to each step and my ascent is measured in reluctant clicks. From below I hear the sounds of discordant music from a man hammering a clapped-out piano, and the low laughter of plague dodgers, while above, my brother's heart is clearly breaking from the eerie howling noise he makes. I see the cause as I enter the attic room. A young woman lies in the bed and I can tell that she is dying. Peter is now murmuring, 'Love, oh my love.' I did not know he had a beloved. I have never met this lady. Although soon to die, she is so alert to all around her that I want to run and hide. She is in shocking pain, that much is sure. But looking out from within her shrunken, pain-wracked body is an intelligence and awareness of her state and, although her eyes are glazed, her thoughts are coherent and are all for Peter and his welfare.

'I am sorry to leave you, love,' she says.

Her skin is blue and tough, her lips darkened and her nails a livid purple. By the bed are shitty rags covered with a strange rice-like, watery stool. Death is stalking the bed and the living smell of fear.

The only other man I have seen cry is my father and he never thought that I did. I watched him bury my mother's

225

stillborn bundles many times in a field by the house under cover of darkness. She would take to her bed at those times and lie facing the wall, not interested in the living and mourning the dead who had never breathed of their own accord or seen the blessed light of day. Sometimes when her belly swelled we got a brother or sister but more often we did not and then it was the sight of my father in the dark with a spade in one hand and a small bag of bones in the other, his head bent in sorrow and secrecy.

All Peter can say is her name over and over, 'Abigail. Abigail.'

I fold myself against the wall, praying for a miracle. We get the next best thing God has to offer us, which is the Reverend Whitehead. The sight of the holy man is a comfort to the dying girl, although she bends double again and again with the pain of this scourge. I cannot help but think of the glories God has given the world, like the animals we saw at the Zoological Gardens, and wonder why He also made so much that is bad, like cholera. Does Man need to be tested so?

The Reverend performs some rites and Abigail breathes her last. It is a release to her to go, I think, as her pain was immense. Peter slumps across her body and I want to beg him to care for himself now. What if this disease can seep out of Abigail and into him? Eventually, though reluctantly, he lets her mother attend to composing the body for removal. His cries have become howls again and I worry for his sanity.

I have no idea how much time passes as it is bent out of shape here: sorrow is moulding it cruelly and it has all but ceased to mean itself. I am minded, however, that Aunt Nell warned me not to dilly-dally and she will have no idea where I am. I want to comfort Peter in this terrible time but I must also get home. I beg him to come with me but I am not sure he hears my words for what they are.

'She was the sweetest and the gentlest,' he tells me, his eyes hollow and about to roll back into grief again.

'I know,' I say, although I know no such thing but must believe him and have no reason at all not to.

It is hard to credit that the blue cadaver on the bed now was ever anything much, however, and that strikes me as harsh.

'How can she be taken so quickly?' he wants to know, of no one in particular. 'Less than a day ago she was laughing and in my arms.'

None of us has the comfort he needs and the proof lies before us shrouded and ready to make her final journey. Even the Reverend is quiet. He blesses Peter and the family and makes to go.

'Sarah, you should return to the Blake household,' he says gently, as much to release me as to make sure that I am reminded of my place in this distorted scheme of things. I think he wants me to be safe and I am grateful. I leave ahead of him and when we emerge from the narrow stairwell into the sticky night, he touches my shoulder as if to remove any threat that might hang upon me.

I must hurry now but my feet drag as if weighed down with lead. The heat is pressing me to the ground and I want to lie in the street and beg the Lord Our God to take me. I lean against the pump in Broad Street and my thirst is great but Dr Snow said we should avoid drinking all but our own supply of water, and whatever else you might say about him, he is not sick from cholera and has obviously followed his own advice, and if that's good enough for the Queen herself, it should be good enough for a country girl like me. I round the corner of Pig Lane and see Aunt Nell looming in wait. I know she wants to clip me about the ear for worrying her and although I should take this as her affection, I wish she would hold me and tell me that all will right itself. She does not scold me much and when I have told her of Peter's situation she crosses herself, tells me to pray for us all and shushes me to bed. I am glad to climb into my little room and its safe familiarity, but I wish Martha was here all the more.

I am like a ghost as I go about my duties the following morning. The Master is reading from the *Observer*. 'In Broad Street on Monday evening, when the hearses came round to remove the dead, the coffins were so numerous that they were put on top of the hearses as well as the inside. Such a spectacle has not been witnessed in London since the time of the Plague.' He hits the newspaper in agitation. 'The Plague? Well, that should get the populace into a state of high anxiety,' he says.

'Arthur, the people are rightly worried. Many have died. And I wonder if we shouldn't think about leaving while this disease is raging.'

'Isobel,' he says, shaking his head, and I know they have discussed this in private. It seems the Mistress has not triumphed thus far with her plan of fleeing this wretched town.

Her eye falls on me. 'Dear Lord, child, are you sickening?' Her hand is cool on my forehead but I am not burning up.

'No indeed, Ma'am,' I assure her. 'I am sound but last night my brother's intended was carried off by the disease.'

I can tell she is anxious that I may be a carrier now. We know so little about this killer that we must assume it is cunning beyond our comprehension. She darts looks between myself and her daughter, anxious to protect, as a mother should.

'I am well, Ma'am. I am tired, that is all. Truly.'

She takes me at my word but would prefer me gone so I dispense of my duties in double-quick time and hurry away. I hope I have not lied to her, a woman who has been so kind to me, who tries to help me shed my ignorance and school me. I think it is just that I am tired and anxious and not that I have taken on the cholera. If it works as quickly as I have seen, I should be sporting blue lips and the like, and be bedridden too.

I beg Aunt Nell to let me go check on Peter and she allows me out again with her usual dire warnings, all of which are entirely understandable now and suitable to our situation, as there is a killer at large on our streets and we do not know where it will strike next or how it is managing to conduct its vile business. I hear reports outside that hundreds have died, most of them the poor. But here is a strange thing: there are hardly any deaths to report from the Lion Brewery where Peter works. Perhaps it is that they drink some alcohol every day and it has great properties to make a person feel fine, for a while at least. In my experience, however, when people have had too much of this demon drink it disimproves tempers and appearances rapidly. Also St James's Workhouse on Poland Street, which is filled with the poorest of the poor, has had only a handful of deaths from over five hundred souls within its walls, so it cannot really be mostly the poor that this killer wants. It is a curious and vexing thought. This thwarting disease has its own means of choosing and we cannot know its mind.

Peter looks wretched and he is, both physically and mentally

229

so. I ask if there is any comfort I can bring him, unable to suggest one myself as I am unskilled in dealing with death at such close quarters and I have no marker as to what is required of me now. He shakes his head miserably. I smell that he has been drinking even at such an early hour. It is to be expected, I suppose.

'Are you sure?' I press.

He takes my hand and strokes it fondly. 'You're a good girl, Sarah,' he says. 'You are special, you know, and smart. You must waste no time.'

I do not know what he is trying to tell me.

'I am not special in any way,' I say quietly, and it is the truth.

He shakes his head again so I follow on with, 'If I was as special as all that I would not have been sent away.' From nowhere tears spring and roll down my face. We are both distraught now. The blue of my brother's eyes shimmers as his tears are released and he says, 'They sent you away that you might live a different life, that you might have opportunities they could never give you and *be* somebody. You must matter, Sarah. For all of us.' It is the most extraordinary thing I have ever heard and I cannot make sense of it.

I spend the day in a kind of trance, doing as I am bid but hardly noticing the work. I cannot get Peter's declaration out of my head. Why was Martha not given the same chance? After all, she is me too, is she not?

Aunt Nell has been quiet for hours, distractedly thumping out pastry and breads, fretting about cheeses, and plucking and gutting a chicken for dinner. The latter is a job I would normally do but it gives her satisfaction today and I see to the vegetables and other sundries. Dr Snow and the Reverend Whitehead are both to dine with the Blakes tonight and my aunt is intensely proud of such occasions on behalf of our employers. She will not let them down, never has, even when her mind is on other subjects as it so clearly is today. We are sweltering in the kitchen because she flatly refuses to let in the rank air of the streets. 'What?' she roars when I complain. 'You would throw open the house, with all that danger and disease abroad just waiting for an invitation to rush in at us?'

'Not on your Nelly,' I might once have muttered but I do not want a clip on the ear and I could certainly look forward to one for cheeking her. She crosses herself at the thought of my foolishness and also touches the wooden table for luck, just to be sure. I have to admit that, in spite of the punishing temperature, the smells of cooking food are far superior to the noxious miasma of Soho outside and I quit my whining.

Miss Cecily comes to beg milk and biscuits and not even a woman as stonehard as my aunt could refuse her. She perches on a chair, swinging her tiny feet and jabbering.

'Will they put me in a box on a carriage?' she asks. She is referring to the coffins carried away with such regularity. It must be said that she does not seem too perturbed by the idea and I would guess that in her mind it counts as an adventure on a grand scale.

'No, child,' Aunt Nell says, looking aghast at the notion. 'It is only those of low regard who are dying and that's not you.'

'Is it any of us at all?' the young Miss wants to know, her face creasing with the unpleasant possibility.

'No,' Aunt Nell says. 'We are good and clean people here.'

This satisfies Miss Cecily and she clambers down off the

chair and runs off to whatever mischief she can find. My aunt looks almost kindly in her wake so I seize my moment to ask, 'Why was Martha not given a chance to better herself as I have been?'

'Martha needs minding,' Aunt Nell replies, without thinking too much about it.

'Why?'

I get no answer to that even though I leave her enough time to reply. I must press my small advantage here. 'Is she not special too?'

My aunt heaves a sigh as if a great burden weighs her down and steels herself to say, 'Martha was last out and she did not reach the air in good time so she is special but in a different way to you.'

I must look a picture of ignorance because she clarifies herself curtly. 'Your sister, Martha, is a bit simple, child.' And from her expression I see that that, as they say, is that and all I'll get from her on the subject presently or perhaps ever. She may as well have smacked my face. All I have now are questions burgeoning from this news. Weighing most heavily is an immediate, unconscionable guilt that I got out in jig time but may have pushed my loved other back and held her from her due breaths and, therefore, a full and fulfilled life. Dear Lord, what kind of monster am I?

So many things begin to make sense. There are the occasions I can see in my mind's eye when I thought our mother favoured Martha and I kicked up against it, perpetrating a naughtiness for attention. She was simply looking out more especially for her needful child. Martha has never questioned as much as I, on any level or subject. She is uninterested in reaching for more than is ever offered and satisfied with the face of things. We are so alike to see and hear but in the way of curiosity I thought the gap between us simply illustrated differing personalities. I see now there is also a physical attribute to it. This is fascinating and appalling to me, all at once. I cannot fathom how we can be so alike and yet so very different. But if I had not held her back in the first instance, we would be entirely identical surely. So I am a guilty wretch and now I know that I must make my mark for both of us from now on. I must make the imprint of two people on time and the world. And there I was, thinking it would be hard to leave the measure of one. Everything I am has been multiplied by two from birth, I am thinking, and so it goes on from here, in earnest.

When it is time for dinner I am called upon to serve. It is difficult to concentrate on the settings and rigmarole of a meal when such interesting topics are discussed. The gentlemen are at odds about the cholera outbreak. The Reverend Whitehead holds with the Miasmatists, citing the rank air as injurious.

'The atmosphere, all over the world, is at this time favourable to the production of a most formidable plague,' he insists. He looks like a man who would pace the floor were it not for his dinner about to arrive at the table in front of him. 'I must also point to the disturbance of the plots holding the bodies of the Great Plague victims, which were uprooted some years ago. Rumours flew about then that no good would come of it and disease would rise again.' He spreads his hands apart to show the right of this.

Dr Snow looks small alongside the Reverend but he holds

his ground. His squeaky voice steadies as he asserts his authority and it is certain that he is in possession of a great deal of that. 'I have been at the bedsides of sufferers and you must take my word, as a medical man, that this disease is ingested and not inhaled.'

I am poised with the soup ladle held unused above the Mistress's bowl. We all hang on his quiet, confident words.

'Cholera begins in the gut, the respiratory system is unaffected. Therefore it is not caused by the air, rank as it may be, but by something taken by the victim.'

I think of Peter's Abigail and without pause say, 'I have also observed that.' All eyes are on me and I burn in the unwanted attention. I cannot believe I spoke aloud.

'And when was this, child?' the doctor asks. His interest is clearly piqued. He is like a policeman hunting for the truth of a murder.

There is little point in me stopping now. 'Just last night, not two streets away, sir,' I answer. 'My brother's fiancée . . . died.'

'I, too, was at that unhappy event,' says Reverend Whitehead. He looks troubled. 'I find you are right, Snow. She had no difficulty breathing beyond the great pain she was suffering in general, which must have rendered all movement, even clinging to life, intolerable.'

The Mistress has pushed her soup plate away and will not eat well this evening.

'What do you say to the idea abroad that it is the poor who are most affected, especially those living on the higher levels of the tenements?' This is the Master now.

'Simply this,' says the doctor. 'They are dying faster because there are more of them.'

234

It is such a certain and beautiful logic that I cannot believe no one has uttered this truth before.

'I must concur,' says the Reverend. 'There is no class divide to this disease.' He laughs. 'I have a Prussian neighbour, a Mr Karl Marx, who has been disseminating this theory most forcefully since the start of the outbreak. He is a remarkable personality and, I fear, a revolutionary.' His face does not betray any horror at his foreign neighbour, however; Reverend Henry Whitehead believes, that we must live and let live, that much I know.

'There is no moral component to this disease,' Dr Snow says. 'The poor are not dying because of their failings. They are dying because they are being poisoned. The same goes for any class drinking the affected, pestilential water. What we must do is to locate its source.' He turns to me again. 'What else have you heard, Sarah?'

The great Dr Snow knows my name and I feel I will faint at that knowledge. This man has attended the Queen, the highest of the high in the land. And he just called me Sarah.

I gather my breath and try to remain calm but my voice betrays me. I tell of the strangeness that few associated with the brewery have died, nor many at the workhouse on Poland Street.

'The latter information gives further credence to your theory that it is not a disease brought upon the poor by their situation,' the Mistress says.

'Eley Brothers have suffered great losses,' I say, and worry that he will think I am calling the people who work there lowly or destitute. I cannot form arguments and thoughts like those of the educated people gathered in this room.

'The munitions factory does not have its own water supply,' the doctor comments, as much for himself as the company.

'No indeed, sir,' I say and find that I have exclaimed louder than is necessary. My face heats up but I forge on. 'They take water from the street pump. They fill two huge barrels for the workers every day.'

He nods.

'And Mr Eley sends a jar to his mother in Hampstead regularly,' I add. 'She considers it the clearest and best water in London.'

The doctor is thoughtful on the point. 'It does always appear clear and is always refreshingly cool because of its depth in the ground. In fact the general quality of the water from this pump is not in question, I would say. It is some outside agent that has contaminated it, for the time being; perhaps the evacuations of cholera patients somehow making their way into the well has kept the disease virulent.' He is almost thinking aloud. 'First thing in the morning I will establish the health of those drinking that water. It is my understanding that the poorhouse and brewery have their own supplies and are not reliant on the pump.' His eyes pierce through me again. 'It is the Broad Street well to which you refer?' he checks.

I bob and nod.

'Excellent.'

'But for one thing,' says the Reverend. 'I drank from that pump recently and have lived to tell the tale.'

There is a silence then, as if he has stumped the doctor and ruined his theory. But John Snow smiles. 'Not everyone who has done so will become ill and die. You are an exception. Perhaps the one that proves the rule, as they say?'

Then he has a litany of questions as to how much water Mr Whitehead ingested and when. He ruminates while chewing on his chicken and the sight is almost comical, but for the weight of our topic.

'You are a big man,' he tells the Reverend. 'Your constitution might well be such that the small amount of water you drank had little effect.' He pauses to let his mind puzzle the conundrum. 'I feel the time at which you drank that water may be pertinent as it was before the onslaught proper, so perhaps the curse had not taken full hold of the well. In other words, it had not reached its full and awful capacity. The disease is waning now, it must be admitted, through a combination of factors, not least that so many have fled the area, but also I expect that it may have almost run its initial course of life in the well. You were the "before", as 'twere, and we may now be headed to the after.' He shakes his head and chastises himself with the word, 'Conjecture.' Dr Snow looks at the company with an apologetic expression. 'Forgive me, I have lapsed from science. We cannot know for certain what will happen to the cholera as we do not know enough about it in the main. It would be a foolish man who would second-guess its next move without fully understanding its nature. And we do not, at this moment in time, more's the pity.'

The Mistress changes the subject somewhat to the horrid weather baking the town and everyone tries to enjoy the fine meal my aunt has sent upstairs. But appetites have been affected by the heat and the worry of our situation living in this place.

When the guests have left, the Master and Mistress descend to the kitchen to thank Aunt Nell for her efforts.

'I must apologise that we did not do full justice to the wonderful food,' the Master says and my aunt lights up.

'I wonder if you might save the wishbone for Cecily,' says the Mistress, although she knows full well that we always do.

As they turn to go the Master puts his hand to the Mistress's back to usher her safely on to the stairs and I can see how in love they are. I hope to the core of my soul that I will one day feel that too. I love my sister, Martha, and my family, but it strikes me as special to love An Other and that must be part of God's plan for us. He tests us with it too, as I have seen when Peter lost his love so recently. It is a hard road we walk on this earth that we may gain the eternal salvation He offers.

I cannot sleep for thinking of all that has happened and been discussed this night. When the first slivers of morning shy through my window, I get off the bed, fully clothed still, and rush to complete my chores, hoping to fall in behind the doctor as he journeys about the houses to chart the truth of the cholera's progress. The Mistress has given me permission to go about this business and Dr Snow allows it too. My Aunt Nell is horrified that I am pushing myself above my station and loses no time in saying as much.

'She is an inquiring mind,' the Mistress tells her, as if this fact stands up and is to be counted by itself as an entity. My aunt looks as if milk has curdled in her mouth to hear such a thing. 'We must not staunch that impulse. Sarah was most helpful to the doctor last evening and may be the charm he needs to help stop the march of this accursed disease.'

It takes all my strength of will not to hoot at the sight of my aunt and the impact of the Mistress's words. It is not lost on me that this household is a singular one and I know of no other woman in the world but my Mistress who would thrust a girl forward in this way. We are not meant to be at the forefront of public life but here in this house we are encouraged to speak and be of a curious disposition. Here, it is as if we are all Blakes and I am so very proud of that.

Dr Snow stands before the door to the munitions factory. He is in full sunlight as the day is as bright as the mood of the populace is dark. The faces of passersby are crossly racked with lines from lack of sleep, probably due to the high temperature as well as the fear of contracting the cholera. The day is hot as Hell's fire, I am certain. The sulphurous odour of the explosives, which hangs in the putrid air, suits the mission the doctor is on, to track a demonic pestilence.

A black ribbon hangs on the main door and a written notice to the effect that the company is in mourning for Mrs Eley, mother of the Eley Brothers and drinker of Broad Street pump water. Dr Snow is quietly resigned to the fact that his theory is fast becoming reality but it is not a moment to be joyful that he is correct, because of the horror it brings with it, so I am quietly glad for this man who may be able to save lives with his knowledge. Reverend Whitehead joins us, reading the news posted on the factory entrance.

'John, your ideas gather credence with each step.'

'Sadly, this is so,' the physician admits. 'I have been studying Mr Farr's published lists of deaths for yesterday and of the eighty-three he recorded for this area, sixty-one were definitely Broad Street water drinkers. The number might be greater but for the fact that all belonging to the other twenty-two are dead also and we cannot establish firm links as a result.'

'We must act to warn the residents and do something about this infernal pump,' the Reverend insists. 'Even if it is not the definitive culprit, it seems to play some part. Is it not curious, however, that the Paving Board inspected it some months ago and declared it free from contamination of sewer waste matter? So how can it now carry such deadliness?'

'This is what we must establish,' the doctor quietly insists.

'I have parish calls to make,' the Reverend tells us. 'I hope in the course of these I may be able to garner information to bolster your case.' With that he bows slightly to me and shakes Dr Snow's hand vigorously then strides away on his long legs past the well in question which, in spite of the heat, has no one in line to take its water. The citizens have gone to ground or are ill in their beds.

We visit various houses in the area and Dr Snow asks the same questions of each so that his information will tally. Whenever we visit elderly or infirm people who live alone, I am sent by them to fetch water. I know not to use Broad Street. After the umpteenth such occasion, Dr Snow confides in me. 'I suspect, Sarah, the reason those people are still alive is that they had no one to bring them their daily dose of pump water. The children have either been sent away or are being kept within.' It is a fascination to observe how his impeccable mind works through even sundry details, let alone big discoveries like this.

Eventually, we are at the nearby Middlesex Hospital as it is treating many sufferers, over one hundred and twenty since the first day of the month, according to the doctor. It is a strange-smelling place and I ask why.

'The staff place dishes of chlorine and sulphuric acid

240

throughout the rooms to purify the air,' my new teacher tells me. 'To little avail, I must say, as two-thirds of the cholera sufferers have died. Nurse Nightingale will not hear that it is ineffectual, however, and she is a formidable character so we have agreed to differ. I will give her this, she runs a clean hospital and is much given to hygiene, which she regards as of primary importance. She is at the forefront of a change in nursing practices and that is to be applauded.'

I look around me and the strangest thing happens, for I suddenly feel that I belong somewhere at last. It is as if my soul has been lifted high. I want to be a part of this endeavour. I long to care for the sick and indigent on these beds. I want to ease their pain and help cure some of their ills. How can that be done?

The doctor is walking ahead and has not noticed my Road to Damascus moment. 'Here they treat the patients with saline and calomel for the cholera and whereas I feel there is purpose there and some good results, I fear they are using too little of everything as a cure. And of course the water must be of purest origin.'

And then she is in front of us. Florence Nightingale. She is a willowy beauty with a stern aspect and great purpose about her. I look up at her and feel a drool begin to form at the side of my mouth. Then just as suddenly it is so dry I fear I may choke.

'Dr Snow,' she acknowledges. 'How do your findings progress?'

'They increase apace,' he says. 'This is my latest recruit, Miss Sarah Armstrong. She is also a seeker of the truth, are you not, Sarah?'

I murmur in assent but am hopelessly tongue-tied in front of these giants of medicine. I fear I may be the living image of my cousin John Cooper, village idiot and certified fool.

'Would you be involved?' asks Miss Nightingale and I await Dr Snow's reply. Then I realise, with no little discomfort, that she is speaking to me. 'Are you a man of action?' How curious she should use the masculine, but I do not dare question it.

'Yes,' I answer and it is fervent, if quiet and like a kitten squeaking. I want to say that I am sure I have been called to this life, though it is so sudden a revelation I must resist an outburst that would make a further spectacle of myself.

'Come join me in my rounds,' she says to us. It is a direction not a request but all the better for it, in my eyes. I am amazed at this woman, apparently fearless, and so full of life and direction. She speaks to the doctor as if she is, somehow, his equal and he allows it too.

'We are overwhelmed,' she is explaining. 'Cholera patients have had to be referred to University College Hospital, also Westminster, Guy's, St Thomas's and Charing Cross. St Bartholomew's received more than two hundred in the first days of the outbreak, I hear.'

'I will need to ask sufferers and their families about their drinking habits,' Snow replies.

'Certainly. And you may be pleased to hear we have increased our use of saline and hope it will help us as a cure.'

'I await the results with great interest.'

'Young lady, help me here,' she instructs and I am now in the midst of hospital work as we change sheets and remove soiled cloths. I am struck by the amount of liquid evacu-

242

ated by the cholera patients and feel they are correct in their attempts to replace this fluid in the afflicted bodies. She tells me that the salts are important to maintaining the body's health, which is why saline is being used. At every juncture she makes me wash my hands and keep immaculate. I want to tell her about Aunt Nell and her insistence on such things. She would fit into Nurse Nightingale's regime, and be a 'man of action' with her little moustache. I actually smile at that thought but it goes unnoticed, which is as well as I cannot imagine Miss Nightingale laughing. Ever.

I am a little fearful of catching disease but courage must be the order of my day now. As Dr Snow interviews those gathered who have presented with the cholera, and their relatives, I am at Nurse Nightingale's bidding. One poorly man is delighted with me and reaches out to touch my white hair.

'She is an angel,' he says, to no one in particular. 'Look at her halo.'

I glance at my mentor and she gives me a curt nod, but it is not an angry one. I think she is happy he gains comfort from his observation. An hour later he is dead.

After a backbreaking afternoon of work, Miss Nightingale is ready to relinquish me to my original companion.

'Not afraid of hard work,' she tells him. 'Also, quick to learn and inquisitive. If her mistress will allow it, I could use her here.' She turns on me. 'I was called by God to this life and I serve no other now, nor ever will. You should ponder that for yourself.'

Every other chore I do this day is ordinary and dull. I am burning to be of use in the hospital again. Dr Snow is to talk to the Blakes about my future but he is also preoccupied with his investigations and I fear it may be some time before he does anything more on my behalf. It is as if I have been shown the world I must live in and then had it rudely snatched from me. I want to scream aloud in my frustration.

I am lying tossing and turning that night in my hot attic room when Miss Cecily appears at the door. She has been in disgrace for taking to the streets alone without permission. She is strangely pale in the moonlight, more than she might be, and I immediately know there is a problem developing before my eyes.

'I did a forbidden thing,' she says in a whisper. 'Sarah, I drank from the pump.'

Dear Lord God, I silently implore, let this not be true. But I know it is. This girl is incapable of lying and never has needed to in her short life. She doubles over and soils herself. It is the selfsame loose-rice stool I have seen from other disease sufferers. Miss Cecily has the cholera.

Without pausing to think, I throw myself into action. I lay her down on my bed, telling her all is well and that she must stay put for me. Then I rush to the kitchen for our own pure water. Into it I put some salt but also mix in sugar to take the horrid taste off the concoction. Back in the attic, she is in great pain and looks so very tiny. I insist that she drink a lot of my specially prepared water but in sips. At the hospital I saw that those who took too much too quickly spewed it all back up, rendering it useless to them. I change any foul garments and bed linen and carefully set them aside. Then I wash my hands thoroughly. Miss Cecily is humming, then singing, humming again, singing snatches of nonsense like, 'If I had money . . . wild . . . furs, dress you like a queen.'

'Of course, sweetheart,' I tell her and mop her sweating brow.

She is so small I know the disease can be expected to work its evil quicker than usual. There is no time to conjure with, or to lose foolishly in a dither of inertia. I now have the task of waking her parents to call them to the bedside of their only child, who may be carried off at any moment. I cannot do it and instead risk alerting my Aunt Nell. She takes one look at Miss Cecily, as much to check on my ravings as to see the child's, then breaks into a waddling run along the passageway and down the stairs, all shrieks and panic. I would not have thought she had it in her. I sit by this child that I love and minister to her and pray harder than I have ever done in my God-fearing life.

'The boys are back in town,' she tells me. She is humming again. She does not seem mad in her mind but she must be to tell of such things, which make no sense.

'Yes, those boys are back,' I agree, not really caring what it is she sputters as long as she still lives.

I give her more of my salt and sugar water and clean up her doings. I wash my hands again. Her parents are naturally and understandably distraught. The Mistress cannot help but say, 'If only you had been with her, Sarah . . .' and she must know that I feel the weight of that even without the admonishment. If I had been in attendance, watching my proper post, Miss Cecily would never have had the Broad Street water. Instead, I thought only of myself and foolish dreams that can never be. I make an anguished cry at her spoken truth and she adds, 'I myself should never have taken my eyes off her,' and I cannot believe that in this moment this wonderful lady would share blame with me when all is my fault and no disputing it. The humanity of it is humbling and I resolve to make good. If I have to will Miss Cecily alive and exchange my soul with Beelzebub himself to do it, I will, and strike me down if you dare, Lord, for this promise. I care not. I care only that the little girl in my bed with such a gift for joy should live, and she will, so help me God. I explain what I am doing for Miss Cecily and that it must be continued assiduously while I run for Dr Snow.

I do not know how I make that terrible journey to the doctor's home on Frith Street. My limbs are leaden, incapable of progress, it seems, like the nightmares of childhood when I am being chased and cannot escape some faceless, nameless pursuer of these dread-dreams. Now they are made real on the overheated, abandoned streets of this godforsaken Soho. For He has forsaken us. And if there is forgiveness to be meted out ever again, He must stand His turn in line with the rest of us sinners, made to His measure, so horribly in His likeness. I have no alternative plan if Dr Snow is not to be found at his house. And so all along this impossible journey I am cursing God and yet praying to Him to deliver John Snow to me and life to Miss Cecily.

I am hysterical when I reach the house and cannot put words to the crisis. My breath is cutting me with each gasp as surely as a knife would stab me. It is also insufficient to allow for speech, mixed as it is with tears and wailing. For one moment I see Dr Snow consider whether or not he should slap my face to calm me. It is enough to grant a sliver of respite and I manage to tell him what the problem is. It takes no more than 'Miss Cecily' and 'cholera' to explain the horror. He grabs his bag of medical tricks and we are off out of the door at speed. He questions me along the way as to what is being done for the child and when I tell him, he actually takes the opportunity to praise me for my actions. If I didn't feel so responsible for the situation in the first place I might allow myself some delight that I have impressed such a man, but Miss Cecily took ill on my watch, when I was furthering myself elsewhere, and so it is fully my fault, no matter what. I can fall no further. I will make a deal with God to swap my life for hers as soon as we reach home.

The Reverend is praying over the child when we return. Dr Snow examines her and proclaims himself pleased with her progress. He makes certain that she is being given her fluid and is good enough to laud my interventions again. I return to my post to nurse Miss Cecily and pray with the Reverend. The Mistress is upset in the extreme but keeping her emotions in check in front of her baby. The Master looks haunted. Cecily is singing about falling in love with someone you shouldn't have fallen in love with. It seems she is raving although that is not one of the usual symptoms of the disease.

Reverend Whitehead takes the doctor aside and tells him he may have located a possible source of contamination. Sarah Lewis, whose baby was one of the first to die, lives at 40 Broad Street and she cast the sick baby's evacuations and foul doings into the cesspool at the front of the house. This is adjacent to the pump and just might have been able to somehow contaminate the well. Only the smallest of fissures would be needed for the poisonous cholera to make its way into the water supply. Dr Snow is excited but cautiously so.

'We must declare this to the Water Board and have them take the handle off the pump,' he says.

'Agreed. We will both see to that as soon as we can. But for now we must pray and minister to this house and this sick girl.'

'Will she live?' asks the Master in a hoarse whisper. It is the question none of us wants to ask, lest the answer be unthinkable, and yet it must be uttered.

'Sarah lost no time in ministering the best of medical care available,' says Dr Snow. 'Now it is up to providence and the child. She has a lust for living that may stand to her.'

'And she's a Blake,' I say. I want to invoke that specialness now. I want to try anything at all that will keep this beautiful girl on this earth to bring it joy. I will lay down my own life for her if needs be. I will build Jerusalem.

On the bed, my beloved Cecily reaches into the air and exultantly says, 'Yellow.'

It is then I hear the music too. It seems to me to sound like a heartbeat, two base notes high and low beating steadily, and above them somehow birdsong in notes also trilling and swooping along and, yes, it is yellow. A harp begins to sound another tune with its glittering notes and I know it will save the child on the bed. An angel plays it and we are being watched over. Miss Cecily is not called to heaven today but is to be left to adorn this earth with her happiness. My own heart, beating strangely now, soars along with these odd and welcome sounds, for they are freedom and release. We are delivered from our woe.

then

Then the few whose spirits float above the wreck
of happiness
Are driven o'er the shoals of guilt, or ocean of
excess:
The magnet of their course is gone, or only points
in vain
The shore to which their shivered sail shall never
stretch again.

Lord Byron, 'Stanzas For Music'

october 1947

I never thought of myself as special. That is to say, I was not special once, when I numbered two, but I am now, being singular. And I am a number, still, but we all have those for our ration books and certificates. However, my tattoo is special to me, of course: mine alone. I did not choose it. Some people opt to adorn themselves with ink, I know, though rarely as plain as what I have, or as deadly and potent a symbol. I had no such choice in the matter, it is true, but I will now display it, and with some survivor's pride too, for those who did not make it out.

It was done with a single needle and blue ink on my left forearm when we arrived. Nothing to be truly proud of, you understand, but it explains a lot and it is significant now. It tells of a horror that words can never approach. It is my mark, and a mark on this time of ours too. In some ways I was lucky to get it as it meant I walked in the right direction for life, not like so many others who went immediately the other way and to their deaths. I had to show my number at all times then and I want to show it all of the time now. We must never forget what happened. It is unthinkable that we might or could, ever, but humans do not like to confront their darkness and I am living proof that mankind is as dark as remotest hell. I have my letter, then my digits; this is my number, this is the sorry tale of these years and what we all allowed to occur, whether victim, perpetrator or bystander. It is the story of all history and the fact that we always declare it can never happen again, even when we know it might or probably will. No, this time it must not. This time must count as the last time. This number speaks of death and sorrow on a global scale but also the dividing of me, of leaving me lone. I am Natalia.

I see the woman only once, when the pigeon comes. I have stepped out on to the metal gangway in front of our little flat. From it I look at our small square patch of sky. I won't glorify the space by saying that we look over a courtyard but if I was fanciful, and I am not any longer, I might suggest that. The piece of sky is everything, the infinite and unattainable faraway. It is my only journey just now, out of our rooms to check on the canopy sheltering us in this London. Today it is steely grey to match the cold.

The pigeon is a beautiful bird but looks like food to me and if it knew that it would surely fly quickly away. The woman saves its neck with her arrival. She looks pale, worried and full of problems, perhaps, but who is not all of those things? She is beautiful but wearing a uniform and I cannot be close to such a thing now; its fastidiousness and all that it might stand for alarms me. I flee. I know I will not see her again, but cannot explain why I am so certain of this.

The man is different. He, too, is diminished and a survivor but I know he is here to stay. And, strangely too, he is here to be with me. But he will need to take time to achieve this and I will need to be sure that it is the correct thing to happen. Caution and cunning are two of the lessons hard-learned in Auschwitz, among the many hard lessons it bestowed. I almost crumple to let my mind even whisper the name of that place and with it open the portal to the horror it bestowed. I cannot waste the knowledge got there and the memories I carry with me now, with the debt I owe to the others.

If I was not wearing this dress the man would see the very essence of me: skin, bone, blood coursing through my veins and not much more. The workings are clear; I am reduced to basics. It has its own honesty, I suppose.

Papa sits in our small apartment and cries all day, which is no surprise. He feels guilty to be alive, guilty to have been separated from us in the first place, guilty not to be able to atone to those of his family who did not survive.

'Live,' I tell him, 'that is our best atonement.' Our best revenge, I think too, but I do not say those words. The world is sad enough without adding vendetta. This is not to say that I don't boil with rage at what has happened to us, and so many more; millions, we now hear. Millions! All those numbers, all those noughts.

The sound of his crying is a comfort, proof of life, and a noise I am accustomed to. Late at night in the camp, when those not entirely exhausted after another horrific day realised that the world had given up on us, the sobbing would come, softly so as not to alert the enemy that we were even weaker than they knew. The day sounded of nothing much, a loud silence with some shuffling, a train whistle in the near distance, dogs barking or a stray gunshot if someone was despatched quickly for some perceived slight. These were the sounds of resignation.

London is devastated and therefore suits us, but it has sound. I have heard birds singing somewhere out there, as if to say, 'It is over and we will make this city great again.' It will be a challenge. All I can see is rubble, faded splendour, and dust, so much dust. I can hear the children play on the street, hopscotch and chasing, cricket and hide and seek, football. I see them sometimes on one of my infrequent forays to the outside. They are filthy and dressed in tatters but they are carefree and safe, those ragamuffins. Someone plays trumpet close by and other times I hear the strumming of a guitar and the gentle voice of a man wondering about falling in love with someone you shouldn't have. Falling in love seems such an exotic thing in comparison with the basic fight for life.

Unhappiness melds one day into another. This endless stream of misery is an ordeal of cold order and seems impossible to escape from. With it also is the thought that to allow it is to wallow but there is no summoning happiness if it is unable or unwilling to impinge. And so, hopeless, helpless unhappiness gnaws constantly but it is an affirmation in its own right. On such a day as this, an ordinary day of base sadness, I get to wondering, if I died, would that be my time wasted, let slip away? Yet the ordinary has its heroics too. It grinds along and must be admired for sheer, calm cussedness. And if time were to seize this small day of my life, if there is such a thing any more, would this be the one that would be replayed forever, boringly simplistic yet illustrative of existence? Would that be so bad? I did no harm today. I may have left a little happiness by being with my papa and therefore a small comfort, a human touch for him. Would that count as good enough?

I am hungry and cold but I cherish these sensations. They are what I have brought with me to my new life. They bear witness. They are as real as my tattoo. I touch it and almost savour what it stands for, because it is not a Nazi mark now. Now it is mine, it is my number: it is the measure of me. I wonder how the Man will feel when he learns of this. And when I tell him my story. And then he will see that number every day and he, too, will be a witness and tell my story to many more. And in that way I hope we can stop that sort of evil ever happening again.

We are aliens here in this London, Papa and me. We were aliens in the camps too, as everyone was. That was why we were there. We were undesirable, the Wrong Sort. My crime? I am a Russian Jew. It was enough. Which is to tell you also that my story begins in Russia, the beautiful country that made me and then could not hold on to me safely. We had moved about and were punished for it. When the scourge came, we were in Belarus, White Russia, and closer to the Hun. 'Asking for it,' Elena would joke, and it did always raise a smile from me. Elena, the beautiful Russian Jew and the better part of me, the better half, always. So, why then did I live? But that is to skip ahead and deny her journey, ours, an ordinary story that must never be forgotten among nations of the world although we were just two Russian peasant girls. And Mama. Yes, Mama too. She played her part.

The Man appears next day when I am outside the door to our flat, listening to Papa cry, drinking in the dusty air that smells of freedom and safety after all we have been through. He stands uncertainly at a distance, unsure how to proceed. I let him look his fill that he may mark me in his mind, know my shape and signs, take my number. He may not know what it means now but he will. He sees a thin woman of nineteen years who has lived so much longer and harder than that, with blonde hair and a sunken face with burning eyes. I look disarranged and maybe a little mad, I am sure. I am these things, in all probability. I am also very much alive and filled with a desire to use that to full advantage.

We will have difficulty in communicating, this man and me. I speak little English and I would be surprised if he has Russian. We will find a way. I nod at him to acknowledge his presence but do not speak. He nods back and gives a small smile that seems foreign to his face, as if he has not done this for quite a while. It is clear he has lost someone. When you have been through that sort of separation and grief, you recognise it fresh in others. He is scored through with it. He holds my gaze and I think he recognises our connection. He hesitates, forming nervous words in his mind, but decides to leave me be and walks to his door and through it. I do not fret; we have time. For once, time may be on my side.

We were lucky when we arrived off the train, strange as it is to say that. The journey had been as hellish as was possible, more than anyone could have explained or warned of. We were packed together, standing for days, with no comfort whatsoever and the certain knowledge that we were doomed, one way or another, when the train stopped at its final destination. My family had been on the move for so long we had ceased to resemble one another but were just bundles of bones in flesh. If you had seen us you would have assumed that mere coincidence had brought us together and not genetic ties of family or the love we had for one another. Elena had cut her hair off and the stubble was filthy enough to look dark. I could not bring myself to do that, as if doing so was the final frontier of giving in. People died upright in the fierce cold of that journey and remained in situ freezing further against the barely living. Cold; so very, very cold. Cold enough to halt decay amongst the deceased, although we all smelt rank and as if we were slowly decomposing. We had been rendered barely human. The dead were almost lucky, being spared any more of this torture. We starved and froze and worried about our fate. There was no resignation for me, just an ultimate, agonised fear that informed every hurtful breath of my precious life. But I was breathing, still am, savouring the pain, making it matter.

The White Angel was on the ramp when they opened the doors. He was a glorious sight, handsome and healthy. He smiled as if to welcome us. His purpose, of course, was far from that. Josef Mengele wanted twins and so a call went out for 'Zwillinge'. Was that a good thing? How did one gauge this in an instant? And it was certainly a snap life or death decision, we both felt that. I could hear Elena's heartbeat as clearly as my own, feel it just as forcibly, thunderously trying to keep its rhythm and help make the correct move. Without speaking, for we did not always need to use words, we walked apart and miraculously were chosen, separately, to walk left for Life. Even more of a miracle, though looking back I think it was probably the result of a harried guard's error and pointing at the wrong line in the commotion, Mama survived the selection. If Mama had not made it through, the result could have been so different.

'You can trust no one. You must not trust anyone.' That was the mantra our mother tried to drum into us. And, worst of all, she followed it with, 'Not even each other.' This much I know, we never would have betrayed the other. But I did see many break under pressure and choose their own lives above a beloved's. It was a time of war, a time of uncertainties and fear, and deep down most wanted to live. I understand that we are human and frail. I understand why we fail. But I still say Elena would never betray me. I will never test this, but I must believe it.

Fear. The smell of fear is a distinctive thing. The taste of it is distinctive. The feel of it is unbearable, especially when it is the life and death fear that no one should have to endure. That is what we lived with. And, always, the cold. Our bunks, in the shack we were billeted to, were bare. We were late in and no one had any spirit left over to help us. We clung to each other but had so little flesh left that we had precious little warmth to offer or share. We were so insubstantial as to leave no indentation on soft earth as we walked it, I suspect. I longed for the forsaken comfort of warm, wet grass beneath my feet but that was a lifetime ago.

We had to speak to those we were flung together with and therein lay great danger. Everyone was gathering what information they could to survive. We never told them we were Zwillinge, especially after hearing what Uncle Josef was doing to twins in his special laboratories. We were sisters, no more, no less.

If he had known we were precisely what he wanted, those special, intriguingly identical ones, we would both have perished horribly and immediately. As it was, it took a little longer than that. In the meantime, we heard of the blood-taking, the endless hours of measurements. We knew he tried to change eye colour to blue with dyes and painful injections. We heard how he infected one twin with disease, using the other untouched one as a barometer of his barbarism, all in the name of science. He even sewed children together, conjoined them, and studied the awful results.

Then a sniff of what we were must have emerged, in spite of the extreme care we took to disguise our bond. One word borrowed another in that place, one lie begat another, building and forming catastrophe for someone. And language is gesture as well as the damnation of utterance. Even a wary look could kill.

'Trust no one,' Mama said, again and again. 'Not even each other.'

But together we were strong.

Whatever happened, it got out because one day he came to where we worked. Mengele sought us. I don't know how we did it but we managed to be remarkably unalike that day, as if we were willing the other to be wholly different, and succeeding too; we were sisters, simply that. He was so persuasive, charming, not easy to dissuade. He could mesmerize you with a smile, a direct look that made you feel as special as he definitely wanted you to be. We were lucky, too, that Elena was wracked with a vile chest infection and accompanying cough. It doubled her over, made her unattractive to look at. Mengele clearly disliked it, found it irritating that she was sick. I had heard of him beating people to death for less and could see him check his inclination to lash out at her. He wanted us to be his Grail, more Zwillinge. It was as if he needed us more than we him, for the briefest moment.

261

I thought my heart might never beat faster than it did that day but the more you live in extraordinary times, the more you realise there is always another level of terror, another level of misfortune. He left, but we knew he would be back. The simple fact of time being itself ensures that. Time repeats, it threatens more of the same and then adds some new digressions on its theme while it is about it. It cruelly delivers on all of these. Mama saw this too.

We were in our cold, oh so cold, shack the night of Mengele's visit. Mama did not live in it with us but managed to get news to us that she would visit. It was made known that she was a neighbour from home as we could not reveal kinship. Any connection was dangerous. We were overjoyed that we would see her. When she got there, her instructions were simple and repetitive: 'Trust no one, not even each other.' Then she demanded that Elena always display her illness, even if she felt better, though we all knew it was almost impossible to recover from lice even, when so challenged with hunger and impossible conditions. When I dissect this visit, as I often do, I realise she had decided what must be done. And even if I had known it then, there would have been no dissuading her.

Mengele sent a doctor the following day, one of the Jewish camp inmates with a medical background, whom he used to do his mundane work for him. The woman measured us and I was glad that Elena had become less tall, for one thing, through worry and illness. She was different to me too because she had also broken several toes once when we were children during a hectic game of hide and seek. We were playing it now with such high stakes, my breath almost lost the rhythm necessary to sustain me. We were physically similar but not identical. We seemed to be just the sisters we insisted we were. This was the news returned to the White Angel and we lived another day.

He may have been distracted by other train deliveries, and we heard he had selected new children, but he was not entirely diverted. I have thought about little else for so long and now opt for the idea that he may have seen us as viable repro- ductively. He had many young children to experiment on but few identical twins that might reveal the secrets of life in the womb and beyond. I will never know for sure.

Mama was still watching us closely too. And Elena was getting sicker and not having to dissemble much in that regard. I would love to be able to name you the day Mama came again, so that we might always say it was a Wednesday, but days, and the naming of them, had ceased to matter long ago. This is a feature of peacetime that is new and hard to fathom: we name things, we decide what they are to be called. It aids regularity, conformity, consensus. In the camp there was only day and night, life and death.

Mama smothered Elena with the meagre lump of hemp we had called a pillow. She chose to sacrifice her so that we might be separate and non-identical, and one of us would be safe. She chose that I would live. That is the great weight I carry each day. Mama died some days later, gunned down while running at the barbed wire as if to escape, but I don't know how many days because it was months before I learned of it. I do not know if it is true because I was not at the event. I choose to believe it. Those who told it to me were perhaps kind in their version of how my mother left the world. People sometimes want to help after the fact, to issue words that will soothe, a legend that those left behind can live with. She may have been torn apart by one of the guard's dogs for all I know: that was a common enough occurence. Why waste a bullet on a stick-thin woman, little more than a skeleton, when the wire would kill her anyhow? Whoever might have shot her wouldn't exactly have panicked to see a skinny Jewess about to throw herself to her death. What matters is that it was an escape, in its way, though not the one the Nazis thought they were punishing. I may even have heard the shots that reportedly killed her. Why don't we say she died on a Saturday? It's as good a day as any to die.

I feel Elena still, like the ache of a limb long gone. I feel her heartbeat. And my heart beats for two now, because it must.

I was a child before the war and am now a woman after it. It is how I will always mark my life: before and after. The leap happened atavistically as I had no choice but to let it. Before, when I was a child, I was selfish as all children are. There was me and my world which I shared as a matter of course but valued as mine. I took things for granted, complained when I felt my due was not delivered to me. I demanded life and its embellishments. I knew no different.

We had music, laughter, books. Papa was a painter, though this was regarded as dangerous, which we found sometimes a little hilarious. That is to say, Elena and I thought the notion comedic. Mama knew better. We could not conceive how his art might tempt revolution. It is expression, of course, that frightens dictators especially when they are lacking in it themselves. They fear books, ideas, musical notes that can enervate minds, spur them on to a higher theme. We didn't know

264

what true danger was then, and almost mocked the notion that Papa's canvases could be taken as such. We know all about danger now. We have lived through even worse.

Papa blames his art for what happened to us but he is wrong about the why of it. We moved around so as to escape the scrutiny of the authorities and, yes, that was because of his work. This is how we came to be in Minsk when the Nazis swooped. Papa was out of town and not swept up with the rest of us. His art had merely got us to that location, it was not the cause of our downfall; the cause was the fact that we were Jews. If I were a mathematician or a scientist, I could now declare QED. We just happened to be in the right place at the wrong time for the Germans to capture us. We had enemies with a sweeping brief to eradicate us. Papa did not make that country and its leaders the homicidal monsters they were. And he was not responsible for the fact that weak people in that city told of our whereabouts in the hope that they would be left alone.

We were not a conventional family; conventional is a sad, sorry state and so it had no place for us. I now fantasise of a past that might have been soaked in convention and perhaps have kept us safe. And there was our religion also, the curse of being Jewish. I am not religious any more; I have too many questions that it cannot answer. For instance, how can being a Jew define me utterly, I would like to know. How might it have been enough to want me dead? But it is the burden placed on my people and always has been and His way of testing us. Sacrilege it may be, but I think He may have gone a step too far this time. Papa still prays, it gives him comfort. I cannot. Again, we could not swap or deny our heritage, nor would we have wanted to, but how envious I am on occasion of those who can slither out of all we could not. Yet freedom is all in having survived, to have lived to tell our tale. It is time for Papa to paint again.

I find that I, too, need to. The woman who is now Natalia, who never showed such application before, has much to offer with paint and brush. The urge is growing, consuming my thoughts and making my hands itch to begin. We must celebrate what we have achieved and break the world's heart while we are at it. Simple storytelling should do that and it is all I will attempt. Mine is a simple story, after all. I will need tools and do not know how to go about this just yet. But there may be a way already shown to me.

The third time I see the Man I decide to make contact. I say 'Natalia,' and point to myself. He says, 'David,' and points to himself. That is all. We stand and take the other in. He is quite lovely. Sad, blue eyes in a gentle face, with aquiline nose and a red tint to his curled hair. He is taller than me by a foot, I should think, and it is pleasant to look up at him. I like the angle from which I see him. He is unafraid to meet and hold my eye and I like that too. I think he sees that I am of a kind with him. He hesitates then very, very slowly reaches out an elegant hand and touches my number with his long fingers. I allow it. I want it. Now, he is mine and I am his, whether he realises it or not. He has touched the most personal of my marks. There is no turning back. We have fallen in love with each other's sadness. It is a start.

Papa has decided he will labour on the rebuilding of London. He has no desire to be more creative than that. He needs the harsh scenario of long days hauling bricks. For me that is too like the camps but I hold my tongue. He feels this will help with his atonement and I will not begrudge him that. We must all find the velocity at which we can get by. Papa needs the punishment of the hard slog. It also gives a shape to his day.

The city is ruined and needs attention so he is well placed to help. Hitler and his architect Albert Speer developed a concept of 'ruin value' when their defeat was clear and a death wish took hold. They would erect models of buildings in the Lüneberg countryside, of stone and concrete, and then have them bombed to compare which would look most impressive in the aftermath of war. They will not rebuild Germany but the British and my father will restore London to this new nation of ours. Papa has made an interesting friend, called Niklaus Pevsner, who is also clearing Blitz damage. This man is an art historian and a Russian Jew so they have much in common and it is good to know that Papa has someone to talk to. I hope Papa will discuss art with him. He cannot turn his back on it totally, surely. Pevsner worked in Germany and once supported Hitler, till he was made persona non grata and had to flee to England. So many are turning up here in London.

I am learning English with the support group who brought us here and helped us settle. Growing up, we learnt French as we felt a kinship with Europe, if only because it was part of the same landmass. It seemed accessible, possible. French is of no use to me in England. I am still uncertain why London was chosen for us but even random acts can offer hope and the move has brought David to me. The group is puzzled by how particular I am about the words I want to learn. I need only plain ones, as the intricacies of language are not for me any longer. I have no time to twist meanings with fine rhetoric, or to indulge in ambiguity. There is the truth and it is straightforward and needs no embellishment. It must be spoken in the light and in colour. As well, I need to know who David is, what he does, and if he can get me brushes and paints. After that, all I need is surfaces; scrap wood will do, paper, anything.

The dream happens every night and I wonder if it will be with me forever. I am running after a train but my legs are leaden and I do not make any progress. It hurts to breathe and I feel held down although my limbs seem unrestrained. The back door of the last carriage opens and an angel appears, dressed in white. He opens his arms wide to welcome me and suddenly I am gaining on him. But I know that when I reach him, as I must, I will die. Then his face changes and it is Elena and I am filled with a sparkling happiness. I cry out her name and in response she opens her mouth and issues forth an ear-piercing scream. The scream becomes an actual stream of red travelling from her towards me and I know it is her life's blood. Then a shot rings out and I fall to the ground, dead, except that I awaken then in a pool of sweat, alone and bereft, tears running unchecked from my eyes and my whimpers filling my small room. I am lying there one night, exhausted after the nightmare, when I hear a child's voice say, 'Yellow,' excitedly, but I have no idea why that is.

I step out to check on the sky. There is a man there I have not seen before. He has an ephemeral quality to him and it imparts safety. He is not exactly flimsy, just gentle. I must learn to trust again and hope that my instincts are sharp in this regard and that he is as kindly as I find him. His eyes are clearest blue and without guile and the soft lines of his face speak of a man quick to smile and praise. His hands rest on the metal railing and are long-fingered and fine. They look as though they might heal. We gaze at a pink and red dusk.

'Where are the stars?' I ask in my new, halting language.

'Oh, they're out there somewhere.' He smiles.

'Do we know that certainly?' I tease, or at least I hope I can put that sort of texture into this new tongue I have.

'We trust in it. They shine on, out there, somewhere.'

'They are hiding?'

'Although they have nothing to hide,' he points out.

We are playing now and it feels good and comfortable.

'Like a rainbow,' I say even though I do not know why this may be true. I hope it is, as it is a lovely idea and smacks of happy fact.

He laughs a little. 'Yes, I suppose. And I've always felt a rainbow had a lovely tune to it.'

'Yes,' I agree. 'A happy song.'

'They've promised us a rainbow for tomorrow. I haven't seen one in ages. It will be a treat. I think it will be a momentous day.'

'It is something to look forward to,' I say. It's nice to have something to look forward to, I realise. I tend to live in the past in my mind and the present in my body but have paid too little attention to the future of late.

'Teddy,' the man says, stretching his hand in friendship.

'Natalia.'

He sees my number and looks into my eyes. 'You are an Other.'

'Yes,' I confirm. 'I am Other.'

David knows a man called Rawley who is willing to help. I understand that I cannot speak of his method of supply or question it. I am used to the illicit furnishing of commodities so this is nothing new to me, nor is it a problem. I learnt a lot about getting by in the camp. I care only that I have my means of expression and with each day the need to get these feelings and images out of me grows more acute. I say images but they are more scratches and colours, patterns of inhumanity that have no identifiably figurative shape. All I know is that it is imperative to commit them to another medium outside of my head or else I will go mad and they will never be seen and taken on board by anyone else.

Papa is quite silent on the subject. He knows what I intend. He is busy breaking his hands down so that they are little more than rough-hewn blocks capable of only the most sweeping actions. He has fallen out with art. He blames it for much of our unfortunate family history. I wonder if we will ever see any of his work again. He fled the war with the clothes he wore and lost most of those along the way. He was delivered back to me in an altered state, lesser in every way. He had some photographs of our past life but those are the only mementos we have. One is a black and white of my parents and their baby twin daughters. It rests on the ledge of the fireplace, leaning against the wall, without a frame as we don't have one and cannot afford one. I sometimes look at the people in that picture and find they are strangers.

Papa likes David but is wary of Rawley. I think he feels Raymond would sell anyone on for his own gain. I do not feel this to be entirely the case, not when it comes to us. There is something of the underdog about us that appeals to him and he does have that famous British sense of fair play, however submerged he may keep it in general. David wears his heart for all to see. I know about Jane and their baby. We all carry a sadness. Some day, I want to tell him, we will have a child. I know this. It is not time to let him in on that secret yet.

Raymond can only get me tins of paint. I don't care how crude the pigments are. I am so full of anguish, I can work with anything to begin with. These things inside me won't go away easily so I can hone whatever needs to be honed in years to come. And I don't want to make my painting slick or toothless, necessarily. I want people to gasp. I want them to see the world through new, disturbed eyes. I want to move them. This is my uncomfortable gift.

My first attempts are on wood. The planks remind me of the hard bunks in the camp. I let red soak in, like blood. Then I darken the stain so that it looks just like the hard bed did when I spent my time on it with Elena, adding to the residual sorrow and pain left by others before us. I take nails and bang them into the board. Some are flush with the surface, others jagged, to tear at anyone who gets too close. I place some fabric on these and tug, leaving behind threads and scraps of rag. I gouge out small sections. I submerge the piece in water to weather it. I place it outside the door for the wind and rain to deal with. I take it back in and kick it around the room. I am happy with the result.

David sees it and puts his arms around me. 'Well done,' he says.

Raymond nods when it is shown to him.

Papa takes the picture and hangs it in his room.

then

No sun – no moon!
No morn – no noon –
No dawn – no dusk – no proper time of day.
No warmth, no cheerfulness, no healthful ease,
No comfortable feel in any member –
No shade, no shine, no butterflies, no bees,
No fruits, no flowers, no leaves, no birds! –
November!

Thomas Hood, 'November'

november 1979

Dad is standing at the door when I answer it. He is gazing at a piece of sky, admiring the clouds. This is the square patch, visible through other higher buildings, that has looked down on the flat for as long as I can remember. It is a fine, frosty day and the clear blue we see sets off the fluffy white of what he tells me is cumulus mediocris.

'Not mediocre, Frank,' he qualifies, in case I mistake his meaning, 'merely medium sized.'

My dad loves his clouds. I know he has always admired the way Constable painted them and frequently makes little forays to visit those works in the gallery, if they're not in the room he's watching over. His favourite is a view of Weymouth Bay near where the artist spent his honeymoon, followed closely by 'The Cornfield'.

'Constable called the sky a keynote and the chief organ of sentiment in his work. I've always thought his skies a lot more interesting than his landscapes below.'

We stand looking up, happy to feel the sun touch our faces although it can give little warmth in this chill November air. It's welcome, all the same.

'I wonder if those sort of shapes will always be there in the sky for mortals to see and appreciate? Will there come a time when there are no clouds?'

'There'll always be weather,' I say. 'As long as there's an atmosphere around the earth.' I feel like a pedant. There is no poetry in my words, no joy at the natural world.

'It feels like life's been a bit grey of late. Blackouts, strikes, it reminds me of the war and after. Grim. All we're missing is rationing, though I think hard times are imposing those at family level.'

'They say it's our winter of discontent.'

'A winter that has taken a year so far,' he points out.

'Yes. I think the papers and chatterers need their buzz words to describe it, a lazy phrase to explain things for the hard of thinking. It's a "there's your hook, job sorted, we know what we're dealing with" type of thing.'

Dad points at the railings. 'That's where I first saw your mother,' he tells me and launches into the formal soliloquy I have heard many times. He has honed this memory and it is now delivered almost in a patter. 'I thought she was a ghost. She was a grey apparition and the thinnest creature I had beheld in some time, which is saying a lot because we were all still grimly starving in the aftermath of war. Victory was a poor place in many practical ways. She had her pointed, bony back to me and a gentle breeze moved a shapeless, rough shift she was wearing around her body. Even without seeing her face I knew she was in another place, a separate world. There was a set to her that spoke of suffering and the burden of surviving. A pigeon roosted by her side on those very railings and she seemed to be watching it closely from the angle of her head. When she turned at the sound of me, one hand travelled to the other arm and touched the number etched on her skin, the way that some newlyweds abstractedly worry the rings placed there by their new contract. I was caught in the beam of black, haunted eyes. The sight of her beauty actually pushed the breath from my body. It was gaunt and stark but startling. My immediate instinct was to go to her and take her in my arms to protect her. However, I knew that she'd bolt if I made any such sudden move. She didn't know me so flee she most certainly would. The bird cooed and fractured the moment, and she granted it a fond glance. Then she made for her door and disappeared from my view. I had missed my chance to speak to her or even to hear her name. It would be weeks before I got another opportunity.'

We spend a moment remembering my mother.

'Weeks meant nothing to me. They passed quickly. I had been a widower six years by then. No, weeks were nothing.'

'She'll never know Mengele died this year,' I say.

'If you can believe the reports. He was in Brazil, they say.'

'Tea,' I suggest. There are some British traditions that abide in this little Soho household and that is one of them. Besides, it's too early for a beer, even with my wonky body clock.

He stands looking at the wall where his print of the Arnolfini portrait still hangs. When he moved to the suburbs he left it there and I didn't move it because I have always been fond of the painting. He is rubbing his hands together in that distinctive way he has when something uncomfortable must be dealt with. I saw it when he tried to explain the facts of life to me, for instance. We never had the foreskin talk because that was the one Jewish thing my mother did for me: I am circumcised.

'I stole that during the war,' he says, gesturing to the portrait.

'I didn't know they had prints like that then,' I say.

'No, I stole the original.'

I really don't know how to react to this. It's preposterous. I am immediately struck by the fact that my dad may be displaying the first signs of his dotage. He's getting on now, after all.

'We all did things then that we may have come to regret. Some have bigger regrets than others. That's not one of mine. I couldn't bear to see them bury that painting for years in a Welsh quarry. Of course I realise it makes me as much an art looter as your next Nazi, but there you have it.'

Something about this is ringing true to me. I am gobsmacked. If I was ever pushed to explain the subtle difference between my parents, I would have ventured that my father always strove to do the correct thing whereas my mother tried for the right thing. Yet, here he is telling me that he stole a national arte-fact and had it on his wall as the shit was being bombed out of London in the forties. Way to go, Dad. I start to laugh.

'You old bugger, you,' I say.

He is pleased with the moniker. 'See? You never thought your old man had it in him, did you?' He nods. 'Audacious. I never knew I had that sort of lunatic instinct. I greatly fear there may be a dreamer in us, genetically, son, and we are powerless against some of the more wilful acts to come of that. As long as you've got your mother's bravery as well, you'll be fine.'

But it was Mum's tiger heart that let her down and stopped long before any of us wanted it to.

Mama always called Ray Rawley 'Raymond' and he loved her for that, and a whole raft of other reasons too. He is my unlikely ally in the construction of my music machine. I've always taken him for granted. He has been part of the fabric of my life forever, as my godfather but also as friend to my parents. He grew up with my dad and they have Soho traits and history in common. Rawley has always known someone or someone-who-knew-someone-else who could supply or help out with whatever you might need. He understood my project better than most others from the off because he could see things in colour, just not music.

'Here's how I knew I was different, Frank. I was, what, seven or eight maybe, and I had this little weekend job at my dad's printers, just cleaning up and whatnot. Small beans but pocket money, you know? Anyhow, we all had to explain our hobbies one day at school and I thought I might talk about my weekends and the excitement, the kick I got out of doing a day's work. I said I counted the days off till purple. What I meant was Saturday but I wasn't thinking and I called it by its colour for me. I took a lot of stick for that and I learnt not to mention it or draw attention to it again. So I get that some people might understand music in colours.'

'You are a synaesthete,' I told him.

'Easy for you to say.' He shifts about a bit and I hope I haven't embarrassed him. He has a certain reputation as a hard man and this wouldn't fit the description at all.

'Not to be too lardy, synaesthesia is the condition of seeing music or days or words in colour. Neural patterns and trails remain in some people's heads from childhood that aren't shed or streamlined by the brain as it matures, so you get left with this strange ability. For my money, it makes your brain a lot less inhibited than mine.'

281

It intrigued my godfather. From there on he has championed the work. It's crude because the technology I am using is young and what I've done is that *I* have chosen colours to match notes but I am beginning to realise they differ from person to person. One might see G as red while another sees it as brown, and so on. There are some broad strokes I can lean on. Most agree that they see lighter colours for higher sounds, that louder tones are brighter than soft ones, and lower tones darker than higher ones. Ultimately, all I want to do is make an entertainment for someone who cannot hear, so that they can enjoy the spectacle of a piece without hearing the music itself. My thinking is that the choice of colours for notes is probably unimportant in this context. This scheme will have to do at this point, in the absence of a better idea. It would be different if I were tailoring it to an individual who already had a chosen palette. Some day, sophisticated systems will deliver everything I can only dream of, but this is 1979, we're living in recession, and resources and know-how are limited to me.

My grandfather, Papa Konstantin, told me about a Russian composer called Scriabin who worked on the same idea. He, too, chose a spectrum of colours and decided which would go with the notes, writing deliberately contrived music based on a circle of fifths. He didn't ever get to make his machine, a colour organ, but as far as I can ascertain, an engineer did for a world trade fair some years later, working with the composer's rules. If it's a mad idea, I am not the only one to have had it.

Rawley got me a home computer, a Sinclair ZX80. I am trying my best to understand what it might do for me but it is Eric who is the wizard on the thing. My head is wired for music, his can manage technology too. All I have to put up

282

with in return for his expertise and doggedness is him ranting about Thatcher and how she'll break the country, or at least the unions. He hates the ZX80, says it has shit memory capacity, extremely limited basic language and a horrible keyboard. It also crashes frequently and even I get frustrated then. We are keeping the pieces we play short and simple as a result.

'What we need here is an Apple or a Tandy, or an Atari.' His eyes lose focus as he invokes the name Atari and I know he longs for one of those. 'Does Rawley know anyone in America? They're way ahead of us. I'm not sure we can achieve much, if anything, with this heap of shit.'

It was all triggered by the Chinese girl who walks her brother to the school around the corner each day. She is clearly deaf and they communicate with signs. From what I can see and appreciate, it's a veritable Tower of Babel between them, though through signage. I will probably never tell her what she has done for me, what she has set free as an idea. She is the beautiful and distant catalyst for a lunatic notion and it might disturb her to know what she has unleashed.

Recently I asked Rawley if he still sees the days in colour.

'Not so much now,' was the scant reply.

I knew he was hedging, but also wanting me to get off-subject: he's not a man comfortable with talking about feelings. No villain is, I'm guessing. He's suppressed this part of him, unwilling to admit to a brain differently arranged to the accepted norm. Fair enough.

'Ray Rawley got his hands on a camera and film early on in the war,' Dad says. 'He took a photo of Jane and me that you might find interesting. It was accidental but intriguing. I must hunt it out for you. You like the Arnolfini painting so you'll appreciate the photograph.'

He clears his throat. My father wants something more than this off his chest.

'I met Anthony Blunt, you know, more than once. He visited the gallery lots of times, naturally enough. I've always admired him as an art historian.'

Dad did a night-time degree in history of art. He is captivated by the subject and sometimes writes papers for the various journals that might be interested. He seems, to my uneducated readership, to have some foxy theories about provenance and style although, as I say, I am no expert. I have always enjoyed his articles as they reveal a secret David Johnson, one filled with a passion no one could guess at if they meet and greet him briefly. Having said that, I think there are a lot of his regular acquaintances who'd be surprised at his passion for his chosen academic subject too.

He's looking at me now as if he has unlocked a mystery for me but I have no idea what it is he's telling me.

'Have you seen the papers? Heard the news?'

'Dad, it may not be big or clever but I am working lates as a drag queen in a seedy Soho club. Unless Blunt came in and performed a lewd act in front of me in the wee small hours, I wouldn't know what he's up to.'

'He's just been outed as a Soviet spy.'

'Really. I never knew a background in art history could be so filled with intrigue or important as a prerequisite for passing secrets of state.' I let him pace a bit. 'Have you had the tap on the shoulder?' I tease. 'Is that what's up?'

'Facetious, Frank,' he says. 'I wonder if I should have known.'

'OK, you've got me, I'll bite. How in hell might you have known?'

'Well, I don't suppose I *could* have known really but it turns out his code name was Johnson and sure enough, one day when we were discussing the Arnolfinis at the gallery, someone called my name and we both turned round.'

'That sounds to me like the honours syllabus in spotting spies.'

'He's the fourth man after Burgess, McLean and Philby, the Cambridge lot, you know? Thatcher has just exposed him in parliament though the authorities have known for years. Apparently he confessed in nineteen sixty-four but they sat on it. He's been stripped of his knighthood.'

Although this is all very intriguing, and I love a good spy story as much as the next man, I wonder what it has to do with us exactly. There is something in my father's manner that tells me it has set off a reaction in him none of us might have predicted, possibly even him.

'He worked for MI5 during the war.'

Ah, we may be approaching it now: the war.

'See, here's the thing. I was always appalled by Nazi actions but when it came to something like them looting art, I felt a hypocrite because I stole the Arnolfinis for myself at that time. I was no better than them in that regard. And now here's a man who loves art also, and it turns out he is a traitor to his country. It's betrayal, Frank, plainly speaking. I, too, betrayed my country.'

My father has tears in his eyes. It is unbearably touching to see how worked up he's got himself over this. And very, very funny. I try to be gentle.

'Dad, I think you're overreacting here.'

He is a relic of old decency and I think if Britain had more solid and sensitive types like him, our world would be a better place. It is very hard not to laugh, though. I wish my mum were here to enjoy this lovely moment.

'You gave the painting back,' I say, adding a worried, 'didn't you?'

'Good God, yes, Frank. What do you take me for?'

'You did no harm then. No one knows. It hasn't impacted on anyone's life. You're fine, Dad, relax.'

'Lighten up,' he says and nods.

When I was growing up I knew that other houses had arguments about football, whereas we had more highfalutin discussions about art. It wasn't odd, it was just how we were. It also meant that I could score football talk with friends but have my head tickled at home. It was a desperately embarrassing fact during my early adolescence but I got over it, and myself, quite early in all of that hormonal stew.

My grandfather held passionate views. 'Art is a mischief maker at best,' he would say. 'At worst it is dangerous. Plain trouble. To be avoided.' He always hoped if he spoke forcefully and succinctly enough that it would end the matter.

'It will outlast us all,' my father would say, taking up the baton and running with it.

'It gifts a legacy, certainly, whether benign or otherwise. My experience of it has not been positive. I curse it.'

'It charts man's achievement, honours creativity. It separates us from the animals.'

'Does it? David, you are a romantic.' Papa Konstantin usually said this fondly while shaking his head but there was a rub to it too, as if my dad couldn't fully know art and was naive about it because he had not suffered for it.

Mama's contribution to all of this was to continue to paint.

'We had a strange courtship by any standard,' my father tells me. 'I always felt she knew what was in store for us. She had a calmness, a certainty, about her that I think came from her knowing we would be together. I was a lot slower off the mark.'

I have heard all of this before but he likes to tell it and I like to hear it.

'We both recognised the damage and sorrow in the other and that was a good thing. However, that didn't make either of us victims on the rebound. We had new lives we needed to lead and fate brought us together in this little complex of flats. Your mother might have been sent to another town but she was sent here and to me. This place survived the Blitz almost unscratched, which was just as well, considering it was giving shelter to the Arnolfinis.'

'I still find it hard to believe you took them.'

'I know. What class of lunacy was I up to, putting them on the wall? Anything might have happened to that painting.' He shivers to think of his actions.

'I wanted to provide for your mother but that was hard in a time of rationing. It was just as bad after the war as it had been during it. Food was always a good gift but what she really wanted was paint, brushes. I tried my best and Rawley outdid himself. Papa Kostya would bring what he could from the sites too, offcuts of wood and so on.'

This is why there are some very interesting shapes of work from Mum's early period. They turn up now and then and fetch great prices at auction, which would surely amuse her.

'I wanted to be romantic and give her flowers, say, but they were such a luxury, frivolous almost. Sometimes, if I visited Jane at the graveyard, I would walk in the woods close by and pick some wild flowers but they hated being plucked from their natural home and wilted quickly in any pot back here. Your mama finally asked me not to bring them because they made her sad when they keeled over and died. I did manage to find chocolate occasionally and she loved that.'

'She had a sweet tooth.'

'Yes. I trawled the town for chocolate and waited to hear her story. She took a long time before telling me. It wasn't that she didn't trust me, no, it was that she found it hard to choose words that would do it justice, especially in a new language.'

'I suppose you could say everyone had a new language after the war, nothing was the same any more.'

'Oh, yes,' my father agrees. 'What was incredible was that she learnt to trust again. That she would allow it was a mammoth leap after all she'd been through. I was thinking about that today, trust, you know? After the whole Blunt thing. Wondering who you can trust.'

That is what's bothering this lovely man.

'But you must be open to all experiences, I think that's what your mother taught me. That way you can reach judgement in an informed way. That is how you learn.'

It's strange to hear Dad sounding abandoned. It doesn't quite match him outwardly, being high-pitched; he looks a lot more rooted and stern than that. I have brought him to the club this evening to meet Sally and he is taking it all in his stride, even if he clearly thinks it's some sort of other side through a looking glass, a looking glass surrounded by lightbulbs with graffiti written on it in lipstick at that. This man is amazing, with much credit to the woman by his side for taking him this far out of himself. Or perhaps he's always been this far out and I have never seen it before.

I have no idea what Sally has said to him but he is taken with her. That's Sal, I want to tell him, she can talk to anyone and make them feel at ease. She has a gift for people. She's a communicator.

'I'm coming to the show this evening,' he tells me.

I have no cogent response to this. I am lost for words. How will my elderly father react to his son in drag?

'I think you'll enjoy it, David,' Sal says. 'Though I rather suspect Frank won't, given the green gills on him now.'

They enjoy my discomfort, partners in gentle crime. I don't mind. Here are two of the people most important to me and they are getting along just fine.

By performance time my nerves are in shreds. My hand shakes too much to do any good with my eyeliner so Sal assumes make-up duties. When she is done, I look fantastic. We stand in front of the mirror and she tells me I am 'magnificent'. I all but crumble to hear the belief in this woman's voice. For my part, I cannot believe my luck to have her in my life. She holds my gaze in the mirror and kisses my cheek. 'Your dad is going to be knocked out.'

'That's what I'm worried about. He'll have to be one big character to take this baby on.'

'And he will. He's already bursting with pride that you're his son. He says you're endlessly inventive and positive. He can't say it to you because he's your dad and he's a man and an Englishman at that, and you're a man and an Englishman too.'

'Just not tonight,' I point out. 'I never realised what a weird family we are.'

'Hardly weird. How does "alternative" sound?'

'I can roll with it.' I try to breathe more evenly. 'I think I'm going to be sick.'

'You're not. You're going to use that nervous energy to kick ass, as our American brothers and sisters would say.'

The management sends a bottle of dodgy house champagne over to Dad's table and I experience a warm glow for Garibaldi till I remember he knows that Dad and Ray Rawley go back to the year dot so his altruism is business-related and not because the father of an esteemed member of the company is in the audience.

I have a buzzing in my ears for the whole performance and cannot hear myself or the band properly. I am glad of the curtain of eyelashes now because they obscure my view of the audience and, in particular, my father. Caesar goes out of his way to shimmy close to him any chance he gets and I am convinced the others are making a beeline for him too. I am rooted to a spot and dare not budge in case I fall over or wet myself in fear. I do stumble as we take our bow and Eric grabs me in a playful embrace that mortifies me. He'd have let me tumble into a void normally but judges this to be a better wheeze by which to embarrass me. I take extra care to regain my manliness after the performance and am scrubbed red-raw by the time I face my father. He looks around us and down at the ground a lot, but with a smirk on his face. I don't know what to think.

'What would Mum have made of it?' I ask him, for want of better.

He looks me in the eye an instant, then away. 'She'd have been singing along, I reckon. She loved to see people happy, you know. Did you feel the delight in the room?'

'But what would she have thought of me, her only son, in a frock and make-up?'

He grins and I see a young piece of mischief under the layers of calm and age; I see a happy person, the sort Mum liked to see. 'Above all things your mother understood that you use what you have at your disposal to get whatever you need, day to day. That's exactly what you're doing here and leaving a smile on a lot of punters' faces while you're about it.' He pauses.

'What?' I ask.

He shrugs, reluctantly. I steel myself.

'What, Dad?'

'I'm just not sure pink is your colour, son. You should maybe look at a green gown next time out?'

Everyone's a fashion expert round here: he's not the first to have mentioned this and he won't be the last.

Love is risk, through and through. Frank knew this. So he knew he must, and would, expose his innermost self to Sally in order to prove himself. To secure her, he decided to show her the music machine in action.

'It will be the simplest of tunes,' he warned. 'The system can't handle anything complex.'

'Most things worth experiencing are essentially simple,' she said. 'Stop making excuses and show me the marvel.'

He took the Arnolfinis off the wall and set the projector in front of it. He attached the wires from the machine to the computer as Eric had shown him. They had written notes on the keys of the pad and it was programmed to show a corresponding colour when he pressed them. He pulled the curtains to dim the light in the room. He was not a religious man but he muttered an intonation that could have been construed as a prayer. 'Please don't expect much,' he said and began to play.

Two soft pulses of deepest red appeared on the white wall, then were repeated. He continued them as a base and played yellow, green, blue, indigo, yellow. He repeated the sequence twice and rested.

'That was beautiful,' Sally said. 'Was it the opening of your show?'

'Yes.' Frank felt tears prickle.

They stood before the wall, holding hands now. Quietly, she began to speak. '"What a piece of work is man. How noble in reason, how infinite in faculty, in form and moving how express and admirable, in action how like an angel, in apprehension how like a god." Christ, don't look so surprised, Frank, I am a trained actor. I may never get to play Hamlet, but I do know some of the lines. And before you get too excited, he does go on to say man doesn't please him nor woman neither.'

He waited.

'You composed that music from the birds sitting outside this window and then made it into a fleeting, extraordinary picture. For me.'

'Did you like it?'

'I loved it. I love you.'

now

Hold Infinity in the palm of your hand,
And Eternity in an hour.

William Blake, 'Auguries of Innocence'

december

Another year gone, Karen thought, but this time I have climbed out of an emotional hinterland I didn't even know I was part of. She was amazed by her life but suspicious of her good mood and fortune. More time-wasting, she thought. Why not just grab at it and enjoy? Why are we programmed to a default position of mistrust?

She loved to see London all lit up. Throughout the year, Soho had more than its fair share of neon, and those single, naked, red bulbs glowing in plain windows, improvised to signal a body for hire. Now, the whole town sparkled with strings of lights joining both sides of every main street.

Karen was delivered two Christmases by her new circumstance, an unexpected turn of events. She didn't much like the traditional English one and was uncertain how she felt about enduring double from now on. Russians had their celebrations in the New Year so, in the aftermath of her annual festive time out with her parents, she was preparing to join the extended Bulgharov clan for more.

Soho was mild and showery today. She watched the weather from her window, following the clouds across the sky, taking little bets about which would weep on her street and which would travel elsewhere.

Until this year she hadn't been a woman known for taking stock of life but that might have been one of her problems all along. She was paying more attention to her surroundings and situation now. For too long she had been detached, letting things run away from her. It was time to take charge.

It was natural that Tony be on her mind. A year ago they had ripped up the season and, while hung-over and wasted on Christmas Eve, had even contemplated not returning to their parental homes.

He'd said, 'Pointless small talk, a vague smear of disappointment in the air, pretending to have a great time? I'm way too exhausted for that.'

Remembering it now, it seemed such a mean analysis. He had been a bitch about so much. It had been hilarious at the time, of course. He went home, in the end, as did she. She wondered if he knew it was his goodbye visit to his family. Had he chosen gifts that were extra special, therefore, or just what was handy in some airport he was dragged through? The Dash highlight had been her mother's triumph with the sprouts. For once they were crunchy.

'It was an accident,' her mum admitted. 'I simply mistimed them.'

Ah, timing, thought Karen. Whoever could get that right at all? What did it profit us to come around the right corner at the right time? And how could we be sure we had? Perhaps all of life was the act of turning the wrong corner at the right time and vice versa. As Tony pointed out, there are no rules. And that was the problem. We were cast adrift, possessed of a little kindness, with only our initiative and common sense to rely on and that was usually not enough to get by. But when luck kicked in, we had a chance.

Was that what had happened to her?

Karen was unconvinced that sheer, lucky accident was what steered Queen Beatrice off course and into her Soho life. There was something about the quality of the air when the bird was around that puzzled Karen. It was an unfathomable rhythm that was out of kilter with the norm, as if the light was bent and events out of joint. Fanciful, she knew, but it was what she experienced. Tony would have said it was chemical afterthought brought on by wine or other stimulants. If it had a solid explanation, then she hadn't worked it out just yet.

The latest shower had stopped and a fragile rainbow was staining the sky. She thought of the little girls she had met outside and the colours the youngest saw. 'Good tune,' Karen said of the arc on blue.

She hoped taking stock was not a depression waiting to pounce. Had Tony assessed twelve months since and found his lot so lacking that he decided to leave? It was a year and yet only a breath ago. She was struck by the fact that as Tony died in her bath twelve months ago, he was still alive in New York, which was hours behind. She said as much to Alex later on and he quoted an eccentric Irishman called Sir Boyle Roche who held that a man cannot be in two places at once, unless he was a bird. 'It's something the pigeons understand,' he said. 'Especially Queen Beatrice.'

She sat by her window watching office parties go by. If she stayed here long enough the theory was that everyone she ever knew might pass. She took in her reflection in the darkened glass but, instead of herself, she saw her grandparents and parents and countless other family members who'd gone before her all stare back from her face.

Frank took charge of clearing his father's belongings after his death in 1984. The old man would have appreciated that he had gone in Orwell's mighty year, and also that it came and went without any of the apocalyptic mischief predicted.

'Fear is what we need to avoid,' he had said often enough. 'When good people become afraid, they cease to act on their principles and bad things happen.'

There was the usual bric-a-brac to decide on. He felt guilty throwing away anything his father had used regularly, as if there was still an essence of him attached. He allotted an hour of every day one week to sort through the dead man's possessions and looked forward to spending time with him then. They reminisced together, even if one of them was permanently absent now. He found Rawley's photograph on Wednesday.

He had bagged some jackets and trousers from the wardrobe, having selected a few to keep to wear himself, when he saw the brown woollen sweater, hand-knitted and worn, folded neatly in the corner. Frank had seen his father wear it only once a year throughout his life, sometimes sweltering on that day if the weather was hot, as the date dictated it should be. He knew the jumper his father wore on 10 May was made for him by Jane, his first wife, as a Christmas gift in 1940. He knew that his father had always suspected Rawley had supplied her with the yarn but had never figured out when or where she'd had the opportunity to knit it.

But it was the photograph underneath that made Frank's heart leap. This was the accidental shot his father had made mention of but which Frank had never seen. This was the photo Rawley had taken of them during the war.

It was a small, black and white portrait of David and Jane. They stood side by side, her right hand holding his left while her other hand lay on her belly. She was looking at the floor. David was caught in time as he lifted his right hand to signal something to the photographer, who was reflected in a mirror behind the couple and had the unmistakable shape of Ray Rawley. His supply of fruit to Jane lay on the window sill by her husband's side. Beyond the pane of glass a sleek grey pigeon sat in the light. David and Jane were captured in their moment as the Arnolfinis had been five hundred years before, almost identically. All that was missing was a scruffy little dog.

A ghost cannot exist unless it is recognised by the living. So it is with history, particularly the personal. If no one knows of a person's life, might they never have existed at all? Sarah Armstrong's 1854 diary was found by a builder in 2125 as he renovated the old Blake house, which had become Claxton Court. He stripped those original features still in situ to be used in Golden Square which had been designated a theme park to celebrate the nineteenth century. When he pulled up the ancient floorboards, he found the small book, in remarkably good shape considering its long sojourn beneath the planks with little protection. The journal was handed in to the British Museum, checked for mites, worms and fungi, fumigated and wrapped in a protective sheath. It was then placed in a box with others of its kind where it remains unread to this day. It covers her life in service in London, and includes an account of Cecily Blake's remarkable recovery from cholera in the September 1854 outbreak. It contains several poems that she loved as a young girl, living and working in Soho.

Sarah would fill another diary with her later adventures and this is entirely lost to the world. So, it is likely that no one knows she trained with Florence Nightingale in 1860 when the famous Lady of the Lamp set up her nurses' training school in St Thomas's Hospital. Five years later and aged twenty-three, as one of the first trained, Sarah began her time as a nurse at Liverpool Workhouse. Thereafter she returned to her birthplace in Kent, married and had seven children, including two sets of twins. Sarah Armstrong died of tuberculosis in 1880. But maybe along her bloodline her spirit and genes persisted, all the way to the twenty-first century and a man called Colin who thought he had killed his twin and whose clone loved clouds as Martha, Sarah's sister, had.

But even if Sarah Armstrong never lived, her story is no less valid than that of John Snow or Henry Whitehead or Florence Nightingale.

Her early charge, Cecily Ffrench, née Blake, died in childbirth along with her first baby in 1868. They rest in a cemetery high above London close to the spot where David Johnson buried his first wife, Jane, and their unborn child in May 1941.

Alice was my first love but Louise is my true love. I am a lucky man. To have encountered either one of them in my life is a miracle, let alone both. Just as my life is something of an accidental miracle. If Colin and Alice had not made me, I would never have known this happiness. I would never have known a thing. I would simply never have existed. It is an idea I find hard to contemplate. How could such energy as I have, and such thoughts as I think, never have been? It is why I cannot figure death at all. How can this wonder that is life just end? How does a mind stop? What if it does not? This last idea is a terrifying one. It speaks to me of a formless soul alone in a nothing blackness with no touch to look forward to or rely on, no tangible contact with any others.

Louise says I must not let this fear encroach. The fact is that I am alive and wildly, happily so. And when it comes time to leave, that too will make sense. She says I will leave behind an essence that will flavour time. I hope she's right. She bases this assertion on Teddy's life and his work with our brains and inner beings. She says if there was a problem with moving on, something we should know about it, he would surely have come back to tell her. She believes love can do that, give signs, even if there is nothing we can understand beyond our own present, breathable, life. In the meantime we must love where and how we can, allow ourselves to be loved, and try to live well.

I woke up to a world already ordered. I had memories, plenty of them, but no experiences to speak of. So it was that I could touch velvet in delight as if for the first time yet know it felt right because that was preordained for me by Colin. Now I am learning so much more with each day. And I have Louise. Without Teddy's death and Colin's grief I would never have been contemplated. There is a reason for everything, however obscure. I would like to figure out more of the world's randomness. Louise teases that this is my own version of Theosophy and there really is such a thing. It's a kind of ancient faith, practised from the nineteenth century till now, that marries the mysteries of religion and science. The idea is that we live a number of times on the earth, studying all branches of thought so that we can become perfectly wise and good. She tells me I have an elegant mind, like Teddy. When she says this, I remind her that Colin does too.

I stand outside the Soho apartment now and look up at the sky. Beyond the murk of manmade pollution it is infinite and ultimately unfathomable. I feel small in comparison but I know that I matter too. I hear a dog growl and a bird coo and some music begins nearby. It is a trumpet voluntary of some sort, followed by maracas and strings. It sounds heavenly. I turn and go back into the apartment, accompanied by the music, and continue my packing up to leave.

This would be their last December in Soho and so they began their farewells. Other people would come to enjoy the shelter of this home when they left. It had been a rickety sanctuary for many centuries, a dwelling place recorded on the spot from the time when such documents were begun. It had sheltered many.

The little family would see out the year, relocating to the suburbs a month before the baby came. This was their second chance at life, their opportunity to make good on their promises to themselves. Alice and Colin would share the miracle of giving life again, this time to the child growing in her womb. It would be their continuity with the future and acknowledgement of the past.

How human we are to want to mark this love, Alice thought, not just of one another but of life itself. She rubbed her expanding belly, to make contact and feel the quickening within her. Humans would always have the same preoccupations handed down through time: the need for love and the imperative to love being the greatest. Or that is what she hoped. Hope was what they were dealing with every day. It was a good place to be.

Beyond it all was the compulsion to create and express the feelings of everyday life through whatever medium you were gifted. And to contemplate the bigger ideas of what it means to be alive in time, your time. But were there definitive answers to these dilemmas, could they ever be satisfactorily explained?

Alice was on the cusp of realising her dream, giving birth. That was her contribution to the sweep of humanity.

Theo was the first to ask the obvious question. 'Is it one baby?'

She loved him even more for that. 'Yes, just the one.'

'Plenty?' he said.

'More than enough to be getting on with.'

Colin was swelled with pride and emotion. He heard Wordsworth's 'still, sad music of humanity' every day, for sure, but it was beautiful with the promise of new life. Teddy would always be with him but he had so many more added to his world now. He felt excitement, properly, for the first time in years. He would be a father, a concept that was as terrifying to contemplate as it was thrilling.

Theo joined him to pack a box of fabrics.

'Would you mind if we kept the lozenge cushions?' he asked his clone.

'You mean the cholera series,' Theo said, giving it provenance.

'Yes. I'd swap you some of my shirts. If you're going to live with Louise in the suburbs, there's no need to show your number all the time. It can be up to you to choose when you share your story. People make assumptions when they shouldn't. They jump to conclusions. I know I did. It's lazy and ignorant.'

'It's a great leveller, ignorance.'

'Yes, but no excuse.'

They worked together silently, side by side, identical echoes of each other but each whole now, not shadows of a dead man. Colin felt their intimate connection, knew it was special, but he also felt within it the exquisite relentlessness of time and its repetition and how he would continue it with his own child. It was a cry out to life, to be delivered into time and its fabric to make a mark, an addition, to it no matter where and when. He felt its emphasis. He felt its joy.

Alex held Karen close. 'There is something you should know if you take on a Bulgharov for life,' he said. 'There is an unknown in our family history. We have a genetic whisper.'

Somewhere close by a trumpet began to climb a scale. A car alarm wailed lonely in the December air. A gaggle of women ran past on the street, sending shrieks into the night. A dog barked.

'My grandmother's Auschwitz story didn't end with Elena's death or their mother's. Mengele took his revenge. Someone betrayed the sisters' secret. Mengele was incensed to have been done out of his pair of identical twins. So he turned up, immaculate in uniform, and took Natalia away to his facility, letting his German Shepherd dog snap and bite at her all the

way across the compounds. He put on a fresh and crisply laun-
dered laboratory coat and became the White Angel, and
pumped her full of anything he could lay his hands on. What
she remembered most was not so much the pain of the injections and the drips forced into her bone-thin arms, although
they were excruciating, it was his cold, silent rage at her. He
performed all of the procedures himself with great precision
and maximum pain. She said he smelt so clean, of soap and
minty toothpaste. The camp guards all stank of alcohol by
then. They knew the war was lost and sought to anaesthetise
themselves against their fate; history honouring the victors,
and all that. Mengele made no notes of what he had put into
her system and told her so. She would just have to spend the
rest of her life wondering, he said, smiling calmly as he spoke.

'She didn't remember liberation when it came soon after,
and never would because she was in a biochemical fever when
it happened. We don't know if any of that is relevant to the
fact that she died young. She never wanted to do the battery
of tests that were suggested to her because she thought they
would be just as bad as what Mengele had done, and if the
news was tinged with fatality, she might let herself die early
of fright and worry and that would be a waste, she said. In
the end, her heart gave out. It might have anyhow. We didn't
delve any deeper than she had, she wouldn't have wanted us
to. What we believe is that brevity comes through the
Bulgharov line, be it something that was always there or something triggered by Mengele. We have always accepted it and
take whatever time is granted us. That is what you would also
be in for, Karen.'

'That's why you took the name, isn't it?'

'Yes. I wanted to acknowledge my lineage. Sergei never married or became a father, that we know of, so it might die out with him otherwise. We may not have a lot of time together and I know that's a lot to ask anyone else to take on. I'll understand if you can't or don't want to be a part of it.'

'I'll take it, Alex,' Karen said, 'and gladly. I feel I've waited all my life for you, without even knowing it, and now that you're here I am going to hold on tight.'

'I love you, Karen Dash, for that and so much more,' he said.

'Well, selfishly, I'm doing my calculations and it seems to me that even if there is a family whisper there it gets diluted with each generation so I probably have more time to look forward to with you than your mother had with your dad, or David did with Natalia.'

'We evolve, eh?'

'Yes, I guess we do, whether we like it or not, or even whether it's useful or not in our particular circumstance. We dilute some deadly traits and introduce others. A sort of sod's law.'

'We should drink to that.'

She sat on the sofa of her Claxton Court flat and waited for her lover to join her. The air around her began to fizz and change. It filled gently with the ring of music and sighs; with the beginning of life's breaths and those that were final; with the noisy bustle of a town; with the quiet of a man's mind given over to wonder. And so, as Karen Dash lifted her glass in salute and forgiveness to a dead friend,

Frank played trumpet,

Papa Konstantin cried in his room,

Louise stood at the door ready to return,
Sarah Armstrong began to run for John Snow,
Teddy fell to his death,
David lifted his hand in anger to Jane,
Natalia spread paint on a board,
Alice felt the baby take hold inside her,
Sally watched colours on the wall,
Alex put the pigeon in its box,
Theo stood reflected behind Colin,
Tony took a last gentle breath,
and Cecily Blake cried out an exultant 'Yellow'
in the space that is time and the place that is home and the
city that is, perpetually, London.

author's note

Most of the poetry and longer Bible quotes used in this book are from the Poetry on the Underground initiative, which wondrous thing has made many journeys on public transport enjoyable for Passenger McLynn over the years.

I have taken a small liberty with John Snow and Henry Whitehead and allowed them to meet a few weeks before they actually did in 1854. The great irony of the brilliant doctor's life was that he suffered chronic poor health, including kidney disease. He became incapacitated by a stroke shortly before he died, on 16 June 1858, at the age of forty-five. Today a pub called the John Snow stands on the site of the pump in what is now Broadwick Street.

Henry Whitehead remained at St Luke's in Soho until 1857 after which he left the area and went on to another curacy. He was instrumental in dealing with an outbreak of cholera some years later, in 1865, in the crowded slums of east London. His experience of the Broad Street outbreak meant he was listened to as to the cause of the disease. He died on 5 March 1896 in his seventy-second year.

Karl Marx and his family lived in Soho for some years during the 1850s.

The Savitsky Museum in Nukus, Karakalpakstan, houses the largest collection of Soviet dissident art in the world. The wonder is that it exists at all and survived so many years of Soviet repression particularly during the reign of Josef Stalin.

To the best of my knowledge no one stole the Arnolfini Portrait during the World War of 1939–45.

The art historian Niklaus Pevsner did serve in the rebuilding of London after the Blitz of the Second World War.

many and heartfelt thanks are due to –

Angela Cook for her wartime remembrances; Lawrence Till for Thatcher and King Lear; Stephen Threlfall for music (especially Scriabin); Louise Grundy for unicorns and sequins; David Gholam for the Savitsky; Sally Carman for general ballast; Ian Mercer for the epileptic fit; Victoria Smurfit for South Africa and her ability to inject poetry and passion into the everyday; Jane Heller for another great copy edit; all of the regulars to my website who offered such valuable encouragement when I thought this one would not get finished; and, finally but not least, my wonderful Top Trio of agent Faith O'Grady, editor Clare Foss and husband Richard Cook without whom it might all have floundered.